# Unloved, Misfit and Misunderstood

*Donia Ray*

# Table of Contents

# Dedication

I want to dedicate this novel to my beloved daughters, Sienna and Arianna. I am so proud to witness Sienna embracing her own passion for writing down her overflowing imagination.

# Acknowledgements

I want to thank my sister, Flory, for all her support and encouragement over the years. She is my number one fan and my number one critic – she made me wish to become better to make her proud. Special thanks to my dear husband for putting up with my unusual hobby and for discussing with me certain situations when I feel stuck. Finally, I want to thank the publisher for all the efforts made for 'Unloved, Misfit and Misunderstood' to reach the public.

# About the Author

Donia Ray is a Romanian-born author residing in the UK for over 16 years. Since her teenage years, she loved reading, writing little stories and poetry in her native language. She loves love stories with a side dish, either thriller, witchcraft or magic. She wrote her first book in English in 2016, Against All Odds, published in 2017. Unloved, Misfit and Misunderstood was written in 2021. Donia loves creating strong female characters who complement their male counterparts and end up fighting together for a common purpose. Although the main character in this particular novel doesn't seem strong, she proves resilience and a composure that make up for her shortcomings.

# Chapter 1

Nolani had a feeling in her gut that this was a bad day from the start. The phone call from her mother resumed strictly to 'When are you going to sell that f… house? I want my f… part of the money!' was just the beginning. She still had that feeling despite the fact the part with selling the house was promising. Considering the size and the value of Jacaranda, she thought it was going to take months of advertising to attract prospective buyers. The house reached the market in just a week, and she had a meeting with one about 3 p.m. who wanted to see the house. Eloise Burton, her estate agent, sounded so pleased on the phone about this buyer, Mr Wiseman. Of course, she was short on luck today; Eloise was away for the rest of the week and asked her to show the client Jacaranda. She made a point that she didn't know how to present a house to a potential buyer, and she could throw out on the window a chance to sell her grandmother's property, but Eloise said that Mr Wiseman took his entire day off, which was unheard of, to solve some personal problems and to see the house. That being said… it was down to Nolani to make the presentation, or the client might look elsewhere.

Then came the dreaded phone call from Sunrise Nursing Home. Vanda suffered another psychotic episode; she refused to wash and change even if she was in a poor state. Altogether, she needed to leave work and rush out of Dallas to see how she could help. Vanda's room was devastated by her violent outbreak. The family pictures so beautifully displayed on the window sill were smashed against the walls, the clothes were scattered everywhere, and Vanda was screaming to the staff at the top of her lungs' obscenities. The image broke Nolani's heart. Her otherwise proud grandmother, who was hosting high society parties, waltzing full of condescendence between politicians and business people, was hard to recognise in that room. Nolani never heard her swearing while she grew up. She was full of hate and judgemental; she could hurt really bad telling somebody how unworthy they were, but she never swore. Now she was, maybe for all the years she kept it in. The unwise decisions of her mother and later her own ruined the image Vanda tried so hard to keep in society. Her aristocratic British blood was tainted. Her dementia took the best of her.

'Vanda, in half an hour, the Arringtons are coming, my darling,' she said from the entrance. She could notice how her grandmother paused, looked at her without any acknowledgement of who she was, then passed her small fingers through her hair. 'We need to get dressed and, in the lounge, until they are arriving. We wouldn't want them to come to your room, don't we? Plus, Lucas told them, how wonderful his fiancée is, and they are eager to meet you…' Vanda turned her beautiful, blue eyes towards her, and for a moment, Nolani thought she might have recognised her. That moment passed, and that recognition has never been displayed. The good part was that Vanda agreed to a shower and left the girl to help her with the dressing. By the moment Vanda went to have her breakfast, she completely forgot why she dolled up and was so excited to follow the staff towards the common area. Nolani remained in the room, trying to salvage as many of the family pictures as she could, while two members of staff were changing the bedding and arranging Vanda's clothes back in the wardrobe.

She was preparing to leave when Rita, a very sweet lady residing in the nursing home, observed her from her favourite corner in the common area and waved at her with a huge smile on her face. She paused, looked discretely at her watch, then crossed the area to say 'Hi.'

'Rita, you look gorgeous today,' she smiled before sitting in the chair next to the lovely lady.

'My grandson is coming to see me today,' Rita explained, while her eyes were expressing how happy she was at the prospect of seeing her only grandson. Her cell phone was in the pleats of her blue dress, and her fingers kept caressing the device through which she received the good news. 'Terry said he has even better news when he is going to arrive. He said he's going to be here about 11, but it is passed 10 and no sign of him. I'm sure he is on his way.'

'I am glad for you, Rita. You haven't seen him by… how many years?'

'Two. The day when he helped me move in here.' Rita rushed, though in his defence. 'He is a very busy defence lawyer, you know… He travels a lot…'

'I'm sure he is, Rita… Maybe he is going to take you out for a meal together?'

'I don't think he has a wheelchair-friendly car…' Rita sighed, trying to fight with the bitterness of her condition. 'Even if he has, if I need the toilet, what can he do to help me? And I cannot disrupt the Home by requesting two carers to go out with us just for me to enjoy a meal out with him… It's unpractical…'

'I didn't know you need the help of two carers…' Nolani said sadly, biting her lower lip.

'They use the machine to move me from one chair to the other. The hoist, you know… My knees are not good at all. I'm on Morphine patches because of the pain…'

She could see the expression on Rita's face changing from resolved to ecstatic in a split of the second. Her green eyes were looking somewhere behind her, and Nolani turned her head to see the person whose presence made Rita so happy.

In that moment, Nolani realised what a bad day she was having. The blood disappeared from her face, and if she hadn't been sitting, her knees would have given in, looking in disbelief at the man who entered the room analysing her with eagle eyes. Few strands of black hair were falling over his thick eyebrow. His green eyes were identical to Rita's, but they were analytical, stabbing, bitter. His suit was like made for him, his low-cut trousers underlining his maleness and, at the same time, strongly presenting his 'all about business' allure.

How she managed to keep her composure, Nolani did not know. If ever the lessons of how to behave in the society of Vanda were put to use, it was now. Her fingers squeezed the leather shoulder bag; she forced a smile, which she was hoping to look as genuine as possible and stood up. 'I will leave you, Rita. I need to go back to work…'

'No! No! No!' Rita cried. 'Let me introduce you… He is my grandson, Terrence… Terry… she is the lady I talked to you on the phone about… Nolani…'

'Pleased to meet you,' she whispered, wondering how her small hand finished in his. 'Now, I really must go, Rita… Terry…'

Nolani forced another smile towards both and fighting with a wave of nausea in her stomach and wishing to just disappear, she rushed towards the door. How she did not stumble on her high heels, she didn't know. She pressed the code onto the door panel and rushed out like chased by wolves. The hot air of a very dry day hit her right in the face, and she grabbed the handrail to make sure she could climb down the entrance stairs safely. She heard the door behind opening and closing and prayed that it was another relative going out. She did not turn her head while she walked towards her car because she wasn't feeling like initiating, not even a silly conversation like how nice the staff organised the Easter Party… She sat next to Rita that day because Vanda decided to put herself to bed that afternoon.

She unlocked her car and opened the door, when she realised that she was not alone. She turned her head, and her heart made a somersault, discovering how close he was.

'Listen, Miss… whatever your name is…' he grunted between his teeth. 'Rita told me how often you are visiting her… every day I am calling she's like 'Oh, she came to see me… and she was looking lovely today… and she's got me a new dress… oh, Terry, you should see how my new blouse fits me… It's gorgeous!' he mimicked, visibly unimpressed. 'I don't know what it is with you and why you are doing all this, but if you are after Rita's money, it's bad news for you!'

Nolani looked at him in a stupor for more than one reason. Did he just accuse her that she was after an old lady's money? The other reason was too deep and personal to even acknowledge.

'My own grandmother is residing in the same home. I do not come here to visit Rita, but my own grandmother. What do you want me to do? When Rita waves to me, she seems happy to see me. Shall I ignore her? She looks so lonely and deserted!'

'I know she didn't have many visitors for a while…'

'She never does. How do you think she feels when everyone gets to be visited regularly, and she doesn't?'

'She knows what the situation is…' At least he looked guilty about the loneliness of Rita.

'It doesn't make it any easier!' she replied, lifting her chin up.

'This does not explain why you are buying her stuff!'

'She needs brassieres, she needs underwear, new clothes, continence pads, cosmetics… Who else was there to buy all these for her? I am a lady; she feels comfortable to give me a list of what she needs. Otherwise, all the transactions are more than transparent. The receipts are all in her file and the manager signed as a witness. You can check with Mr Thompson in the office, before you accuse anyone of having a run for Rita's money! Plus, if her body lets her down, her mind is sharp as steel. You are nowhere close to say any different.'

'Well, even if it is how you say, Miss…' he said, pushing his hands into the pockets of his trousers, a gesture which attracted Nolani's attention towards their fly. She lifted her eyes on his white shirt, the V created by the two undone buttons and his dark skin towards his strong chin, carefully shaved, his lips and those eyes… The look there was so dangerous that Nolani turned her eyes away toward the parking lot. 'I'm around now,' he announced with defiance. 'I'm around and I have every intention to stay around. I want you to keep the distance. Rita doesn't need your charity visits from now on. Is that clear?' he asked with a patronising air that Nolani found despicable.

'I'm glad for Rita that you will be around.'

'Is that clear, Miss?'

His whole arrogant attitude reminded Nolani of her childhood. Vanda was like that. To challenge Vanda's decisions was futile. The choices she could make were limited. Even the way she was allowed to dress was limited. What she was eating, it was Vanda's choice. She was forced to accept these decisions for her, and the feeling was suffocating. Rita's grandson was giving her the same feeling of helplessness. He was right, though. Rita was his grandmother and he could take that position or whichever he saw fit. The only unravelling thought was that he had the intention to remain around. That thought was more suffocating than the one that she was not allowed to visit Rita anymore. Her heart was aching for Rita due to their closeness, but he didn't need to tell her twice to keep the distance. She didn't want to be close to him or even to be in the same room with him.

'You've been more than clear…' she answered with a low voice, before turning on her high heels and sat in her car.

He made a few steps backward, to leave her room enough to manoeuvre the car out of the parking spot and then out of his sight. Somehow pleased with his decision, he returned to the home to talk to Rita. Her green eyes were full of acknowledgement when he made his way towards the chair the lady sat on when he arrived. 'I told you she was beautiful,' Rita said with a shy smile.

'Yes, you did, Rita…'

And she was. Ash blond hair, blue eyes and overall elegant and stylish, yes, she was beautiful. The features of her face were all sweet, but her attitude was reserved. She never shouted at him, she talked with a moderated tone, highlighting to him the needs of Rita, even if he felt she acted like a cornered fox.

'But you forbidden her to come and see me, didn't you?'

'Forbidden… no…' he said diplomatically. 'I just told her that I am around now, and it is not necessary for her to… bother, so to say…' Rita preferred to look at her hands but at her grandson right then.

'How long are you planning to stay around?' she asked, playing nervously with her cell phone.

'This was the surprise I promised you this morning,' he smiled, all charming. 'I am opening my office in Dallas. I made all the arrangements for Laura to move with the school locally, and I have plans even to buy a house, fifteen minutes' drive from here, Rita.'

Normally, the news would have been a blast for his grandmother. Whatever reasons were behind his decision to move from New York with business, child and all, this was supposed to make her happy. Rita lifted her head and smiled, then looked down to her lap again.

'And since when your plans started through pushing my only friend away?'

'You have many old friends… lifetime friends… real friends, Rita,' he reminded her, feeling uncomfortable. 'You told me you are writing to them…'

'But Nolani was posting my letters for me…'

'Thing that I can do from now on…' he bargained.

'I like her… and I was convinced that seeing her, you will be smitten!' she laughed bitterly.

Terry looked at her carefully. He refused with a gesture a member of staff which offered them a drink. Was Rita playing the matchmaker? He smiled, amused by her naivete and moved his head in disbelief. Rita always had a romantic nature. 'You will never change, Rita...' he chuckled with a low voice.

Rita refrained from giving him a sour answer. She was happy to see him. She was happy that he decided to move closer to her. She was not happy with what he had done in the first ten minutes of his arrival. Being rude to Nolani. God! She shivered, only imagining how cruel he could have been.

'And how is Laura? Is she happy to leave New York behind and move to Texas?' asked Rita, watching him carefully. She was very perceptive, so he put on one of his most charming smiles. God, he was so deceptive he could go into politics!

'Yes, Rita. She is very enthusiastic about the move, the chance to make friends... plus she is only six. It is an age when children are adjusting easily to changes... We found a very good school where I can leave her on the way to work... I can work around her school hours. I signed, the first hour this morning, the rental contract for an office eighth floor, very elegant, very stylish...'

'And the house?'

'It is in Angel's Marsh... I did not have a chance to see it yet, but looks very promising. I must say, the move seems to be as smooth as it can be. I saw some pictures. The house has been beautifully redecorated by the last owner, and it seems they are in a rush to sell it as I am to buy it. It might turn out pretty well. The price they ask is very appealing as well. It seems a lot of house and land for the money.'

He continued the chat about how the pictures of the two acres around the house were looking and how that would benefit Laura's upbringing away from the big city. He was happy Rita didn't bring back the subject of that friend of hers. After he parted with her, he went into the office. The small conversation he had with the manager proved that Miss Nolani didn't lie about the transparency of the transactions. She was bringing in the shopping and the detailed receipts and Rita was giving her the money back with Mr Thompson as a witness. All the paperwork was straightforward and could not be challenged.

Pleased with the results of that last conversation, he left.

He gave a phone call to the childminder, Mrs Talon. Laura was enjoying a day out; she had ice cream, and they were preparing to go and watch a movie at the cinema. He even talked to his little girl, and she was sounding chirpy.

He had a look at his watch. He decided then to return to the hotel, to have a shower and change before taking his dinner in the hotel's restaurant. During his dinner, he analysed the documentation regarding the property he was about to see. Everything was looking fine. If everything was going smoothly and the seller was agreeing with everything, he could see himself moving with his little girl in a very short time. Laura didn't like too much to live in a hotel. She badly wanted her own bedroom, decorated with her favourite Disney Princesses.

Terry had a look at the other properties brought to his attention by his assistant, but none was even close to that house in Angel's Marsh. Everything recommended that that house was the perfect choice. It was not in Dallas, but close to Dallas. He didn't need to redecorate.

Big rooms. Air conditioning. Functional fireplace, very charming, original features. Apparently, the house belonged to a congressman or something. That piece of information was not written anywhere, but it was what the Estate Agent told his assistant.

# Chapter 2

Nolani needed a lot of time to recover after the meeting with Rita's grandson. The impact was so intense, she needed a couple of painkillers to fight a headache. She tried to get busy working on some projects but realised quickly into developing them that she wasn't in the right spirits for work. She looked over some sketches she worked on the evening before. They seemed decent and it was more in harmony with her client's wishes.

By the time she reached the property of Vanda, she was more relaxed. The bad dream passed. She needed to concentrate on selling her property. The money would help in paying for Vanda's care. Her needs were increasing; her fees as well.

She talked with Vanda's lawyer. Her mother could make the biggest scandal. The money was intended just for Vanda's fees. Only after her passing, depending on her will, the money would go wherever Vanda wanted. Nolani passed her fingers on the shiny surface of the piano with a sad smile on her face. Possibly the local church or something. Anyway, she made sure before putting the house she grew up in on the market that she had the power, as the only next of kin of Vanda, to sell the house, not to create unwished delays in the process.

Like showing the house herself, Nolani sighed.

Of course, she knew that house inside out. She redecorated that house throughout. She had memories in every room, in every corner. The restricted and lonely childhood. Listening to Vanda damning her mother for making a child aged seventeen and abandoning it in her arms. Vanda raised her more from a sense of honour rather than love.

When she did the same crime as her mother, less the abandonment part, Vanda went ballistic. She had to leave. She had to remove herself from the house and away from Vanda's fury, ugly accusations, name calling and such to ensure a proper environment for then her unborn son. She had to return actively to Vanda's life a year ago when Vanda had to be removed from the house because, due to her mental deterioration, she was in danger of burning the house down with her in it.

It was then that the bell sounded in the elegant rooms, a sign that Eloise's client had arrived. Nolani breathed in to calm her nervousness. Since the ugly encounter with Rita's grandson, she couldn't get rid of her anxiety. She opened the door and remained numb, looking aghast at the same man who caused all that confusion. Her heart sank while she fought with all her might to regain control. He looked as surprised as she was.

'Mr… Wiseman?' she asked with a low voice.

'Jeremy Wiseman is my assistant. Terrence Morgan. And you are the Estate Agent…' he concluded, not at all enthusiastic that he had to deal with her.

'No, Mr Morgan. I am the granddaughter of the owner. I am the one who sells the house. Miss Burton is away for a few days. As you insisted on seeing the house today, she asked me to show it to you. It is ok if you want to arrange another day somewhere next week. I am sure that Miss Burton will be happy to assist you…'

She offered a good plan of action, and he was more than tempted to take it, until he remembered that he was planning that somewhere next week already to have all the paperwork done.

'No, it's fine, Miss…'

'Nolani Arrington…'

'So, the house has been recently renovated by Forever Inc.,' he remarked, entering the hallway. He made a sign towards the panel exposed in front of the property, before closing the door behind him. Nolani felt very vulnerable at that moment. She was willing to negotiate a later date when he could see the house with Eloise. The whole plan was for her to stay away from the entire process of selling the house. And from now on, she was… but why did she have to be so unlucky to cross paths with him twice in one day?

'All the plumbing work, electric wiring and woodwork has been checked, and it is up to standards. The kitchen area has been renovated completely. The furniture is completely new. The same the kitchen appliances.'

'I saw the company. The offices are on the second floor in the same building where I rented the space this morning to open my own offices.'

He was trying to make conversation, but Nolani's heart stopped. Because her hands started to tremble, she crossed her arms around her middle. She could not say a word. What act of fate was this that everywhere she would go from now on, she would bump into him? Their grandmothers were residents in the same care home to start with. He was intending to buy this house from her. He was about to work in the same building as she was. God Almighty! What mistake did she make in the past to deserve that? And for the moment, the worse didn't happen! She pretended to look at the beautiful wooden floor and closed her eyes, fighting to assert some control over her trembling limbs.

'Is this the original furniture of the house?' he asked, looking around impressed.

'Yes, but everything can go, to make room for your personal furniture.'

'Any further plans regarding it?'

'I talked to an antiquity shop if they can sell whatever item is not wanted…'

'So, the asking price does not include the furniture…'

'I wouldn't impose it on anyone…'

'Definitely, I want to keep some of it. This room, for example, is exquisite, exactly how it is… It would shorten the time to move in as well…'

'As you wish, Mr Morgan. You can take your time to a later date, make an inventory with what you want to keep, and I can work out a convenient price for both of us.'

Nolani tried to remember what Rita had told her about her grandson. She told her that he grew up in North Carolina, close to his mother's family. That he was a very successful lawyer in New York… Did she say anything about a wife? She was struggling so hard to remember, she completely lost sense of what he said to her.

'Sorry?'

'Do you play piano?'

'I used to. A lot. My grandmother was expecting me to entertain her guests every time she was hosting a party. I'm not doing that anymore. I was teaching for a while…'

'Do you want to take the piano, or I can put it on the list?'

'It can remain if you wish…'

Terry sensed that even if she was polite, she was very tense. The accusation he threw at her in the morning made this meeting even more awkward. It did not stay well with her. He was not the kind of person to apologize, but in her case, he did pull the wrong conclusion. It made Rita extremely unhappy and added a lot of bitterness to his potential to buy this beautiful house for himself and his daughter.

'About your grandmother… when did she move into the nursing home?'

'A year ago, Mrs Watkins, a lady I was paying to come from time to time to check on her, alerted the police and the fire brigade when Vanda left the pan on the cooking machine. The food was burnt, the place was full of thick smoke… she was sleeping. She was very confused. I was put in the position to make a decision for her safety. I've been told that Vanda was more forgetful, dressing inappropriately… accusing Mrs Watkins of coming in to steal from her… a purse that was hidden behind the toilet seat… She's been diagnosed with frontal dementia and Picks Disease, which is progressing rapidly. She was mentally sectioned, so I take care of all her financial affairs.'

And she was not taking care of her grandmother's bill, stealing from Rita. She did not continue, though, even if she felt tempted to.

'Your parents?'

'Not around,' she said evasively.

While they were talking, she showed him one of the most beautiful rooms of the house, an office, all leather and wood, which appealed to him a lot.

'Was the office belonging to your grandfather?'

'I think so. Vanda never used it. Personally, I never met my grandfather. He died when my mother was ten, I think.' She introduced him to Vanda's favourite room of the house which she used intensively to entertain her guests. It was a bright room, enormous compared with the lounge. White columns from place to place were ensuring the upper floor's stability. Architectural, the house was a piece of art. Few French doors were facilitating the access towards the park where there was a gazebo, an even lawn well maintained… Terry looked around for something.

'Did you grow up here?'

'Yes, I did,' she said, remaining in the door frame. His whole physique was impressive and very handsome. Her heart was drumming in her chest, and her breathing wasn't very good either.

'Is there a swing? A tree-house? A playground for a child?'

'Do you have a child?' she asked with a very low voice.

'A little girl. Six.'

Nolani swallowed slowly, fighting her nervousness and lifted her shoulders, looking randomly at the trees in the park. 'I am afraid there is nothing like that. But it can be done. The park is huge and there are many trees strong and fit to hold a little suspended house.'

'You never had anything like that…' he concluded, turning towards her with curiosity.

'No,' she answered, returning inside. God, maybe Eloise could have talked to him more about the advantages of a big park and how this could benefit a six-year-old child, but she couldn't say anything more. The emotional baggage was too large and was leaving her confused, exhausted and lost for words. Only being around him, trying to act like it didn't affect her, it was affecting her tremendously.

She heard him closing the door behind him, and she looked around, struggling to remember what to say next. 'This saloon can be used for private parties, birthdays and so on. There is a corridor directly towards the kitchen. Do you want to see it?'

'What are those doors at the end?'

'A special bathroom for the guests. There are about six private toilets. Are not separated like in restaurants for males and females, I'm afraid.'

He looked in. There was a huge mirror on the wall above three sinks, soap dispensers, paper towels… The floor choice was pleasant, and overall, everything looked new, modern and practical.

She invited him back into the piano lounge. He liked everything he saw. The kitchen, the quiet lounge, what she called another room which was inviting to lay on a sofa and enjoy a TV program. Nolani went then upstairs where there was another lounge with access towards three of the bedrooms. 'There is another small bedroom at the end of this corridor, she said. All the bedrooms have ensuite bathrooms. The small one has a shower. That one and the two bedrooms with the windows towards the back have balconies. The master bedroom has a walking wardrobe. Will Mrs Morgan see the house at a later date?'

Terry entered the master bedroom, very impressed with what he was seeing. They were looking impressive in the pictures handed to him by the Estate Agency, but they were larger than he imagined, gorgeously decorated and elegant. The master bedroom was not feminine at all, but the decorators managed to make it suitable for a woman or a man equally, or a couple. The good taste was up to the highest, in his opinion. 'I'm divorced,' he answered when Nolani did not expect any longer for an answer.

Nolani wondered then if he and Mrs Morgan shared joint custody of their child or if the child remained in his custody only. She couldn't dare to ask, even if the answers were so important for her. She needed to know. She didn't say anything after.

One after another, he entered every bedroom, checking cupboards and drawers. What he couldn't find anywhere in the house was a sign that she was still living there. 'Did you move out before ordering the redecoration?' he asked while walking towards the exit door.

'Long before that. I live in Dallas.'

'What if I request all the furniture to remain in the house?'

'I have no problem with that.'

'Do I still have to make a list?'

'I do have a list of the items. I can look at it and establish a sum,' she said, following him out on the porch. 'Are you going to contact the agency once you make up your mind?'

'I've made up my mind. I take it. Of course, if you still are agreeing to sell it to me.'

'Why wouldn't I?' Nolani asked, even if she knew the answer.

'Because of how we started the day?' he asked, lifting an eyebrow charmingly.

'It has nothing to do with me selling you the house. I got the message clearly, and you were in the right position to make that decision. Even if it hurts, I will respect your decision.'

'Why did you started buying stuff for her?'

'She asked me to.'

'I was wrong to accuse you of trying to manipulate my grandmother for her money. My assumptions were wrong.'

'If this is an apology, it is accepted. How fast do you want the approximate for the furniture?'

'As soon as possible. We both hate to stay in a hotel.' He smiled. She went livid, not exactly what he expected. His smile usually was attracting females, not making them turn ghostly. If she accepted his apology, it was just a façade. She did not forgive him for that.

'From now on, every aspect of the process will be ensured by Miss Burton. She will let me know if there is any change in your decisions.'

'Is there any number I can contact you directly?'

'Miss Burton will be more than happy to assist you in anything you need,' she answered politely with a gesture of her head. The headache returned and was pounding in her temples. She didn't want to sound abrupt in interrupting this meeting here, but for God's sake, how she wanted to throw herself in her car and run!

He got the message. No number. 'All right. I'll wait to hear from you and to see you somewhere next week when we can sign the deal.'

Nolani nodded, then got herself in the car and closed the door. The heat was unbearable, so she activated the air conditioning. She looked in her purse and got out another two pills for her headache. The water was warm but at least it could help her to swallow the tablets. Her self-control ran extremely thin, and her eyes filled instantly with tears. She took a tissue, fighting a sob and risked another look at him. He was leaning against his own car, thoughtful, staring at her. Obviously, he noticed her tears; he frowned. In a minute, her car was nowhere to be seen.

❀ ❀ ❀

'I shouldn't have let you talk me into showing the house myself, Eloise,' she said after an hour of crying in the bathtub. She analysed and overanalysed both encounters with him on that day. She calmed down. Thinking that his office would be in the same building as hers made her freak out again. Then she realised that the mutual animosity between them would keep him easily away. So… she decided to cook. For many women, this activity was strenuous and boring. For her, it was therapeutic. Tate was having plans with his best friend to sleep over that night, so she didn't have to worry too much that she was looking like she just cried buckets.

'Was Mr Wiseman okay?'

'Mr Wiseman is the assistant. Mr Morgan is the client.'

'Oh! Okay… so how is Mr Morgan?'

'To put it mildly, arrogant, patronising…' Familiar, she added in her mind, cutting vegetables.

'What did he say about the house? Did he like it?'

'Yes, he wants it with all the furniture. As soon as possible.'

'Then what's wrong, honey?' asked Eloise with a sweet voice.

She hadn't seen him in nineteen years. He was gorgeous and dangerous, and he was buying her grandmother's house. Rita and Vanda were residents in the same nursing home. He was to work in the same building as she.

Suddenly the vegetables in her hands become all a blur. It was good he did not remember her. She was far from the shy girl he saved nineteen summers ago on the beach in Florida. Then she really started to cry. He did not remember her…

# Chapter 3

Now he had it. He went to a great extent to get Miss Arrington's number. Eloise Burton from the Agency was more than reluctant to give it to him. She said she couldn't give him the number of her client without permission. She also said she would ask for it and come back with a phone call. The next conversation he had with her was for her to say that she sent him via email the list of items remaining in the house and a total. She instructed him to call him back if he agreed with the total sum, which, in her opinion, was a fortune. She added, 'The piano costs half of that sum…' All friendly and professional to a fault, Miss Burton didn't even mention about the private number of her client.

He went to visit Rita over the weekend, and apparently, he missed her twice. Rita was in tears because both times she saw her friend from her favourite chair and she waved at her, but she went out without even looking towards her. She seemed upset. Terry asked the staff if everything was all right with Vanda, but they all acted evasively, and nobody said anything. Terry sighed. She took verbatim what he requested her to do and ended up hurting badly his own grandmother. He felt like a criminal when he requested Rita her number 'to apologize to her.' She gave it to him with all her hopes up again.

He survived an entire weekend with Laura dreaming out loud about how she wanted her bedroom and asking a million questions about the house. They lived all her life in an apartment on the 20th floor. To have a garden to run and play was sounding amazing.

He wanted to call on Sunday evening as soon as Laura went to bed, but he couldn't find a reason strong enough. Should he tell her

Rita was in tears because of her behaviour? Whose fault was that?

Terry went to bed restless and struggled to concentrate on the numbers on the pages he printed from his email. The sum was more than acceptable. He emailed back to the agency that he would hand out a check to Miss Arrington, especially for the furniture, during the meeting arranged to sign the contract.

On Monday morning, he had an email from Miss Burton that the meeting was agreed for Wednesday morning, asking him if he agreed to it. He wanted today. He replied that Wednesday was perfect.

❀ ❀ ❀

'He agreed with everything, honey!' Eloise said through the phone while she and Tate were having breakfast. 'I don't know how arrogant and patronising he was, but he loved the house and wants it exactly how it is. His little girl might want some changes in the room of her choice to make it more girlish, but otherwise, everything goes faster than any selling I ever made in my entire career! You were good!'

'I very much doubt that, Eloise. I think he just wants no fuss and wants to move as soon as possible. I am not living there, so he doesn't have to give me time to move out or anything. That's the reason, not because I was any good. I was awful at it. I don't even remember what I told him that day.'

'Anyway, the meeting for the contract was established on Wednesday at 11 in the morning in my office. Take your lucky pen with you…'

'And Vanda's lawyer…'

24

'That too,' Eloise giggled.

Tate smiled while Nolani closed the conversation.

'If everything goes well, you don't have to struggle anymore with the bills of your grandmother, isn't it?'

'Yes. The lawyer said that I can keep the money from the furniture in return for renovating the house and raising its value on the market. If that is possible, by the end of the month, I will be able to buy you a car, Tate. You cannot continue to take rides from Jake or from me when you already have a driving licence. I'm sorry all this story with the house consumed all our savings.'

'It's ok!' he said joyfully, drinking his chocolate milk. He was passed eighteen but still was staying away from coffee. She collected the dishes, rinsed them and placed them in the dishwasher, while Tate wiped the kitchen table. 'I hope you are going to give me a lift today, mom. Jake can't make it. He just messaged me…'

'Sure, honey.'

She collected the keys, her handbag and together left the house. Her phone rang as soon as she sat in front of her wheel, ready to take off. The Bluetooth made the call sound in the car like an ambulance siren.

'Hello,' she answered manoeuvring the car into the traffic.

She recognised the voice from his first hello. Tate looked towards her, curious.

'Do I disturb? I needed to talk to you, Nolani.'

'I already talked with Miss Burton. She said you agreed to the meeting on Wednesday morning, and you also agreed with the total I estimated for the furniture…'

'That I did… What I need to talk to you is about Rita. Do you think you can meet me sometime today?'

'I'm not sure. I have a crazy day ahead…'

'Don't forget you have to pick me up at four, mom, after my football training,' Tate added.

Nolani sighed. She never restricted Tate to talk. Why would she have started now? Okay, Mr Morgan found out she's a mom. She squeezed the wheel nervously.

'What about your lunch break? Can you meet me somewhere in that time?'

'One o'clock? Across the street from our… from the office you rented, there is a nice coffee shop with a terrace. I think I can meet you then, Mr Morgan.'

'All right, I will be there…'

She closed the conversation and parked the car on a side, close to Tate's high school. She knew that the kids were not very proud to be seen with their parents, and she didn't want Tate to feel embarrassed with her. The feelings of her son, though, were completely the opposite. He couldn't care less who was seeing him with his mother. He was proud of her in all aspects a son could be proud of the only parent he knew.

'Was Mr Morgan the gentleman who agreed to buy the house of your grandmother?'

'Yes,' she sighed, turning towards him.

'And Rita?'

'Rita is that lovely lady from my grandmother's nursing home who became my friend. She is the grandmother of Mr Morgan. He had an issue with our friendship…'

'Did he tell you not to visit his grandmother anymore?'

'Something to that extent,' she sighed.

'But he wants to buy the house of your grandmother,' said Tate thoughtfully.

'We didn't know that until he came to see the house… anyway, we passed our differences, and we managed to close the deal, not because I am an exceptional house seller, but because he is desperate to move in the house as soon as possible. Now it's time for you to go,' she reminded him, gesturing towards the gate. 'I can see your friends from here.'

'Ok, mom, good luck with that lunch with him.'

Yeah, she needed a lot of that. 'It's ok, Tate. I'm a big girl; I can deal with Mr Morgan. Good luck at school. See you at four. Shall I be at the football field gate or here?'

'Football field gate. Thanks, mom!'

'Don't mention it! Love you!'

Tate closed the door on his side, and Nolani followed him with her eyes until he met his friends and shared handshakes and man hugs. Her little boy was a man. Nolani smiled from behind the wheel. A very handsome, energetic, kind man, ambitious in his studies with big plans for his future. He was respected by the boys and loved by the girls. She talked with Tate about the subject. His candour was shocking. Yes, he did have his success with regard to girls, but he was not making empty promises and he was always using protection.

Tate confided to her he had never been in love. Every time they were touching this subject, he was opening the subject of his dad. Nolani knew that his questions with regard to his paternity were consuming him. She had grown up with that as well, and it was tearing her apart that she couldn't protect her own child growing like that. She knew no mother or father. Vanda was all she knew. She talked with Jessica Arrington on the phone multiple times. Most of the time, her mother was demanding something else. She never told her, *'I'm sorry for abandoning you.'* She never seemed to acknowledge her as her daughter. But she could tell a little girl eight years old by the phone, when Vanda refused to talk to her, *'Tell that hag to go and kill herself.'*

All that bickering backwards and forwards between her mother and Vanda confused her deeply. The level of hurt inflicted on her was all-consuming and was affecting not only the way she interacted with people but also the way she dealt with the secrets around Tate's paternity.

Nolani sighed and rolled the car with care on the very busy street. School hours could be a nightmare. She could watch from behind the car's windows, parents with little children walking towards the gates of the elementary school Tate used to go to when he was their age.

Her eyes detected between the parents a particular one, a man close to forty, tall, massive, elegant in his smart suit, black hair… He was holding the hand of a gorgeous little girl. Her long black hair was carefully plaited, and it was touching her waist. She could only imagine that her eyes were the same colour, a definite trait of the family, deep green. Her heart sunk looking at him, taking his child to school, chatting, laughing, looking at her with adoring eyes.

As soon as she found an opportunity to emerge into the traffic she did, relieved that he didn't notice her.

In ten minutes, she sat at her desk with a more unsettling thought deep in her mind. The enormity of it took her breath away. Even their kids' schools were so close to each other! Years ago, she didn't even know his name. His nickname was Stampede, apparently having something to do with his ability to play football.

Today, he was a lawyer. Criminal defence attorney. She dared to smile, looking through the window, lost in thoughts. Far away from professional football.

Tate loved football. Tate wanted to follow law school. He wanted to pursue family law. Oh, God!

The office got animated with the arrival of her employees. They were all laughing, sharing an internal joke while turning on their computers and organising their projects for the day. The door opened, and her assistant smiled at her with an energetic 'Good morning, boss.' 'Had a great weekend?' she added, leaning with her shoulder in the door frame.

'I had a weekend…' she smiled.

'I have a voice message on the phone. Nick Logan said the work on Simons' property goes as planned, and there are no signs of delays.'

'Did he check everything? The Simons' complained of that awful gas smell…'

'All gas pipes checked. He still looks where the trouble is. He says there is no smell of gas on the property…'

'Tell him to double-check, Marina. If there is a gas smell on the property, it's a serious issue.'

'I will call him in a minute, boss.'

Another wave of laughter rose in between the desks. She looked at her assistant, intrigued.

'Jada spent the weekend visiting her fiancé's parents. She spent it playing Cinderella. From cooking, cleaning and serving dinners to 'You are not allowed to talk when the men are talking…' kind of thing. Funny enough, Brian found everything okay, he had a lovely weekend, his parents absolutely loved her, and he wants to decide the wedding date…'

'Oh, dear…' Nolani sighed, feeling sorry for her.

'And Jada broke the engagement. Don't worry. She seems in good spirits. Now she just mocks the parents. After the reality show this weekend, which served instead of a cold shower, she very much made up her mind…'

'It's not like he treats her like that, or she is supposed to live with his parents…'

'This is the problem. Brian wants, after marriage, to move in with his parents because they are growing old and they need all the support of the young generation… He is the only son… bla-bla-bla…'

'I did not expect this one,' Nolani mumbled. 'I trust Jada knows the best… Back to business now.'

Her assistant came closer, and Nolani handed her a new project. Seemed a pretty forward one; the family wanted a nursery for a new addition. She talked only on the phone with them, and everything seemed 'I don't care, I just want a cute one…' She knew the real challenges were met by the interior designer in asserting what they wanted and agreeing with each other in every aspect of the project. She had many projects like that during her ten years of career to know that none was as straightforward as it seemed when they first contacted Forever Inc.

Marina took the project and asked the team who was willing to take it. Jada said that two of her projects were almost ready to give the key; one was in full redecoration stage, and she was free to get a new one.

'After the 'you must cook for me because I conceived such a wonderful man for you' experience, are you sure you can deal with pregnancy hormones and 'I don't really care, but I want it blue' project?'

Nolani smiled. Marina could not portray better the challenges ahead of that project.

'I am all professional. One has nothing to do with the other. Just because my wedding plans are gone to heaven, it doesn't mean that I am willing to lay my career in the same coffin. I can deal with it,' Jada said.

She was very sweet and patient, and maybe that's why she passed with flying colours during her weekend with Brian's parents. She has known Jada since she finished her architectural studies. She was one of her most talented designers. Plus, she was experiencing a personal dilemma. Personally, her life turned upside down since that morning in Sunrise Nursing Home when she had that encounter with Mr Terry Morgan. She couldn't take a holiday just because she was an emotional wreck. Jada didn't want to be pampered, either.

'Marina, Jada can take the project,' she said when all the others started to comment their own opinions on the matter. Jada sent her a glorious smile and took the file from Marina's hand.

'Are you sure about this one?' Marina asked, entering her office surprised at her decision.

'Yes, I am, Marina…'

'You don't know what it means to deal with a broken engagement while smiling to soon-to-be parents pretending everything is okay, when last week Jada said she wants badly to be a mother!'

Nolani looked at her assistant with a subtle smile. She never entrusted her personal life to anyone. Her only witness and support when she hit the bottom and she fought her way up was Eloise. That meant, though, that her allure that 'everything is okay, I never experienced hardship in my whole life' was more successful than she ever thought to be. Being a mystery to all those around you had its own merits.

Nolani intertwined her fingers, observing the combative posture of her assistant. Marina grew up as the only child of two loving parents. They made all the efforts to ensure a bright future for her. She married a few years ago her high school sweetheart and had a two-year-old son. She wasn't just assuming that Marina had it all easy. She said it herself. She did have it easy. She could not grasp the thought of someone not having a stable childhood. Everything out of the perfect picture made Marina overdramatic about it. That was embedded in her personality and Nolani liked her for that. She was very passionate about protecting the unfortunate. That was the reason why she was so surprised by her decision. It was not because she didn't think Jada could do it but because she wanted to protect Jada from heartache.

'You don't know what it would mean for her to deal with this personal baggage when facing family bliss, a couple expecting a child and so on…'

'And you do know…' she said with a low voice.

'No, but I know that if I were to break up with Sunny, I would be a wreck.'

'Brian is not Sunny, Marina. You are going overboard in putting yourself in someone else's shoes. Your Sunny wouldn't let his parents boss you around all weekend, tell you off, show you your place, cook and clean their house and decide to wed after!'

'No, he wouldn't…' Marina acknowledged hesitantly. 'Even so, she loved the guy, Nolani. She has to be broken-hearted!'

'People are different, Marina. They react to different situations differently. Not everyone loves fully, crazy, all committed, full speed ahead, trusting blindly and receiving it all back with the same passion and devotion as you do, Marina. You are a lucky woman, but not everyone is so fortunate. Do not assume that Jada experienced her love story, engagement and her dreams for her own future in the same way you did. She is hurt, I know, but I trust she can continue working, functioning to the best of her ability.'

Marina nodded. Nolani could read in her body language that even if she was ready to back off, she didn't really understand. 'Can you please contact Nick about the Simons' house again and tell him to double check that gas leak they complained about?'

'Ok, boss…'

With Marina out to do what she was asked, she could return to her work, dreading the passing hours and the meeting she agreed to during her lunch break.

# Chapter 4

Nolani paused when she entered the cafeteria at five to one that day. She should have established another place to meet him, to avoid office gossip, but now it was too late. There was a table where all her employees were laughing and chatting. At another table, on the terrace, under a white umbrella, was sitting her worst nightmare. His suit was impeccable; the sunglasses were hiding those amazing green eyes pointed at her since she arrived. He was looking good. He was looking like a cinema star, a women's idol with that hair falling charmingly on his forehead, sitting nonchalantly in his chair sipping his icy cola.

Nolani moved slowly. In the moment he stood up and pulled her chair, a certain chatter in the cafeteria subsided suddenly. Nolani's heart was beating fast. She answered with a low voice to his greeting and put her handbag on the chair next to her. She ordered food, but she couldn't see herself able to swallow anything.

'Have you been to Sunrise today?' he asked taking his glasses off for her to be able to see his unsettling eyes.

'Not on Mondays. I go only if there is any emergency.'

'I've been this weekend to see Rita. Twice. I missed your visits in a matter of minutes, Rita told me. She is very upset with me. For you avoiding her.'

Her blue eyes met his for a short while, before moving towards the napkin on the table. 'I was too upset to say *hi…*'

'On me.'

'On Vanda's psychotic episodes. She will be seen by the Mental Health Team soon to adjust her medication, I hope. She is not well at all.'

'Well, Rita was very upset with me because you didn't even look towards her,' he sighed, playing with his own napkin. 'I'm sorry about your grandmother. If you wouldn't be so upset because of this situation…'

'If I would have said *hi* to Rita? Of course. I wouldn't have stayed to chat with her as I usually do… You've been clear when you asked me to stop my charity visits,' she underlined with a bitter nuance of her voice. 'That, though, wouldn't make me act so rude, not even to say *hi* to a dear friend.'

'I want to take that back,' he shuffled in his chair, while his eyes feasted with her beauty. God, this lady didn't seem to have sweating glands. Her hairdo was all professional, and her whole appearance was entirely feminine, elegant, and sophisticated. Her beautiful blue eyes met his for a couple of seconds before moving slowly toward her perfect manicure. 'I'm sorry for my behaviour that morning. It wasn't a good start at all, me pulling all those conclusions and being so… rude. For Rita's sake and for business' sake, I want us to be friends.'

'On Wednesday morning, the business ends, due to you and me leaving aside all our differences. I don't need to be your friend to call on Rita from time to time.'

Terry looked at her, really taken aback. He did not expect her to be so clearly antagonistic to any idea of friendship between them. He did not expect her to declare so clearly that she wanted nothing to do with him.

'Ma'am, you do keep grudges…' he sighed, leaning against the back of his chair thoughtfully.

'It's not grudges. It's not about the other morning with you taking position as the only Next of Kin of Rita. I understood that. I accepted that. It hurt, but I did. I accept the apologies as well. But…'

She stopped as the waiter brought their order. His green eyes locked with hers, shaded charmingly by the long, black eyelashes. As soon as the waiter was gone, he asked, thumping in a certain rhythm his fingers on the table. 'But?'

'Beside the house I am willing to sell, and you are willing to buy and talking for five minutes to your grandmother when it happens to visit mine, I do not see any ground for friendship, that's all.'

'Does your fine education, prevents you from telling plainly a '*go to hell*,' Miss Arrington?' he asked sarcastically, leaning forward over the table, in a way Nolani found equally aggressive and attractive. She shuffled uncomfortably and sipped a bit of her Cola. He smiled. As a response to his smile, she went ghostly again. God, definitely, this lady didn't hear that when a guy smiles at you, you should get wet, not faint. The thought was not amusing, though. Not amusing at all. He never had this effect on any member of the opposite sex.

'I did not imply that, nor did I want to be rude. Friendship is a serious relationship you grow into, and you commit to, not a statement you make five minutes into meeting someone,' she replied.

'Ok, I take that you are a relationship expert. Does your expertise come from being a Miss with a child?' he asked cynically, digging his fork in his lunch.

Nolani wondered then what made him change in such a bastard. He used to be a lovely young man, all good versus evil, full of dreams. With a slow move, she looked into her bag, got out a note, and put it under her glass, before standing up from the table and leaving the terrace without a word. He looked after her dumbfounded. Ok, he offended her badly. He knew nothing about her to throw that question. His grandmother never told him about any children, her social status, or anything like that. Again, he pulled some wild conclusions and ruined what could have been a nice lunch with… an acquaintance.

Nice lunch for hell. She didn't touch her food. She barely drank something in what should have been her lunch break. She was not comfortable at all around him to eat and drink but to accept his friendship proposal. And to counterattack after with his sarcasm was low of him. It took him a second to decide what to do. He added some notes to her one, and he ran after her. He needed to sort this out before it could aggravate Rita's situation more. Or the sale of the house. He was planning to move his little girl into that house as soon as possible. Her game that she had nothing to lose if he withdrew his offer could be a rouse, but it didn't mean that she couldn't say on Wednesday that she didn't want to sell the house to him. She didn't seem so desperate as to play his friendship game until the contract was done. He managed to catch up with her in front of the building he was working into opening his office. Maybe she had her car parked there? In a few steps, he could throw his arm around her middle, halting her from entering the building.

'I take that back. It was uncalled for,' Terry said while her whole body collapsed against his front. She didn't make a sound, she didn't scream, she didn't turn around to throw her bag in his head. She was frozen, completely frozen, taken by surprise, and she gasped for air.

'I don't know any of your circumstances. I was just being a jerk. Sorry if I offended you, Nolani.'

To feel his breath on her neck, his nose touching her loose hairdo, his arm around her, and her whole body against his, she felt like fainting. Gently, her bloodless fingers moved over the back of his hand, trying to convince him to release her. People were passing by. She knew some of them. She could die of embarrassment. This kind of show in public was unacceptable.

'Let me go, Mr Morgan. I have to return to work. See you on Wednesday morning,' she said breathlessly, trying to collect her chipped self-control.

'Not until we sort this one out.'

'There is nothing to sort out…'

'I offended you…'

'You are very perceptive. You said the truth. I am a Miss with a child. There is nothing to add to that. Let me go.'

He mumbled a self-deprecation before guiding her gently to turn her face towards him. 'I didn't mean to be hurtful.'

'Yes, you did. You are just used to ladies who are ready to give you everything because you are rich and handsome. You throw punches, and they bounce back. I duck. I run. I stay away. So, stay away from me. I do not need your sarcasm, your acid remarks, or your attitude anywhere around me. I don't bounce back. I do not find your aggressive way cool or charming. It doesn't stay good with me. Now let me go!' she demanded, taking a step back.

Terry pulled his arm from her waist. She turned on her heels and entered the building. He could see her through the window, marching on the black marble towards one of the elevators.

There was something aristocratic about her that appealed to him from the very beginning. He understood, through the way she looked with the end of her eye to some people passing by how uncomfortable she was feeling of this public display. He met many ladies who were very well educated, with a huge pride in being fortunate and precious. Many grew up selfish; many came from rich families, which taught them a disproportionate sense of self-worth. They could throw tantrums, make a scene in public, behave immaturely and demanding, considering everyone under their level. This was the only woman who really inspired him to have a true sense of aristocracy. She was proud. She was precious. She was exercising a level of self-control that he found charming, elegant, but infuriating. Because even if she accepted that he was perceptive regarding her situation, he couldn't read her thoroughly. She was perceptive, too. His aggressive way of being was once too many times considered part of his charm. He was used to get away with it. He never said sorry to anyone.

Good, he just did, twice in one day. And he didn't feel forgiven.

Okay… make it three, he thought, when he lay in his hotel bed that night, pressing the call button on his cell and moving it towards his ear. Nothing.

He mumbled something and sat upright in his bed, trying to call again.

Then he really got angry. 'Very mature of you, Miss Arrington,' he growled, throwing the phone across the bed. Miss 'I don't want to be rude' just done it. She did something which never happened to him.

She blocked his number. He growled with frustration. And when he realised that it shouldn't matter and he could live a good life away from *'Miss Sensibility,'* he growled even more frustrated. He jumped out of bed and made a few turns through the room with the air of a lion in the cage.

He dated many ladies. It was not always milk and honey. With some, the relationships were quite rocky. Never, but never happened to him to have his number blocked. It was not like he was pursuing her romantically. It was nothing like that. He was giving her that, the lady was very pretty. Okay, gorgeous, he corrected, pacing at times before turning to make another circle. He pushed his fingers through his hair. He shouldn't have said anything about her boy. That pissed her off badly. She turned all her claws on him and declared him the worse of human race. He never judged a woman for having a child unmarried. What made him say that?

❀ ❀ ❀

The atmosphere in the elegant office of Eloise Burton was perfect for business. He was there with his assistant, Jeremy Wiseman. She came accompanied by a very tall man, with a long beard, cowboy hat and dressed all in black. She presented him as Ian Wilson, the lawyer of her grandmother, Vanda Arrington.

'Did anyone change his mind regarding the Jacaranda property?' asked Eloise after she invited everyone to have a sit.

Eloise Burton was a lady in her sixties, quite robust and short, abounding of energy, and extremely pleasant. Her smile was genuine. Her violet hair was not. Terry smiled, admiring the outrageous colour which, amazingly, suited her. The two ladies seemed to be very close, as they hugged and kissed when Nolani arrived. In comparison,

Nolani looked her best in a pale blue suit and an embroidered blouse around the neck. Her skirt was long to her knees. The shoes were white with very high metallic heels. Amazing how easy she seemed to walk around with them. Her hair was collected in a ponytail down her nape. Her makeup was impeccable. Her attitude was reserved. God, she was beautiful. He smiled towards her. Yesterday, apparently, she passed by; she said *hi* to Rita and chatted for a little while. Rita was in heaven when he visited her with Laura at about half past three in the afternoon.

This time, she didn't go all white with dread. She leaned towards Miss Burton and whispered something. Eloise smiled. As an answer to her question, he answered simply, 'The offer stays put.'

'What we do need, though, is to negotiate the price Miss Arrington is asking for it,' added Wiseman, planting his elbows on the table. Taken aback, Terry looked at him with an expression of 'Where did you brought that from?'

'The price is more than reasonable, considering that Jacaranda is an eighteen-century building which kept throughout all the original features…'

'I don't know about that…' Wiseman said, pulling out a few pictures from his file. They were looking like cut-offs from old newspapers. He took the papers first, examining them with a frown. The walls were looking outrageously opulent.

'Golden silk or actual gold?'

'That was actual gold,' Nolani said, realising, without looking, what he carried in his hand.

'So, you are aware that the state the house is now, even if it is good looking and whatever, does not respect the original features…'

'And… what makes you believe, Mr Wiseman, that those were the original features of the house?' asked Nolani with a delicate smile on her lips. 'The house has been renovated by the new wife of Congressman Lucas Arrington shortly after their marriage in 1956. She was, or so she was convinced she was, British duchess blood of some sort, connecting to a high level of very influential people in Europe. Maybe she was, I'm sure she wasn't, but that is not the point. Vanda Arrington, nee Percy, wanted to prove to everyone around that she was aristocracy, and one way of doing that it was to show it. Redecorating the Jacaranda to show glamour and a high lifestyle was one of her ways to brag about her impressive origins. That does not make Jacaranda original. I don't think Mr Morgan would have looked twice at a house dressed in gold and silk. *Forever* brought back the original features of the house, as the glamour is there, through the very architecture of the house, its large rooms, and the details of the woodwork. I did my research as well, way beyond Lucas' marriage with my grandmother, and this is what I sell. An old house with original features but modernised to today's standards.'

Wiseman nodded his head, taking the paperwork from Miss Burton's hand. Then he proceeded to analyse the content.

'Please, excuse my assistant, ladies… Mr Wilson. He did not discuss with me any of this. I would have discouraged him to do so. I saw the house, I liked it, I agreed with the price…'

'There is something else,' said Wiseman interrupting him. 'Are you sure, Miss Arrington, that your legal status permits you to sell the property of Mrs Vanda Arrington? I did hear you… talking about your grandmother... but to the littlest research I made, Vanda Arrington regarded you as not being her blood, and she was caring for you out of the goodness of her heart.'

'You dug up the dirt in my family... for a house...' she whispered in disbelief.

'A three million house to be exact,' Wiseman gave her his shark smile. 'What do you have to say about that? Or, to be more exact, do you have the paperwork to give you the right to make financial transactions in this old woman's name?'

'Before Mr Wilson gives you all the paperwork to prove that I am in the position to sell the house in the name of my grandmother, I have to say just two things, Mr Wiseman and Mr Morgan. My grandmother is not old at all. She's just 72. She was a woman who considered the opinion of the society higher than her blood relations. It did not stay well with her when her seventeen-year-old daughter made a baby, then ran away from home and abandoned it in her arms. She had big plans for her only daughter. I don't know... so big, like becoming the First Lady of the country. Having a child unmarried and without a father on the birth certificate, it was outrageous. Her tactic about it was understandable. She denied it happened and came up with all kinds of scenarios to make her look good and pose nice. It was cruel, especially for the child implied, but it doesn't mean that I do not have all the adoption papers in order to prove that legally I am Vanda's daughter.' Terry realised that it was not easy for her to say that. She must have had a horrible childhood growing up with a woman who was seeing her as the biggest mistake in her daughter's life. He recalled the park lacking any facility for a child to play. He could easily imagine, growing up in a house with gold and silk walls, that her childhood was very much divided between high society education, piano lessons, and God knows what else she had to learn to be up to her grandmother's standards… with constant reminding that she was unwished, abandoned and a huge mistake.

To corroborate her words, Mr Wilson handed him the legal paperwork, which proved that she was appointed to take care of the financial affairs of Vanda Arrington, her Mental Section decision and so on.

'In this case, it is a surprise that your grandmother didn't give you to somebody else for adoption or something, considering her efforts into hiding a blemish on her name's reputation…' Wiseman commented, analysing the documentation thoroughly.

Terry could notice her face going white, her delicate fingers going gently in a tiny fist, and her breathing becoming fast and erratic. He was wondering now if her, having a child herself unmarried, was a comeback against her grandmother's vanity and ill-placed pride. No, considering her reaction when he brought that up, it was not a decision she took willingly. She was abandoned with a child by her son's father.

'Wiseman, this was cruel and uncalled for. Miss Arrington is not a witness in the stand; she is the lady who agreed to sell me a house. Back off!' he grunted. 'The documentation is more than all right. Let's proceed, please, without further delay!' he ordered, pointing to his assistant.

'My opinion the same,' intervened Miss Burton. Her attitude was not as friendly as at the beginning of the meeting. She was frowning, was a pack of ice, and seemed ready to show them the door.

Unfortunately, in the equation was a house worth three million and they were not ready to leave the chance of selling it flying out the window. Wiseman seemed to have given up and he could finally discuss the contract and sign it. Again, Wiseman tried to negotiate the sum of the items remaining in the house as they had not been actually assessed by an antiquity expert. Nolani handed him a file that proved that they had been assessed, as she was planning to send some to the auction and some to an antiquity shop. The sum they were worth was double the one she asked. 'Thank you… wise… man…' he grunted while he signed a cheque with the whole sum.

They left soon after all the proceedings were done, him with a nice house and land in his hands, Wiseman with a huge smile on his face.

'I loved the little haunted expression on missy's face in there,' Wiseman commented, walking next to him towards their cars. 'When I heard what their family friends were saying… the old witch convinced them all the girl is not related…' he chuckled. 'I had a blast when I saw that they were related, proving the skeletons in their cupboards; that's why it was nice to bring it up… High society, my ass!'

'So, you saw Miss Arrington's birth certificate…' he mumbled thoughtfully.

'No, it was hard to get it in such a short time… I found her in the school register. Miss Nolani Ariel Arrington, born on the 2nd of November 1976. The daughter of Mrs Vanda Arrington was Jessica Augusta Arrington… Do you know her mother was not eighteen when she must've given birth? Hm, apparently, the family friends never saw her pregnant. Vanda was away as well for over a year. She came back with the child and said that because Jessica wanted to move out, she decided to adopt this one. Oh, I love family secrets and the dirt they hide! Did you know that Miss Arrington done exactly the same thing? Just past nineteen, she gave birth to a boy, Tate Nicholas Arrington.'

The curiosity was eating at him badly, the reason why he decided not to jump at his friend's throat for the way he behaved during the meeting. 'How old is the boy?'

'He turned eighteen last week.'

'Dad?'

'Nothing. The girl repeated the story of her mommy,' Wiseman laughed cynically. 'Family friends were saying Vanda flipped big time. She tried to convince the girl to give the boy for adoption. She wouldn't have it. Then she moved from Angel's Marsh in Dallas.'

'Her grandmother was a piece of work… Why did you have to bring this up in the meeting, though?'

'To crack her face a bit. All that demeanour of being a respectful lady was just a piece of crap put on display…'

Terry nodded and then stopped by his car. He was impressed with the detective work Wiseman done on her. The information was flying towards him without being necessary to ask, but his request for them being friends was completely compromised now. First, he acted like a jerk, attacking her for having a child, unmarried. Now Wiseman brought up her ugly abandonment story. She could easily think he ordered the check on her. He sighed, unlocking his car.

'Here is all the research I have done on her,' Wiseman said, giving him the file. 'Everything went well after all, isn't it? You got the house you wanted…'

'Yes, ending up paying the full price on all the furniture, thanks to you. What was that anyway? I approved the asking price!'

'I was hoping she was unprepared for it and she will bring the price down. I did not expect her to have requested an expert evaluation… One can only try… Sorry for that. She said though that you should pay just the price you both agreed. Why did you sign the cheque for the whole sum?'

'You wanted to crack her face, and you ended up cracking mine. I have done it to save some of it… Ok. Is the office furniture coming in today?'

'Tomorrow at the latest. By the end of the week, we will have it all set up.'

'I'll have to go and see *Forever* again. I'll see you at the office after that. I want Laura's bedroom set up for her as soon as possible.'

'I would recommend you then to work with another decorating company,' Wiseman laughed.

'Why would I? They did a great job ripping apart gold and silk walls!'

'Because I don't think Miss Arrington will be up to discuss business with you so soon after I passed her through the grinder in there…'

# Chapter 5

Nolani needed those few minutes alone with herself. Remained that as soon as the transfer reached Vanda's bank account, to have a meeting with Mr Wilson to complete all the arrangements for paying for her grandmother's care. As they agreed, all the money coming from the furniture were to go back in her account. She argued that it was way over the price for redecorating the house. He laughed, and he said they were well deserved. Investing personal money into the house, she doubled the evaluated price.

She distractedly saluted at her employees, before hiding in her office to play rewind the last couple of hours. She needed time to lick her fresh wounds, to restore and get up again. She didn't hear much from the rumours, but she was aware that people were talking about her having that lunch with Terrence Morgan… corroborating with others who witnessed her being manhandled by the same character. She didn't want to know. It would be just some erroneous assumptions people felt they had the right to make regarding somebody's private life. Gossips. Bad words and mathematics… Vanda dreaded them. She was fighting beyond herself to make people believe what she wanted them to.

Nolani was dreading them, too. She grew up with a cult of keeping a good pose in society. Opposite to Vanda she was not jumping over her head in giving people who had no right in her business explanations as to why that happened and what was really going on. She learned the hard way that no one could control what people were talking about you.

Vanda went like crazy into denying their relatedness, but she couldn't fool people. They played their part that they were buying her lies, but everyone could see how alike they were looking. Still, Vanda wasted her life believing she could manipulate people into believing what she led them to believe.

The blows she got during the meeting today were totally unexpected and painful. The man had her past checked! For buying a house! Unbelievable! He made it look like he had nothing to do with it and it was only his assistant decision to bring up those claims, but she knew better. Why would Mr Wiseman make the decision to dig into her past without him requesting that information?

Nolani imagined that being always prepared was vital in his job, but this was not the case. She wondered what else he could discover in the search of her past. What else did he need to know? Did he remember the little grey rat bullied, harassed beyond aggression he protected in that summer so many years ago? He seemed not to. But did she really change so much from the shy girl with dental braces and skinny legs? For a man whose job depended on having a great memory, this didn't seem plausible.

She buried her forehead into the palms of her hands, feeling very nervous and upset. Marina knocked on her door, then popped her head through and smiled. She didn't notice her curious expression because she was too busy to recover her composure.

'Hi, boss. Sorry to bother you. Mr Morgan is here to see you. It's about Jacaranda.'

Her heart made a flip. Her hands went cold, and her ears started burning instantly. She breathed in deeply and forced a smile. 'Let him in, Marina…'

The door opened to let him pass. 'Shall I bring you some coffee?' asked Marina. Terry said he doesn't intend to stay long. Following that, they both declined the coffee.

Terry looked at the wall where the logo of the company, silver on a black background was looking simple and stylish. 'First time I read on the hall downstairs, the logo of the company, amused me terribly. It still makes me smile.'

'Why is that?' Nolani asked, letting him go on with that little chit-chat to eliminate the tension after their morning meeting at the Real Estate Agency.

'Forever. Inc. It contradicts. One is the definition of unlimited. Then it states that it's… limited. Funny.'

'I wanted to call it differently, but I was not allowed.'

'Jacaranda?'

'Never passed my mind…'

'Isn't it a kind of flower? Tree?'

'Yes. Now… what can I do for you?'

'Laura's bedroom. Castles and Disney Princesses. Lots of pink, red and purple. As soon as possible.'

She paused. She sat down thoughtfully, before raising her blue eyes towards him.

'I will appoint Marina, my assistant, to help you with that.'

'Marina being the lady who just introduced me and who was chatting to a brunette lady that she thinks that you and the guy from the eighth floor might be together and we might have a little argument the day before yesterday?' And, of course, him being here didn't help the rumours…

'Marina, the lady who introduced you and who is an expert in designing Disney-themed rooms for children…'

'I don't want just a designed room. I want the same designer who had Jacaranda as a project. I want the same level of sophistication.'

'You are asking too much, Mr Morgan. I want no dealing with you whatsoever from this point further.'

'Because of Wiseman's little tricks today?'

'You are denying having anything to do with it…' Nolani said it with the air that she did not believe him.

'I never denied something which I did. I did pull the wrong conclusions in the first day and we started on the wrong foot. I did insult you Monday and I am sorry I did. I did not give any order to Wiseman to check on you. Never passed my mind. Your story isn't pretty and definitely not a reason to be bullied for. Did you remain pregnant in spite? Sounds like you did.'

'It doesn't matter. I don't owe you a confession. What I did or I didn't do, it's my life, not your business.'

'Fair enough,' he said, strangely, with a smile. 'So, when can I introduce you to Laura?'

'You won't,' she said with a low voice, sitting down in her chair.

It was a bad idea. He was not only a tall man, but he was equally impressive, and instead of having a superior position in front of him, hiding her nervousness behind her desk, he was quite intimidating as he remained standing. His hands were both in the pockets of his business trousers, a gesture observed already for the second time. Was it a gesture to intimidate or one out of anger? Frustration? She looked to the beautiful features of his face to read any sign of being one or another. No, he was amused.

'I pay extra bonus.'

'I can recommend you another girl if you have something against Marina.'

'They are all gossiping about you, Nolani.'

'It doesn't surprise me at all.' And, of course, he was not helping to dissipate the air of ambiguity around them. 'Taking the project, they will have an extra reason to gossip. Like this, you are just a client who bought Jacaranda and wants a room for his child.'

'Sounds like your grandmother pretending you are not her granddaughter to save her from the town gossip.' That, in itself, had the effect of a slap. She acted like she just got one across her face because she lowered her forehead without seeing anything. The feeling of giddiness was just the first in the whirlpool, which seemed to swallow her completely.

'God, you are toxic…' she whispered, averting her eyes. Tears filled their beautiful colour.

'I don't want to be toxic, Nolani, and I swear you are the last person I want to find me like that. I can be tough on my clients and tough on witnesses in the court, but not here with you. All I want is for you to continue to see Rita because she depends on you and your presence in some respects… I want us to be civil with one another and to have a chat from time to time about one subject or another. And definitely, I want you to design Laura's bedroom. I want her not to be just surrounded by princesses but to feel like one. As for the gossip… who cares? Do what you want to do and let them believe whatever they want. Do we have a deal?'

❀ ❀ ❀

She gave Tate the good news regarding the sale of the house. Of course, as soon as the cheque could be cashed out the plan remained to buy a good car for him.

'I passed with Jake next to a car dealer the other day. Seems to have pretty decent cars in there.'

'It's wise to buy a second-hand car, Tate, but we need someone with us to point us in the right direction. With my knowledge about it, we may end up choosing wrong.'

'Jake's dad can come with us. He really knows this stuff. I'm going to ask him if he can do that, can I?'

'Sure.'

Excited with the idea of getting his own car, Tate ran to give a phone call to his best friend to ask if his dad will be willing to help. In the meantime, she had to answer the door. Eloise rang an hour earlier, telling her she would come a bit later to celebrate. The women hugged and kissed, then Nolani helped Eloise to carry inside the bags she came with.

'Where is my godson? I haven't seen him since his birthday!'

'On the phone with Jake, we need his dad to assist us in buying a car for him.'

'Did you cash the cheque?'

'I did. I can touch the money in few days. The bank will call when the money will get into my account.'

'Ok, good. I am glad you managed to get much more on that old stuff. That Wise Ass stepped badly on my nerves. And apparently, on his boss' nerves as well. Mr Morgan looked like stung by a wasp when he done his cheap trick on you.'

Nolani didn't comment, preferring to look busy with the bags Eloise brought with her. Wine, cheese, grapes, crackers… 'That is for Tate. You know how much he liked my phone. I bought a new one for myself…'

'Eloise, but this looks like a new one as well!'

'I promised my godson that I will give it to him when I changed my phone. The problem is that I smashed mine, so I bought a new one for me, and not to break my word…'

'… a new one for him… Eloise, you shouldn't have! Tate would have understood!'

'You would. Tate is a perfect teenage boy who has dreams and expectations. I would hate to disappoint him.'

'I know the feeling,' Nolani sighed.

'Now… going back to Mr Morton… isn't he a gorgeous guy?'

'He is… handsome...' Nolani admitted, preparing Eloise's favourite coffee.

'C'mon! He is absolutely gorgeous! His physique is impressive, his eyes would melt ice… and the way he looked at you during that meeting made me wonder…'

Nolani nodded her head with a bitter laugh. 'Nothing like that, Eloise.'

'You didn't let me finish, Nolani. Is he Tate's dad?'

If the earth would open then and swallow her, Nolani wouldn't be more shocked. Her heart did a somersault, and she leaned against the kitchen unit to restore her balance.

'He is, isn't he?'

'That is the craziest idea I've heard lately, Eloise. Mr Morgan is from somewhere in North Carolina. He lived somewhere in New York. He has nothing to do with me or with Tate.'

'Tate looks like him…'

'This bothered me too when I first saw him,' Nolani said honestly.

'Is he like Tate's dad?'

'Not at all. Tate's dad was a lovely young man, full of dreams, honourable, and fighting bullies. Mr Morgan is a bully.'

'I was talking about green eyes, smashing looks and all.'

'I don't see the gentleman this way at all.'

'You need glasses. The guy is absolutely stunning, and he seems very interested in you. I'm telling you, if these two will ever meet, the confusion will be up to the high sky, Nolani, my darling, because Tate looks just like him. To a fault. If you would have conceived him with Mr Morgan, they wouldn't be more alike!'

Nolani needed air. She needed to scream. She needed to calm down.

'Are you sure the guy is not Tate's dad?'

'If it would have been something to tell you… I would tell you, Eloise.'

The eagle eyes of her best friend remained fixated on the beautiful face of Nolani. Nolani kept her composure over that long analysing glance like her life would depend on it. Eloise sighed, then laughed. 'Amazing. Changing the subject now. How is Vanda?'

'Very challenging. The Mental Health Team changed her medication. She started it on Tuesday.'

'Can she recognise you?'

'No. She doesn't seem to. Yesterday, she called me 'mother.' She seemed so nervous and tense during my visit; it was like she was afraid I would be cross with her if she made a mistake. I don't think she had a happy childhood either, Eloise. She seemed terrified by her mother. That being me…'

In that moment, Tate entered the kitchen with a wide smile across his face.

Eloise jumped to hug him tight with a squeal. 'God, are you going to ever stop growing, my man? You are huge! Taller! How do you deal with the feminine attention?'

'Wow!' he laughed, not at all surprised by the words of his godmother. She was always loud and outspoken, bursting with energy, saying things he liked to hear or touching subjects he didn't want to open. Like girls.

'I'm telling you, if I would've had a handsome guy like you in my high school, I would have been arrested for stalking, man.' Tate just smiled, saying nothing. 'Do you have a girlfriend?'

'I talk to girls… I walk with none. With all the exams coming, I don't need any distraction.'

'Did you think career? What do you want to do after?'

'Family law. I applied to a couple of universities around, see what answers I get.'

'Nothing too far from the nest, hm?' Eloise laughed, pushing her fingers with eagle-looking nails through his hair. Tate changed a look with his mother and rolled his eyes, a sign that Eloise's comment touched a sensitive point.

'It's not about being close or far from the nest, auntie, but it is about money to the end of the day. I don't want to put extra pressure on mom. Plus, if I would have brothers and sisters, if mom were married, I wouldn't think twice. As it is… it's only us two.'

'If it is about the money, young man, I want to tell you that since you were born, I've put monthly money aside for your education or whatever you want to do in life.'

'Oh, Eloise!' Nolani cried. Eloise always has been generous with them. From the moment when she rented a back room to a teenage girl who turned out to be pregnant, she was there for her. They passed through everything together. The birth of Tate. His first steps. His first communion. She supported her in every way through all the hardships of a young and inexperienced mother. She insisted that they could look after Tate in turns, and she could continue her studies. As for the beginning, she worked for the Estate Agency as a secretary for a few years as well as a piano teacher to accommodate their financial needs.

'As about the second,' continued Eloise, pushing her arms around the waist of the young man, 'I am not laughing because you are choosing to study close to home, Tate. You would break my heart to go away.'

Sharing him with his natural mother was the closest she could ever get to being a mother herself. That was sad, but she learnt to live with it. She had the stability a young mother needed but not a child or even a chance of having one. Nolani had the child and needed stability. It seemed a perfect deal between them. Tate planted a kiss on Eloise's head. She pushed her face into his T-shirt and hugged him tight. Then she remembers about the phone…

Nolani loves seeing Tate, so happy to get his new phone. He laughed, hugged Eloise tight, ran to bring his old phone and retrieve the SIM out of it, and half an hour later, they were still talking about the functions of the new phone. She was surprised Tate liked it so much. It did have all the social media applications he was using to keep in touch with his friends, but a lot more business-related, such as conferences, video conferences, recording a meeting to get the minutes after and so on. He loved all that. He had friends passionate about video gaming and stuff like that. Being an active young man, he was not too interested in wasting time in front of a computer or on the phone. She proceeds to prepare a tray of cheese and crackers, listening to their joyful conversation in the background.

When she passed on the corridor that evening, she could hear Tate talking with Jake on the phone about his new gadget. She prepared for bed slowly, with the ability of someone following a ritual. Her mind was wandering loose from the upsetting meeting in the morning with Terry and his assistant, to the argument they had in her office until he convinced her to meet his daughter Laura on Friday afternoon. She sighed. With slow motions, she applied the cream on her face, looking in the mirror on the wall of her bathroom without seeing it.

She was tired. She was closing him one door; he was finding three more. The question was why. Why was he doing all this circus if he did not remember her? Why was he so persistent in dragging her into another project? She was tired of it. The sound of an incoming message made her check her phone. Her knees buckled, and she cried in silent horror.

# Chapter 6

With the windows opened towards the veranda and the massive park, Terry enjoyed the morning in the kitchen of Jacaranda. They moved in last afternoon as soon as he's been told that the transaction went through. To make sure he was not trespassing, he gave a phone call to Mr Wilson, the lawyer of the Arringtons. The man told him that Miss Arrington agreed with him to move in as soon as all the paperwork was signed, so he saw no problem in him and Laura and the childminder to move in Jacaranda.

So, he did. The ladies were excited. They play the piano with a choir of laughter. Laura loved it. She asked Mrs Talon if she could teach her to play the piano. Unfortunately, the piano was not on Mrs Talon's Job Description or talents list. She said so with no embarrassment.

All was going well. With Miss Talon taking the little lady to school today, he could enjoy his coffee in the large kitchen at Jacaranda. He was planning to install a TV unit on the wall so he could enjoy some TV programs while he was cooking. There was some other stuff he was planning to buy to make the home homelier, but he was happy he bought it already furnished. Moving into his first-ever house went smoother than he expected. His cell phone rang loudly in the room. He picked it up and a look at the screen. He registered the caller with surprise. Hm, was she planning to get herself out of the arrangement of meeting Laura in the afternoon?

'Good morning, Nolani. This is a surprise,' he stated, opening the doors towards a very elegant veranda with a table and four chairs. It was ideal to be used for eating or drinking a coffee in the morning fresh air. The day was promising to be very hot.

'I'm sorry to disturb you, Mr Morgan.'

'It's not a bad surprise. After you blocked my number though, there is a surprise that you called me.'

'I did not block your number…'

'Then what does it mean when it says that the recipient is unable to be reached on a certain number?' he smiled, looking at the beautiful arrangement of trees in the park.

'That I put my phone on "Do not disturb". That is different…'

'And you've done that because…'

'I'm rejecting every phone call after ten o'clock at night. My friends are not calling after a certain hour, and business calls are unlikely…'

'Ok, fair enough. How can I help you?'

'I want to postpone the meeting today. Is that okay if I pass by tomorrow, let's say after eleven to talk with your little girl and discuss the room she wants?'

'Are you working on Saturdays?' he frowned. Well, she was trying to come out of the arrangement for today, but the proposal to come on Saturday was not too bad.

'Not usually, but Vanda had an accident at four o'clock in the morning, and she's been rushed to hospital. I'm at the hospital right now, and I doubt I can make it.'

'I'm so sorry, Nolani. Which hospital is she in?'

'Medical City Dallas Hospital. She just had a scan, and the fractures were confirmed. Anyway, is that okay if I come tomorrow instead of today? You may have plans for the weekend…'

'No, it's fine. Laura is excited to meet you, especially after I told her that you know how to play the piano. You can bring your son over too, and we can have a barbecue in the garden, if you want.'

She went all quiet for some long ten seconds, before she answered: 'My son is away with his friends for some football practice tomorrow.'

'Okay, maybe another time, then.'

'See you tomorrow…'

'Sorry for your grandmother's accident. Is everything okay? Do you need some help with anything?'

'No, thank you…' she said rapidly, before disconnecting the call.

She just had a phone call with the office. Marina was going on and on with the feedback they received on Jada's project. She seemed to completely forget how against she was for Jada to receive that project because she was heartbroken. Now, she was giggling at the amazing review *Forever* received for Jada's work. With the gas smell in the other property, Nick discovered that the whole street had the same problem, so they had involved the Atmos Energy Mid-Tex Division. Apparently, the neighbourhood's pipes are made from cast iron, which is a leak-prone material. With that taken care of, they could finally give the keys to the owner and finalise the payment.

Nolani fiddled with her phone, unaware of the other people sitting in the waiting room. She was an emotional vacuum. Besides the professional success and Tate, she had the feeling that everything else was falling apart. All the good life she had built for herself and her son carefully, the happiness and numerous achievements she gathered from the moment she ran from Vanda's house, were vanishing between her thin fingers. She wanted to grab it to hold it tight, but that quiet, happy life was gone.

Terry was in the picture and he didn't seem willing to disappear. Her mother was harassing her with phone calls that she wanted her part of the money, and she wanted it now! Vanda's accident. The effects of it on her well-being and her quality of life were to be devastating. The doctors were considering that there was a possibility she would never be able to walk again.

She pressed the code into the phone to activate it and opened again the message she had received last evening at half past nine. There was a picture of Terry Morgan, elegant and professional in a smart black suit, followed by a picture of Tate in front of his high school, laughing charmingly to a person who was not appearing in the frame. The message was, '*I know… You know… Do they know?*'

Her hands trembled on the phone looking at it lost. Who could have sent that? The number was anonymous. Only the thought that her son was spied on and photographed by God knows who and with what intentions made her sick to her stomach. She turned off the screen and left the phone to slide into her shoulder bag.

Lost in her thoughts, she didn't notice the man walking towards her with two plastic cups with steaming coffee. She didn't turn her head when he sat down next to her, didn't give any sign that she was aware of him being there, or that the people were looking with curiosity in their direction, acknowledging what a beautiful couple they were making. With her legs elegantly crossed, with the bag hanging loosely by her fingers touching the floor, looking down, shoulders down, she seemed overwhelmed and defeated.

'I brought you coffee, Nolani. Any news?'

She startled and turned her head so fast that her neck could've snapped. The shock of finding him sitting next to her was visible on her beautiful face. When he looked into her eyes, he could see the horror, the fear, the expression of a hunted animal before it's gunned down. He didn't like it. He hoped he was not the cause of that expression because he never ever wanted to cause such a reaction in a woman. Less one he was attracted to so badly. Slowly, carefully, she regained her composure. Her art of dissimulation was remarkable, but he found it deeply unsettling. She didn't want to share her grief with anybody, even less with him.

'What are you doing here, Mr Morgan?'

'Call me Terry. And I brought you some coffee. I thought you might need the company and the support.'

'Thank you,' she whispered, taking the cup he handed to her.

'I thought your son would be here. In that case, I was preparing for a quick exit… Is he at school?'

Nolani looked into his eyes wondering why this sudden interest in Tate. Did he know something? Did anyone tell him something? First was inviting her with Tate to a barbecue. Now, he mentioned that he was expecting Tate to be here. She couldn't find in his green eyes anything more than genuine worry for her and moved her eyes towards the floor. 'I kept Tate away from Vanda. He has no reason to be involved in any of this.'

'Oh…'

'Vanda asked me to have an abortion when she found out I was expecting. Then she came out with the idea to give him up for adoption. Why would I imply in her care a child she wanted dead or away because he was tainting her image in Angel's Marsh?'

'She was awful, Nolani. All that crap she was saying that you are not her granddaughter to save face in her society… Why are you doing this for her?'

Nolani remained quiet for a few long seconds. She didn't look at him when she sighed. 'She did raise me. In her own way, Vanda's way, she did care for me. She cared more about what others were saying, but she did take care of me when my own mother abandoned me.'

'Are you keeping in touch with her?'

'She calls…' Nolani said with a low voice.

'Does she regret she abandoned you?'

'She wants her part of the money from selling Jacaranda. And she keeps asking when the old hag will… you know…'

'God, my family is not close either, but it's not so… evil, Nolani.'

'Rita said she is the mother of your dad. She also said that you grew up in North Carolina close to your mother's side.'

'Yeah, I'm the only grandson they have. My mom has a sister. She has three daughters…'

'What made you move here so suddenly? All your life was in New York and North Carolina.'

'I still have my office in New York. I left my associates to run it, and I decided to move here. I don't know why Rita wanted to reside here, either. She is from Austin. She has many friends she is writing to, as you know well. Practically, I wanted to be close to her, after my dad passed away. And after the divorce I passed through, I wanted a new start for me and Laura.'

Nolani wanted to ask why he had the girl after the divorce. Probably, with his money, power, and connections in the field of law, he had no problem getting full custody of his daughter. She wouldn't be surprised. She sipped a bit from the coffee and remained quiet looking in a blank point.

'If you didn't order any check on me, why did Mr Wiseman take the freedom to do so?'

'Jeremy is a very ambitious detective. He loves being prepared for whatever comes in the courtroom. Usually, I appreciate his eagerness and his detective work. I hired him, especially for his talents. As I was curious about you, I am happy he did it.'

Nolani looked at him, taken aback. 'But you said…'

'I did not order him to check on you. I looked into the file he gave me, though.'

Nolani's hand started to shake uncontrollably, and she left the cup on the side. Were there any pictures of Tate? Anything that could lead him to think… He didn't seem to display any of the reactions she would have expected. Could it have been Mr Wiseman, the person who sent her the message last evening? Would he keep the secret from his boss and best friend if he discovered that the eighteen-year-old son of a lady, he was checking on just to be prepared for a house sale, is the spitting image of him?

'I understand how this would make you feel, Nolani. Usually this kind of work makes people feel uneasy, their privacy being invaded by a meddling lawyer. But sometimes it is necessary. It wasn't in your case. You are not a client or a key witness. I understand it bothers you.'

'So, besides the statements of so-called Vanda's friends, what else do you have on me?'

'Your home address, your landline number, your date of birth, Tate's date of birth… and some statements full of crap of some very high society limited heads who were swearing they were Vanda's friends. I can't see any of them here. As it seems, your grandmother cared more about them than about you.'

'I didn't call any of them. They are not aware of Vanda's state of mind. She wouldn't appreciate me involving them.'

'And you think you own her this.'

'She's the only parent I know. Good or bad, she's all I know…'

He pushed his arm around her. If he had been a venomous snake, she wouldn't have tensed more. Then, one thought passed through his mind. Could her son be the result of a crime? The way she was holding him to an arm's distance, tensing when touched, stating she wants no dealings with him… He looked down to her face. Her simple make-up was impeccable. Her long lashes enriched with mascara were shading the most incredible blue eyes he had ever seen in his life. This triggered a long-lost memory of another pair of blue eyes full of wonder, pain, and infinite trust. He sighed. He lost a lifetime friendship that summer. The memory was always accompanied by suffocating guilt, so he fought that memory with a shake of his head and leaned his cheek against her forehead. His embrace got tighter.

In that moment, the doctor came out and called out for her. He stood up with her and went to meet the professional.

'How is she, doctor Patel?' she asked reading his name on his ID exposed on his chest.

'Not good, I'm afraid. The fractured hip wouldn't have been a problem. A hip replacement surgery, some physio hours, and time would have helped her to be mobile again. She has a spine fracture, unfortunately. This, considering her co-morbidities and general health… it's not good news. It's hard now to say if she has paralysis. She's been given some morphine. Also, we are now conducting some urine tests and blood tests. It's a wait-and-see basically…'

'Can I see her, doctor?'

'Sure. The nurses will let you know when you can go in.'

'Thank you…'

She sighed, looking after him. Terry looked down to her gravely. 'It sounds serious, Nolani. How did she fall?'

'Down the stairs. She had one of her psychotic episodes. The staff there said it was an accident waiting to happen because she was completely unaware of the risks when she got into one. Well, it did happen...'

Soon after, one of the nurses came and told them they can go and see Vanda. There was not too much to see. She seemed so frail, so pale and vulnerable in her hospital gown. She had a drip in her arm.

'Be aware, when she wakes up, she might pull it off,' Nolani warned the nurse. 'Mentally, she is not in the right place.'

'We know what we are doing,' the nurse answered, distracted. Terry frowned, not happy with the attitude, but Nolani just nodded and leaned over her grandmother. With a gentle gesture, she touched her small hand and then looked at her face. She was the spitting image of Vanda Arrington, and Tate was the spitting image of his father. She knew how she was going to look when reaching her age. She smiled sadly. 'If there are any changes, can I be informed? I will have my cell phone with me all the time. I gave the number to the nurses' unit with all the information necessary.'

'What changes will that be? She's not going to get out of that bed very soon and dance…'

Nolani walked towards the door, ignoring the comment. It was already four in the afternoon, and she promised Tate they would go with Jake's dad to look for a car. Terry memorised the name on the ID and walked after Nolani. Another comment from the nurses made him see red. 'They are all expecting us to stay on the phone and give them information, but when they storm in here, they don't stay more than five minutes.'

He turned back and hissed between his teeth just a few words. Left the girls completely livid before he stormed after her. When she entered the lift, he was next to her.

'You had to tell them something…' she said with a very low voice.

'Yeah…' he sighed. 'Do you want me to drive you home?'

'No, thank you. I need to rush. I promised my son to go with him to buy him his first car. After that, I think I will come back to stay a bit longer with Vanda.'

'Shall I come and stay with you?'

'And Laura?'

'She can stay home with Miss Talon. She is the childminder I hired as soon as I arrived in Dallas.'

'I'm okay, but thank you for the offer…' He walked with her to her car, commenting:

'Pushing me away again. I'm starting to get used to it. You are doing it every time we meet.'

'It's not that, it's just unnecessary. My grandmother is not a pretty view, and spending time in the hospital is not a pleasurable pastime. I will co…' Suddenly she halted her walk on her high hills and got out a weak cry in horror.

# Chapter 7

He froze in place and looked in the direction she was looking. He recognized her car; then his eyes moved to what caused her reaction. There was a white piece of paper with red writing on it. The ink was pouring out from every letter like in the movies when criminals were writing messages with blood. "TELL HIM OR I…'

Whatever the meaning of that was, she was white and shaking seriously. There was no threat of attack or something. Was there? Or what?

'Nolani, what does it mean? Did you ever get messages like that?' She nodded frantically. 'Is this why you put your phone at night on 'Do Not disturb?' Do they call?'

She moved her head positively, looking like a ghost. He moved his arms around her waist and pulled her in his arms in a tight embrace. 'When did it start? Tell me!'

'A couple of weeks ago.'

'Man or woman?'

'Whisper. Low growl. I don't really know…'

'Sexual connotations?'

She nodded negatively. With a gesture, he took the piece of paper and put it to his nose. No blood. Paint. It didn't look fresh either. 'Are you into painting? Is this acrylic paint or gauche?'

Nolani looked. 'Acrylic, I think.' She thought it was blood. Now to come to realise that it was just a text written with a finger possibly and red paint, she felt embarrassed for her uncontrolled first reaction.

'I… I need to go. I'm Okay, I need to go. This is stupid. This is childish…'

'But scares you just the same, Nolani. You don't know what is wrong with this person. You should contact the police.'

'They are not threatening my life. The threat is that they will tell… someone… something…'

'No, Nolani. The message is "TELL HIM OR I…" Can be anything. It leaves room for any action. *I will. I will ruin your life. I will kill you.* Anything. Plus, this message hasn't been left in a place you usually go. Work. Home. It means that somebody followed you here to leave you this on the windscreen. Do you know what they are referring to? Tell him… *who*? And *what*?'

'I need to go, Terry. My son is waiting for me. This silly game of someone…'

'Can be dangerous, Nolani. And if you don't tell me, I can't help you.'

'I don't need your help.'

With those words, she opened the driver's door of her car and pushed the key into the ignition.

'See you tomorrow, Nolani. We will talk more about it tomorrow…'

Nolani left behind the parking spot and Terry, feeling numb. There was so much going on, she didn't know how to operate normally. She grew up hiding her emotions because to the display of any of it, her grandmother was saying that she was behaving inadequately. She was bullied in school for not having parents, for being skinny and shy, for being, at times, just the perfect target for pocking fun at. She had no one to rely on telling how she felt because Vanda didn't want to hear any of it. That intensified her loneliness, but what the others were laughing at, was none of her doing. She never felt so overwhelmed with fear like she was feeling now. This time, it was her fault. To some extent, she was deceptive, and somebody out there spotted a great similarity between her son and Terry. Before, with Terry in New York, living his own life, there was never the case, but now with Terry everywhere around her… 'Oh, God…'

Why would someone get to the extent of leaving that sinister piece of paper? That was a bit too much, it was something overdramatic about it. It was meant to scare the life out of her, not just a threat that the truth would come out one way or another. The phone calls at night. It was like the depiction in thriller movies with stalkers and criminals in the shadows. That was nothing funny about it. She was scared. Scared for Tate. Who could tell that this was only about the secret of his birth and not potentially harmful to him?

To stop this avalanche, she could tell them. It would turn their lives upside-down, but whatever the consequences, they could live with it. What insurance could she get that this sinister game would stop?

To function, she learnt to compartmentalize the problems into little boxes she could deal with, one at a time, when it was necessary. Now, it was like all the boxes were open, and she had to deal with all the problems at once. Vanda's accident. Tate's paternity. Terry's presence and his stubbornness to get as many entrance doors opened in her quiet life. The whispering night caller freaked her out. Anonymous messages. Sinister messages. Feeling followed. Having Tate followed. She needed a break from everything to regain control.

A quiet weekend to think about it all, sort all the problems out and close her little mental boxes.

Nolani could just dream about it. For the sake of Tate, she had to close the door on everything and simulate that everything was fine when she met him, Jake, and his dad at the car dealer. She looked at different cars, listened to what Howard Godstone, Jake's dad, had to say about one or another, the enthusiasm of Tate when he found that five-year-old car. Jake's dad said that the car seemed in a perfect state. The dealer said that it belonged to a client who was changing the cars as often as some people were changing cell phones. The price was high, but she was planning to pay even more for a good, reliable car for her son. She bought it. Tate was ecstatic.

Nolani loved to go after and celebrate Tate's new car in McDonald's with the boys and Howard. She indulged herself in the fast, joyful, and effortless conversation.

She was happy when Jake and his dad invited Tate to remain in their house overnight. Tate promised he would call her in the morning, before heading to the football training session and that he would be home Saturday evening. Howard Godstone was an army instructor; he was kind to her boy, and she felt that while in his house, Tate was protected.

She went home alone, had a shower and changed her clothes before going back to the hospital. There, she stayed for hours next to the bed of a vulnerable Vanda, lost in a drug-induced sleep. She used that time to think, to analyse, to sort out her thoughts. It was about three o'clock when she returned to the empty house. She was too tired and moved automatically to unlock her door, disarm her house alarm, and enter her house. She did not observe the silhouette hiding in the darkness, one foot away from her.

❀ ❀ ❀

Wiseman leaned back in the chair, breathing in the scented air of the Jacaranda garden, sipping relaxed, a can of beer. The piece of paper left on Nolani's car remained on the table, where Terry left it for his observing eye.

'Little aristo-cat plays the damsel in distress,' he giggled, nodding his head in disbelief.

'So… you think it is farfetched,' Terry said thoughtfully.

'It's… too sappy? Looks like an amateur job, that's all. Did she touch the paper?'

'No, I did. Can you ask your friend to have a look at it and run it for prints?'

'It has all the chances to come empty, Terry. If the person never committed a crime and is not in the database…' He lifted his shoulders unimpressed. 'You like her, hm?'

Terry seemed lost in a trail of thoughts. 'Sorry?'

'You seem to like her? Or is it just your protective side jumping to save the princess? She may just try to attract your attention by playing a mystery game, knowing that as a criminal defence lawyer, you would not resist…'

'She didn't know I would come to the hospital to see her. She didn't give any message, or any phone call while I was there. The message was for her, not for me. Stop being so incredulous and

76

misogynistic. I know that Kate broke your heart, but don't judge Nolani for what Kate did, ok?'

Wiseman shuffled in the chair, feeling uncomfortable. He didn't like to be so easy to read for Terry. That episode of his life being brought up was making him feel like an idiot. Again.

'I couldn't find a birth certificate, Terry. There is one registered birth. No father. Mother Jessica Augusta Arrington, 1976, but the child's name doesn't fit. The name is…' He got out a piece of paper and had a look at it. 'Summer Arrington… Not Nolani Ariel Arrington. The birth was registered… keep in mind… Louisiana.'

'What does that mean? That she could be adopted, and her grandmother fed her a lot of bullshit? That's nothing to laugh about it. And it doesn't make sense. The two are very alike… Possibly the grandmother changed the name because it was not posh enough?'

'Summer sounds posh enough… There is only one problem. There is a death certificate for Summer Arrington in August 1977. Cause of death… Sudden Infant Death Syndrome, also known as cot death… What do you say now?'

'Why do you keep looking into it? Ok, sounds interesting, and the mystery kills me, but… just to crack her face? Really? What does she have to do with you paying child support for a child that is not yours?'

Wiseman mumbled, visibly upset. That was a painful blow, and other than his nose for mystery and willingness to expose the little Miss Arrington as a fraud, he had no explanation for why he kept digging into her past.

'Clearly, she doesn't know all this,' he argued.

'Yeah, but you are not doing all this to shed some light on her birth mystery. You are doing it to ruin everything she knows, Jeremy.'

'Doesn't it bother you that she might be an identity fraud?'

'Hardly I can accuse a woman who knows only what she's been told since she was in diapers, an identity fraud. Blame the grandmother. Legally, she has been adopted by Vanda Arrington who had her full custody. Wherever she comes from… yes, it is interesting to find out, and I think she would appreciate knowing, to give her some closure, but… as I said, legally, she is not the granddaughter but the adoptive daughter of Vanda Arrington; she has the legal power to represent her financially and in health-related problems. I investigated it when Mrs Arrington's lawyer gave us the paperwork.'

'Hm… this makes me think… how old was the grandma when she… became a grandmother? Thirty-something? Forty?'

'Okay…'

'Miss Arrington said her grandmother hardly can be named an old lady, as she is seventy-two…'

'And this makes you think…'

'What if the image-conscious grandmother had also a child in 1976? What if the so-called adopted daughter was, in fact…'

'Her natural mother?'

'She was a widow since Jessica Arrington was ten. Society would slam her for having a child, unmarried… if she thought she could manipulate society into thinking her respectability was unblemished… placing the immorality on a daughter who anyway was pregnant in the same period of time and, very conveniently, disappeared somewhere in Louisiana… as you said, they do look alike. This would increase the confusion of Miss Arrington… What do you say? Shall I investigate this trail? See what I can find?'

'Yeah…' Terry moaned, placing his hands into his pockets.

'Now, about the problem at hand… I can't promise you anything, but I'll call my friend.' Wiseman extracted a bag from his pocket and placed the piece of paper in it without touching it. With those words, he stood up thoughtfully. 'Did she tell you anything? What is it all about? Who is *him*? *Tell him* what?'

'She wouldn't disclose it to me. She dismissed my help.'

'That can be a fine strategy to catch a nice-looking, successful, rich guy…'

'She doesn't need strategies to catch me, Wiseman. I'm all into her. The problem is that she seems…'

'Well?' Wiseman asked when Terry delayed finishing what he started to say.

'That she hates my guts,' Terry sighed. 'I don't feel like my good looks, successful career, or fortune are enough to impress this lady. I'm having a hard time negotiating every meeting with her. I feel like an intruder. The way she reacts every time I try to touch her… if I would be a croc, she would react more friendly…'

'So… do you think that son of hers… might be the result of a rape?'

# Chapter 8

Terry prepared everything for the barbecue. Laura was running around the park, staying in his sight as instructed. Miss Talon left the house in the morning for her grandson's eleventh birthday party. Dressed in jeans, trainers, and a black T-shirt, he started the fire. It was a little past eleven, and he started to think that Nolani was going to use the hospital excuse to avoid this arrangement as well.

He didn't finish the thought when he could hear an engine and the noise of a car entering the front pavement of the property. He walked fast to have a look at who was coming. Seeing her coming out of the car in her high heels and professional suit didn't impress him much. The invitation was for a barbecue. Her message was, 'I'm here just to talk with your daughter about how she wants the room.' Terry made her a sign pointing where they were and left her to find her way. If anyone knew that property like the palm of their hands, that was her. In a few minutes, he could see her appearing through the veranda and climbing down the stairs towards the barbecue site.

'Hi, Nolani. Any news about the grandmother?'

'She pulled out her needles this morning. The same nurse was there… lots of blood everywhere, and she was frantic that she did not expect such a sweet patient to be so violent… Vanda was visibly in pain. They managed to administer her another dose of morphine. That was ugly.'

'You can make a formal complaint…'

'I don't want to. I enjoyed telling her just, 'You told me not to tell you how to do your job…' Nolani lifted her shoulders with a sigh.

'Really, Nolani. You can make a formal complaint against the nurse. I was your witness. She could have done something to avoid the mess… Did you get the car for your son?'

'Yes, I did…'

Laura was coming running on the field as soon as she managed to spot her arrival. Her long black hair was flying with every move. She was a gorgeous child. Her eyes, as expected, were green. 'Hello!' she cried out of breath when she was close enough.

'Hello, Laura…'

'Daddy, she looks like a Barbie Doll!' said Laura, exploring Nolani's beauty in pure awe. Terry laughed. Nolani blushed. The compliment was unexpected.

'Laura, she is Miss Nolani Arrington, the lady who sold us the house… Nolani, she is my daughter, Laura…'

'Laura Gabriella Morgan,' the little girl recited with pride.

'You wouldn't guess what Miss Arrington's middle name is…' Terry said with a smile. To the 'Huh?' of his daughter, he continued: 'Ariel.'

'That's not right. She is blonde. She looks more like Princess Aurora than Ariel. Ariel has red hair, green eyes, and a fishtail!'

Nolani laughed. Terry looked towards her, amazed by the change of attitude. She was usually so weary of him, he never saw her smiling but laughing wholeheartedly. She moved towards the first chair, remaining graciously on her feet despite the uneven ground.

'So, Miss Laura Gabriella Morgan,' she recited carefully. 'Daddy said you want a princess room.'

'A Disney princess room…' Laura corrected her, coming close and sitting in the chair facing Nolani. God, she was adorable! It reminded her so much of Tate being her age! Nolani's heart made a tumble. She smiled with that precious air of hers, not realising what an impact she was having upon the little girl.

'What is your favourite princess?'

'Cinderella… Aurora… Ariel…'

'Okay… but between them… What is the most favourite of all?' Terry smiled. Cinderella. He giggled when he heard his daughter giving the expected answer. 'Now the question is, do you really want Cinderella painted on the wall or a Cinderella princess room? The difference is that if you ever change your mind and another princess becomes your most favourite, it will cost your daddy a dear price to take Cinderella down and replace it. In the second case, though… your room will look like a precious palace room, with a princess bed, fancy furniture, cushions, and sofa… in which you will feel like a princess. I can add a fancy dressing table… all in Cinderella theme colours, and if you really want a Cinderella to reside in your room, with you, we can get a natural size cardboard cut Cinderella standing… more… I can add ornaments with the pumpkin carriage… the mice… the Fairy Godmother… what would you like, Laura?'

His little girl looked at him, a bit puzzled. Terry thought of something even less extravagant, like a Disney princesses' wallpaper with the whole bunch of them smiling silly.

'What would you choose?' Laura asked with a wide smile on her face.

'It's not about me, Laura. You are going to sleep in it for the next years.'

'I like the princess room… but… no Cinderella on the wall?'

'No Cinderella on the wall.'

'Can it be pink?'

'Do you want it classy?' Laura nodded. 'Then I would go for the pink cherry tree from…'

'From Mulan?!' Laura asked excitedly.

'Without Mulan, though.' She saw Laura ready to add something and said with a smile: '…or Mushu…'

'Is that the funny dragon?' Terry asked, putting the meat on the barbecue grill.

The conversation continued about other ideas, but ultimately, Nolani persuaded Laura into having a princess-themed bedroom in which she was to feel like a princess. Nolani got out a catalogue, and, alongside Laura, they looked through it. Laura said yes to a white canopy bed, a gorgeous wardrobe with sculpted white wood, a dressing table with a fancy mirror… At the end of the conversation, she didn't even want the cardboard-cut Cinderella anymore.

'So… we are redecorating the room just by changing the furniture,' he concluded, when Laura went into the house to use the toilet and bring her favourite doll to show it to Nolani.

'Not really. I will send Pierre to apply a cast frame and paint the cherry blossom tree. That would give her that touch of pink she wants and classy look. By the end of next week, Laura can have her princess bedroom.'

Nolani looked at the watch, and she gave signs she was preparing to leave.

'Laura wants to show you her doll. And I promised her you would eat with us…' said Terry.

'You shouldn't have promised her that. I did not say I will stay.'

He smiled, leaning with a hip against the table. God, he looked good in jeans! His smile left her feeling all giddy. Instead of looking impressed by his attractiveness, she went all cold and reserved. This woman was killing him! He knew he was looking good. He tried multiple outfits before going for this combination. The T-shirt outlined the wide chest and muscles he acquired playing American football in his youth and maintained through intensive sessions in the gym. The jeans… well, were outlining that he was a very well-equipped male. His secretary in New York used to call him a hunk. Miss Arrington was not looking impressed at all. So, he decided to change the subject. 'Other phone calls? I imagined that you couldn't put your phone on 'do not disturb' last night because of the hospital problem.'

She moved her eyes from him to the trees and sighed. 'No. I've been to the hospital until three in the morning. No phone calls.'

'Other messages like that silly letter we found yesterday on your car?' Nolani answered no. He didn't believe her. 'What was this time?'

'Nothing…'

'What was it? Where was it?'

She heard Laura running out of the house, and she used the child not only to end the subject there but to make an elegant exit as well. She excused herself as having to honour another arrangement, and after a few minutes, she was gone. After her rapid exit, he swore he would not run after her again. He had never been so desperate after a woman to pursue her to such an extent.

She was more than clear. She didn't want him around; she didn't want him in her life. Well, then, so be it!

But then, there was that note on her car which was bothering him. And God knows what she received that morning. And the phone calls. And the theories of Wiseman regarding her origins.

'Is she a real princess, daddy?' Laura asked him. 'She looks like a real princess.'

Terry had to give her right. Her manners, her gestures, nothing was calculated. Even when she was upset and mad at him, he couldn't accuse her of bad manners. She was so natural in her demeanour she could very much be one. 'I think she is, Laura. She doesn't live in a palace. She lived in this house. But yeah… I think she is a princess. She plays piano… She dances… She is clever, successful in her business… She is what I call a modern princess. No fancy dress but nevertheless elegant…'

'I have to learn a lot to be like her, daddy.'

'Yeah…' he answered, making a gesture to sit with him at the table in the garden. *And to have a very sad childhood,* he added for himself.

'Can you be a modern prince, daddy?'

'I very much doubt, sweetheart,' he smiled. 'Try to eat something.'

'Do you think she liked my choices for my room?'

'I don't think she has to like them. It will be your room.'

He began to feel sorry he made her acquaintance to his daughter. She left an impression all right on the little girl. The good part was that he could talk about her with someone without making that person question his interest. The bad part was… he talked to Laura about nothing but her for the rest of the day.

❀ ❀ ❀

Tate noticed him for more than half of the game, sitting on the bench, cheering. He did have a good look at the guy. He didn't like him. His instinct of self-preservation was leading him to keep his distance. Belligerent smile. Self-conscious attitude. Good looking, he was giving him that.

The most annoying part was that the guy kept cheering his name. He changed a couple of looks with Jake and crossed his eyes. He didn't look directly at him.

'Who's that guy?' asked Jake when they stopped to regroup.

'I have no idea, but I saw him a couple of times already in the last few days. He was around to the car dealer. He was looking directly at me but mostly at my mom. I don't like it, to be honest, Jake.'

'Got it. I'll tell dad to keep an eye on him…'

'I think he does already. I saw your dad looking at him a couple of times…'

The boys continued their training, listening to the instructions of their coach and managed to mark extra points.

'Well done, Tate! You're on fire, boy! Break those asses!'

'God, the guy is annoying…' Tate mumbled.

Tate did his best to concentrate the rest of the game while ignoring the noisy cheering. Even the other boys asked him who the guy was. The answer was simple. He had no idea.

At the finish of the game, he made sure he went with all the boys to change. The discussion was mostly about the guy Tate saw following him and his mom around. When they went out, his friends made a point that the guy waiting on a side for an opportunity had no chance to be face to face with him. Jake's dad had the attitude of a watchful eagle.

Losing the chance to have the conversation he had in plan with the boy, he shouted at him, willing to shake him a bit: 'You are better than your old man, Tate, my boy!'

Tate paced for a few seconds, before deciding what he was going to do. His first reaction would have been to run to the man to ask what he meant by that. Did he really know his dad? Did he know who his dad was? His mom told him that the guy was playing in the junior division, and he seemed to have great plans to enter the professional football. She told him that his nickname was Stampede, but she never learnt his real name.

She told him that she met him in Florida, she saw him playing football on the beach with his friends, and after the night with him, she felt embarrassed and she ran away. Knowing his mom, he knew she was telling the truth. Why then run to a man he never met in his life to ask questions about his dad? The guy didn't inspire him much respect, less trust, and he seemed slippery like a reptile. With that conclusion, he jumped in his car, said goodbye to the boys, Jake, and left. Remaining behind, the man smiled sarcastically. 'That will shake him a bit…'

# Chapter 9

Nolani sat on the sofa, thoughtfully drinking a cup of hot chocolate. She bent her knees up looking lost in a blank point.

'Mom, have you seen the guy at the car dealers?' Tate asked, sitting down next to her. Nolani startled and looked at him, alerted.

'What guy are you talking about, Tate? No, I haven't.'

'There was this guy. Tall. Six foot three, I think. Big guy. Blond. Goatee. Blue eyes, I think. He was looking at me yesterday but mostly at you. Belligerent smile. A bull-sized bully, to be precise.'

'No, I haven't, Tate. Why?'

'He was today to my football training. Cheering me. '*Well done, Tate boy!*' '*Break their asses, Tate!*' That didn't give me a good feeling at all.'

'No, especially if you don't know the person, Tate,' she said worriedly.

'The thing is… before we left… he shouted at me, '*You are better than your old man, Tate!*'

Nolani started to shake uncontrollably, hot chocolate flying everywhere, her eyes full of acknowledgement. 'Oh, my God!' she whimpered, not seeing any place where to put her cup. Tate took her cup away from her and put it on the table, but other than that, he was watching her carefully.

'Do you know him, mom?' he asked, alerted by her reaction.

'I hope he is not who I think he is,' she mumbled, looking at her trembling hands, devastated. Took her minutes to gather herself together and even more to create a logical trail of thoughts. Her heart was thumping painfully in her chest, her stomach was like a ball of stone, her ears burning. Her life was crumbling between her hands, and the truth was that everything would have been easier if Terry had given her any sign that he remembered her. It wouldn't have left room for silly games with sinister messages, scary phone calls, and threatening stalking. Nobody could give her the insurance that if she would tell them both, Tate and Terry about each other, this would stop. She did not know what that person's real intentions were, but was nothing good. The fact that he was following Tate, was not staying well with her. The description… of course, could be anyone, but she knew only one fitting that description who knew both her and Terry. His nickname was Hammer. She never learnt his real name either. 'I told you that your dad had a best friend who was very mean to me. Your dad intervened, asking him to control himself. They had a massive, violent fight. Hammer, this was his nickname, came over to me, drunk at night, while I was sleeping. He tried to…' She looked at her son shyly and moved her eyes down.

'I got that… I'm sorry, mom…'

'Hammer was calling me names and that I was asking for it… he was there to teach me some manners… something to that extent… Your dad came into my room after him and stopped him. I was in pain, in shock… I know they threw blows very strongly in between, and to the end, Hammer was forced to leave… Your dad was nice, Tate. He remained to comfort me. He did not use it as a rouse to seduce me in any way, I swear. One thing led to the other. I cried a lot that night for my lack of love and my necessity to feel loved. It seemed the right thing to do. I wanted to give myself to him. He was my first. My one and only. Are you okay with that?'

Tate nodded, listening, fascinated again by the story of the night of his conception.

'In the morning light, what seemed so right was causing me huge embarrassment. I was ashamed of myself. He left to check with Hammer. I gathered my things, and I left the resort without looking back. I don't know what happened between them, if they managed to salvage their friendship and repair the rift which put them in two different positions that night. Hammer was a bully with a huge ego. He picked on me not because I was pretty or shy… but because I didn't have the backup of a group of friends. I was on my own, with no one to look after me.'

'And you think the man today…'

'It could be Hammer. I can't know for sure, but the description fits, and he is the only one who knows me and your dad. You are the spitting image of him, Tate. Your dad was a very handsome man, who never knew that on that night… he left me pregnant.'

'Now was enough for the guy to recognise you and to have a look at me to know who my dad is.'

'It just means one thing, Tate. He is up to no good. Please, stay away from him. I…' she moved her eyes away and sighed. 'Your dad moved recently to Dallas, and I met him…' Tate was startled with all his being, looking at her in disbelief.

'You met him!'

'But there is a problem. He doesn't remember me. I couldn't just go to him to tell him he fathered my son because… he doesn't remember me.'

'You could remind him…' Tate said with a low voice.

'I was afraid, Tate, but for your good, for your safety, I will do it. If that is Hammer, it means that he followed your dad here. I don't know if they are still friends or if there are other motives more sinister, but your dad needs to know that Hammer followed you at your school.' She didn't tell him about the threats she received because she didn't want him to panic or to do God knows what.

'What is his name, mom? What's my dad's name?' The expression on Tate's face was full of excitement and expectation. To grow up without a father, pure and simple, because his mom didn't know his name was one. To find out that his mom met him and his name was no longer a mystery was completely different.

'Terrence… Terry Morgan. Is the gentleman who asked me the other day in the car to meet him at the cafeteria… The same man who… bought my grandmother's house.'

'God Almighty!' Tate jumped with his entire being. His face was lighted by pure joy; his body language was chaotic.

'Tate… please… we don't know how he will react when he finds out about you…'

'I can wait,' the boy said with a shy smile. He could barely keep his joy contained. He was like a well-trained dog who wanted to run like crazy on the field, but he must stay low because the order was *sit*. Nolani's heart was bleeding. She adored her child beyond herself. She felt selfish for putting herself first, pushing away the man her son needed to feel complete. She knew how it feels not to know where you are coming from, to be rejected, forgotten, to feel invisible. When Tate pushed his arms around her, she felt lost in that embrace but very much at home. She felt that she finally belonged somewhere.

She couldn't shake the fear away, though. She was afraid of Hammer. What was his pursuit in this game? Why was that night nineteen years ago so important for him?

The following day, after a night, she kept asking herself if she had done well telling Tate about Terry. Everything they talked about was Terry Morgan. His career in criminal defence. Tate investigated on the internet about Terrence Morgan's career and he was impressed with everything he found about him. Lots of pictures, to enjoy his eyes with the sight of his dad, lots of successes registered in court. He was respected, feared, and named as an opponent in court no one wanted to deal with. He was choosing his cases carefully, and he was offering them the best defence possible. He was merciless to any case of abuse of power and if the protocol was not carried out properly.

He found lots of pictures, snaps taken by media coming out of the court, and interviews regarding one case or another.

What made Tate call her with a matter of emergency was an article in the New York Times about a year ago around a scandal involving Terry Morgan, the successful defence attorney, when he declined to defend in court his lifetime friend, Richard 'Hammer' Maddox. He was accused of a series of rapes. Mostly, the family of Maddox accused Terry Morgan of a lack of loyalty toward a man who was his best friend from the age of five. They couldn't comment on what drifted the two apart, but their friendship was broken by years. There was a picture of Richard Maddox next to one of his dads.

'Is it him, Tate? The man yesterday?' she asked worriedly.

'He has a goatee now, but it is him, mom,' Tate answered, scrolling through articles for more information. 'So, the guy made a career from raping girls, and out of loyalty, he was expecting dad to defend him in court. Dad wouldn't have it because he knows first-hand, he did it.'

'Or because he saw him capable of doing it, Tate. It doesn't mean he was guilty, but knowing that he was capable, he wouldn't be able to be unbiased about the case. Did he comment anything?'

'I'm looking specifically for articles regarding the Maddox case. He is on the loose; I mean, he is here, so what does that mean? Was he proven innocent? Did he run justice? Did he follow dad here? If he did, why? How will this affect us? Why is he following me and you? That's not good at all, mom. Dad needs to know about it!'

Nolani hated to give him right. The only thing was that she didn't know how to go about it with Terry. The start between them was not giving her an opportunity to open the subject of their son lightly. Tate's curiosity about his dad was normal. She never hid the truth from him. Ever since he could understand and he was asking her about his dad, she chose the truth over deception. She didn't choose the same politics dealing with Terry.

Tate opened another article mainly about '*the victims of Hammer Maddox.*' The details were gruesome. He was punishing his victims for refusing to have sex with him. He was teaching them "good manners" in ordeals lasting hours. He was beating them, forcing them to please him orally. The contact was so violent, the damage left one of the girls with internal bleeding and fighting for her life. Two of the victims were sodomised as well, leaving them suicidal or suffering from PTSD.

He couldn't find anything about a trial or if Maddox had run from justice. The whole story left Tate worried for the safety of his mom, his own, his dad's and his sister, Laura.

He left the computer to join her for lunch, but he could hardly eat. He could see that his mom didn't have a great appetite either.

'Maddox is accusing dad that he didn't give him the benefit of the doubt, mom, but I'm sure he did it. All I saw in that article with the girls he raped, *teaching them manners…* he did it, mom. And if dad heard just as little as that, knowing what he tried with you years ago, he knew that too. I can understand why Dad refused to represent him in court. Dad standing up to the bully. I like him. I respect him for what he did for you years ago and for standing up for his principles now. Even if he had been innocent, dad couldn't be unbiased in defending his childhood friend, is it? It's not ethical.'

Nolani didn't comment. Her boy needed to see his father as a hero, a good, standing for justice man. He wanted to follow the law. Now, he was even more excited about it, finding out that his dad was a respected and feared defence attorney.

At that moment, she received a phone call from the hospital regarding Vanda. It was the physiotherapist stating that he didn't really have a chance to evaluate Vanda's spinal damage and the long-lasting effect because every time she was aware, she was screaming, she was violent, trying to pull out her needles. For safety reasons, her hands are restricted. Looking at her scan, the physio didn't think she was paralysed from the waist down, but she was in a lot of pain. They were trying to reduce the levels of Morphine because it was keeping her in a vegetative state, and she couldn't be assessed properly. The person on the phone said that it is down to the doctors what they will decide next, but in order for her to be fit for discharge and return to the nursing home… she didn't listen to anything after that.

'Tate, I need to run to the hospital, my love. Either you come with me, or I let you on my way to Jake's place.'

Obviously, she was thinking about his safety first. He did the same when he answered simply: 'I'll come with you, mom.'

In a few minutes, they were both ready and in Tate's car. Tate laughed that he finally had the opportunity to drive his mother around. Nolani took it as her first chance to observe her son's driving skills.

When they reached the hospital, she could say, from all her heart, that she never felt safer in the car with someone else driving. Tate really had a talent for it. 'This might not be pleasant, Tate,' she warned him when she got out of the car.

'Stop pampering me, mom. I'm a big boy. I'll be okay. What affects you, it affects me.'

And she loved him for that. They entered together in the hospital and travelled together by lift and on the corridors. She saw the same nurse on the shift. She's been observed, too. The nurse threw a long glance towards Tate, and the acknowledgement of paternity has been established. She cared very little about who the nurse thought Terry was for her. All the silly reasons which made her duck and run a week before, were not there anymore. No more hiding. No more boxes. With that dangerous man in their shadow threatening her and her son, she had to put on the big girl's pants and take position.

She went directly towards the room of Vanda followed by Tate. Tate observed everything with a care for detail he inherited from both his parents. The similarities between the little lady in the bed and his mom, the machines, the IVs, the catheter bag hanging on the side of the bed half full of urine, the medication smell, the little hands bandaged to stop Vanda from pulling off her needles. Her little, pretty face was full of bruises, but she appeared comfortable and sleeping.

'These are the only moments when she seems to fully rest,' said a nurse coming in the room with a chart. Nolani turned towards her. The cowards sent somebody else to deal with the family.

'Why morphine and not antipsychotic drugs? Why not try first to take the edge of her psychotic episodes and see if the pain is causing her violent outbursts?'

'Doctor's decision, I'm afraid,' the nurse answered.

'I need to talk to him. This lady fell on the stairs Friday morning. To have the physio telling on the phone that they are concentrating on making her suitable for discharge into the nursing home… that's not right.'

'They are thinking that she might benefit from being in a familiar environment… Plus, they need the bed. She can benefit from full nursing services in the nursing home, when the bed can be given to someone younger… and more able. We are doing our best for your grandmother, Miss…'

'Same name as my grandmother…'

'Oh… okay.' The nurse looked at Tate, who was a quiet observer, standing up near his great-grandmother's bed. 'She screams a lot. Who is Jessica?'

'My mother…'

'She calls her all kinds of names. Bad names. Whore… bitch… traitor…'

'I know. They are estranged. I don't know what caused it. She wouldn't say.'

'Is your mother around?'

'She is well away in Louisiana, I think.'

'We need her to sign some paperwork…'

'Why?'

'As the daughter…'

'If you would look into my grandmother's paperwork, you would observe that me, not my mother has legal power to sign for her.'

'Sorry, Miss, I assumed that… you know…'

Nolani smiled softly. 'Of course, you did. I want to talk with a doctor. Who can I talk with?'

'The doctor will come and see her in a few minutes…'

With those words, the nurse went out. Nolani could see her through the window, meeting the other at the nurses' desk and whispering between them. She inhaled some air deeply. It was so frustrating that every person who was meeting her was reading into her soft and sweet demeanour weakness, and they were taking their freedom to trample all over her backwards and forwards! All her life, she had to deal with patronising attitudes. Vanda undermined her all her childhood. She was not allowed to answer back; she was not allowed to raise her voice… to react to injustice. She had to shut her mouth and be graceful about it! Now she could see in it a way of

Vanda ensuring she gets her way every time. If she protested about something, she was ungrateful for all the efforts Vanda was making to raise her well and offer her a good life. Often, she added that she was doing this from the goodness of her heart when she had no duty or responsibility to do all that.

Emotionally insecure, lonely, and lacking the basic feeling of safety, her body language reflected exactly that. She was badly bullied at school. Vanda was saying, *'What doesn't kill you, makes you stronger.'* She never stood up for her, like every other responsible parent would. She continued to bully her at home, shouting at her to stop crying and to gather herself together as a fine high society girl would. She was adding, of course, that her behaviour was proving that she had mud in her veins, not blood. Do not fight back. Do not stand up to injustice. Ignore the bad comments. It is how it is. A true lady uses diplomacy as a weapon, not a bad mouth. Vanda didn't raise a perfect lady. She raised a perfect victim.

If she didn't end up raped and murdered in a cheap hotel in Florida, it was because of Terry fighting for her. She could not expect Terry to protect her all her life, though. She had to protect her son. The only way to do that was to fight against her own education and stand up for herself first.

'Mom, I think the doctor is here,' Tate warned her. Nolani turned on her heels to face the doctor.

# Chapter 10

'God, mom, you gave him hell in there!' Tate laughed, driving back home.

Yes, she was very articulate when she pointed out how disgusted she was by the attitude and the treatment she and her grandmother were receiving in the hospital, considering that they were paying the bills. It was also beyond her capacity to understand how, in the world, all their efforts were concentrated on pushing her grandmother back into the nursing home when they didn't even know for sure how intensive the spine damage was and if the woman was ever able to walk again. The doctor tried to explain to her that it was almost impossible to work with Vanda when she was awake. She agreed that Vanda had severe mental health problems, but if they were less morphine happy and more into giving Vanda antipsychotic drugs, they could actually have a very nice conversation with her and have her compliant with care.

Now, that all that had passed, she cowered into a corner of the passenger seat in her son's car, feeling bad about her outburst. Maybe she could have been… a bit nicer? She rubbed her forehead, then she looked towards her son. He was shining with pride. She was terrified that the doctor would think now about her that she was a bad and rude person.

Reaching home, she made herself a cup of tea, and she lay on her sofa, fighting a headache. Tate went upstairs to talk to Jake about the Maddox guy and his dad, warning him that the guy was not to be approached in any way, as he couldn't vouch for his intentions.

Nolani talked with Rita for a few minutes on the phone. She was excited Terry brought his gorgeous daughter in the morning to see her. Laura talked a lot about her, and she was convinced that she was a princess. Yes, a very rude princess who was shouting at doctors in the hospital! Rita asked about Vanda. She preferred to be as evasive as possible, not to upset her, but she added that she was hoping for the best.

When she decided to go to bed, after she made a raid through her house to make sure the alarm was on, and all the windows were locked, she could hear Tate still chatting on the phone. She knocked on his door, and when he said she could come in, she opened it just a bit.

'I'm going to bed, Tate. Don't stay too late, all right?'

'Yes, mom.'

Nolani closed the door and went into her bedroom. She prepared her bath with no rush, feeling extremely tired after the poor sleep last night and the day she had. She enjoyed a long bath, then she took her time to dry, spread cream over her whole body. She dressed in a soft cotton short and matching embroidered vest and brushed her long hair carefully. The sound of the phone alerted her she got a new message. That reminded her to set it on 'do not disturb' for the night. She opened the screen and checked the received message. Her heart shrunk. A scream died in her throat while she looked at the pictures in silent horror. 'Oh, my God!'

Terry stopped the car next to her little one. He looked at the pretty house. It could not compare with Jacaranda, but it was decent and enough for a single mother of one. He got out of the car and moved towards the door, which opened in front of him, a sign that she was watching through the darkness of the room when he arrived. She sounded terrified through the phone. He couldn't understand much of what she was saying.

'What happened, Nolani?' he asked when she closed the door after him and punched the code into the alarm of the house.

She lighted a lamp and sat down in the first armchair. She was wearing a dressing gown, and her hair was spread loosely on her back, shining in the light of the lamp in nuances of silver, gold, and rose gold. She was shaking uncontrollably. 'Another message?'

'Anonymous sender…' she whispered.

She opened her phone, pressed the password to unlock it; then she opened the messages. Just then, she handed him the phone. In the first picture was Vanda, asleep. The next picture was of a white pillow pushed by a strong hand, male, tanned. The last one was of a Vanda with the head on a side, lying fragile in her hospital bed, but it was hard to say if she was sleeping or she was dead. 'This is not funny, Nolani. Did you call the hospital? Did you call the police?'

She nodded weakly and buried her face in her palms.

'I'm scared, Terry. He followed my son yesterday at his football training. And Tate saw him on Friday at the car dealer when I bought his new car. He said that he was looking at him a lot, but mostly at me. He gave him the creeps.'

'Did Tate have a good look at him?' Terry asked, sitting on the sofa.

'He recognised him in some newspapers from New York, Terry. It seems to be… Richard 'Hammer' Maddox.'

Terry looked at her dumbfounded. 'You are joking me!'

'Six foot three. Blond. Blue eyes. Goatee. Tate says he displays a belligerent smile. He was cheering him yesterday, calling his name. Then, when he left, he shouted at him, *'You are better than your old man!'*

'So, not only did he follow me and saw some connection with you but done some investigations into your past and learnt who the father of your son was…' Terry mumbled frowning.

Her blue eyes gave him an imploring look. She couldn't voice it. She couldn't. 'Or he is just fooling around. That's his favourite game. Nolani, are you sure it is Maddox?'

'Tate is sure. He looked at him. He was not too far. He wouldn't make up something like this.'

'Did these threats start before or after our first encounter at the care home?'

'The phone calls started a few days before…'

'But you have the office in the same building as me. He might have put his eyes on you…' he thought loudly, jumping on his feet and making a few rounds in her little lounge.

'He's going to hurt my son, Terry!' she cried softly, looking at him. 'Laura… us!'

'I will contact my associates in New York,' he said, looking around without registering any detail of her furniture, carpets, or ornaments or how elegant was the whole arrangement. His mind went into overdrive, thinking fast, planning safety. 'I need to know what the situation is. For as far as I know, if Maddox is in Dallas, it means he is a fugitive. The first trial should be in a month.'

'Wasn't he under arrest or something?'

'I will check. I don't know the particulars of the case. I stayed away as much as I could.'

'Tate read in the newspaper you refused to defend him. You were accused of disloyalty.'

'Call the hospital. Ask them to check on your grandmother and update you. It may be a prank to shake you. Maddox is misogynistic, chauvinistic… He thinks he is God's gift for women… but he never upgraded to murder.'

She gave a phone call to the ward where Vanda was hospitalised and asked the nurse how her grandmother was. She's been told that Vanda had a small dose of Morphine because she was in terrible pain and she was sleeping.

'Can you please go and check on her? Somebody was there. They sent me a picture of my grandmother sleeping…'

'Ma'am, I assure you nobody could enter…'

'They did!' Nolani hissed through the phone. 'Please, go now and check her for me. If she is dead, you will have to answer the police who entered her room and killed her!'

'One moment…'

She kept the phone to her ear with an anxious gesture, hoping it was just a prank. 'Are they checking?' Terry asked before removing his phone from his jacket ready to give a phone call in New York. She nodded, then pushed her fingers through her hair. 'Why do you think he is going to hurt your son?'

'Because he thinks Tate is your son, Terry…'

He was busy looking through his contacts when he heard the tremulous whisper in the room. He lifted his green eyes full of amazement; then he chuckled nervously. 'This is stupid…'

Stupid, yes, but it could be serious. Maddox was mad at him. He was a criminal. He was hurting people. If he was thinking that Tate Arrington was his son, Nolani and her son got in a hell of a trouble, which wasn't their doing. He came to Dallas to change the air; he wasn't running from Maddox or anything like that. Maddox coming after him meant he was up to no good. There were too many innocent people involved in that game of his to dismiss the problem with a shake of his shoulder.

Suddenly, he could hear her weak whimper and came closer. She was shaking from all her being, tears pouring out from her eyes, listening through the phone. He took the phone from her hand and put it to his ear. There was a lot of noise, a lot of shouting, and the hospital staff were anxious, in an alert state. That was not a good sign. Suddenly, a male voice came on the line. He was barking. 'My staff said you received a picture of your grandmother in her hospital room! What hour was that?'

'Nolani, what hour did you get the message?'

'About half-past nine?' she answered weakly.' What do they say?'

'About half past nine.'

'Are you sure that somebody…'

'Smothered her with the hospital pillow. This is what the message was implying. Why? What is going on?' he barked loudly through the phone.

'Mrs Arrington seems to have passed away peacefully in her sleep… If this is the case, we need to get the police involved. We need you at the hospital as soon as possible!'

He mumbled a swearing word, shaking his head in disbelief.

'What did they say, Terry?'

'Richard Maddox upgraded officially to murder, Nolani. We need to go to the hospital.'

'You go home. Laura is there unprotected… I will call the father of Tate's best friend to come and stay with Tate while I'm dealing with all this.'

'I come with you. I'll give a call to Mrs Talon to arrange for somebody to join them tonight on the property, her son or anyone, while you are changing. Call that friend to stay with Tate, if you think this is the safest option. Maddox is a brutal force.'

She knew that. She went upstairs and changed fast in comfortable clothes. This meant, in her case, elegant black trousers, a white shirt with pearl buttons, and a smart jacket with two double white buttons, matching the trousers. She brushed her hair, rolled it on the nape, and caught it up with a hairpin. She rang Jake's dad before she even started dressing, so the moment when she arrived downstairs, Howard was already in Terry's company, looking at him astonished. 'Did you use to play American football, sir?' he asked.

'Yeah… in high school and a couple of years in university. How do you know?'

'That weird stranger yesterday said that Tate plays better than you used to… God, I cannot believe how…'

'I'm ready,' Nolani interrupted, coming down the stairs. 'I checked on Tate. He sounds asleep. Thank you so much for coming on such short notice, Howard. About the gentleman yesterday… We think he wants to hurt Tate.'

'I will be vigilant,' he promised.

'Feel free to take whatever you want from the kitchen or the bar.'

As soon as she and Terry left the house, the man locked the door, then made a full round through the house, checking every room. He made his own check on Tate. He was visibly in bed, asleep, then looked around in his room, to eliminate any possibility of an intruder being already there. After he made sure the little house was clear, he sat on one of the sofas and with all the lights off, he waited.

'What did your childminder say?'

'She was still on the phone with me when she called her son on the other one. In a few minutes, he would be there. She will message me that everything is all right.'

She nodded, looking through the window to the street lights. The traffic was almost nonexistent, so they could get to the hospital in half of the normal time.

'I'm sorry for your grandmother, Nolani. I know she was horrible with you, but she did not deserve that…'

'I cannot believe this is happening. Not even in my worst nightmares, I didn't live something like that…'

'In all honesty, I feel guilty for all this. I mean… I do believe Maddox put his eyes on you for all his sick reasons. You are exactly his type. Blonde, petite, blue eyes. From the moment he saw us together, it upgraded to a hell of another level… Mr… Whatshisname in there thought I was Tate's father as well… I wonder why!'

Her beautiful blue eyes, cloudy with tears, looked at his handsome profile, and she shuffled, uncomfortable. What could she say? *Because you are…*

'I'm thinking now about the message you received on the car, Nolani. *Tell him or…* Maddox was referring to me. This was the secret he thought he caught…'

Nolani bent her head, wishing she would stop shaking. This wasn't a case of someone catching a secret and threatening to just reveal it. To harm Tate now, when he didn't know, it wouldn't mean anything. He wanted Terry to know that Tate was the result of that awful night in Florida. After that, harming Tate, he would know that he had his sick revenge on Terry.

She clenched her teeth so hardly it hurt. Her fingers grabbed the sides of the passenger seat of his car and she started to rock her body backwards and forwards, trying to think.

'I gave the piece of paper to Wiseman to have it analysed. It may come up as nothing. It may come up as Maddox, if you are so sure it's him behind all this threatening game…'

'It's him, Terry…'

'I've sent a message to my associate, Sean Brown, in New York. I told him to wait for my phone call to confirm my suspicions, then to alert the New York police force. I asked him also to look into Maddox's case to find out in what stage that is.'

He stopped the car in a spot in the hospital parking lot and brought the car to a halt. He turned in his seat and looked at his passenger, worried about the state she was in and what was waiting for her inside. 'We are here, Nolani. Are you ready?'

She clenched her teeth and got out of the car. He followed quickly and ran after her on the pavement towards the hospital entrance. For a lady in dangerously high heels, she was walking fast. The fact never stopped to amaze him.

# Chapter 11

She stepped right into the fire of the biggest nightmare she ever lived in her life. There was staff questioned by the Police Department, with lots of tears and a lack of understanding as to why a tiny old lady died in her bed and why her granddaughter received the message she claimed she received.

Nolani has been questioned as well. She didn't break into tears even if she looked on the verge of collapsing at any moment. She answered as much as she could. She didn't know who sent the message or why. The sender was anonymous, and even if she had some theories, they could be farfetched, and she didn't have any evidence to back up her claim.

'Did you receive any other message prior to this one?' asked the officer, opening the message and having a simple look at it. 'Threatening one…'

'There is another message with a picture of Mr Morgan, here present, next to a picture of my son, suggesting that the person stalked them both… with the message *I know, you know, do they know?*'

Terry looked at her with a surprised air all over his face. 'You didn't tell me about that one…'

The officer opened the file and looked at it, then raised his eyes towards Terry. 'This meaning what? That they didn't know they are father and son? Or what?'

'Exactly.'

Terry moved from one leg to another, listening carefully. The officer was saying: '… when obviously they know… I mean… the gentleman is here in what quality?'

'Family friend…' she said evasively, moving her eyes away from both of them.

The officer told her that they needed to keep her phone for further investigation into the death of her grandmother. She knew that already. Also, he said that the pictures just suggested that her grandmother was smothered with a hospital pillow. She answered that she knew that too. 'I rang the hospital hoping that it is just a sick prank to shake my nerves…'

Terry's phone buzzed first, and he checked the message. It was Mrs Talon reassuring him that she had almost the entire family gathered at Jacaranda and his little one was safe and sleeping.

Then his phone rang, and he excused himself for a few minutes to take that call. He was obviously annoyed with all these people, assuming easily that *he was* the father of Tate Arrington. The way she was answering their questions was vague and left a lot of room for assumptions. What else could make the officer, God knows what his name was, to affirm that 'obviously they know…'?

Brown, his associate from New York, said that Maddox's disappearance was unlawful, and he was hunted by the police. He gave them a hint of his possible whereabouts, that he's been spotted in Dallas and he may be in the liaison with the smothering of an old lady in the hospital.

'Brown, we don't know exactly he did it… It is just that the son of my friend spotted him following him and my friend around. He recognised him from the newspapers posted on the internet. Also, yes, my friend started to receive phone calls, but she's quite vague as to what she is told through those phone calls. Also, there are some pictures that prove that someone was following her son around and myself and put them together, assuming I am her son's father! Fact, which is impossible because I just met the lady soon after I moved to Dallas!'

'What does the lady say?'

'She's very vague about it too. I know for a fact that judgemental people made her weary about having the boy while being unmarried. She is very private. This doesn't help me to sort this one out!'

'Our cases are made of peoples' secrets, Terry. Do you think Maddox would hurt the boy, if he would believe he is your son?' Terry sighed. He looked towards Nolani. She embraced herself, leaning against a wall. To deal with all this and her grandmother's possible murder seemed to drain her. There were people capable of getting punches from every direction, falling over and then bouncing for more. She was not one of them. She was fragile, vulnerable and sweet, a woman meant to look good in a salon full of fancy people, talking about the latest fashion, not to deal with questioning, death and stalking. How Laura put it, she was a Barbie doll. In his opinion, she was looking more like a porcelain one. If Maddox was involved in this, it was bad news for everyone. He witnessed what Maddox could do to a sweet, vulnerable girl…

'I think he would, Brown,' he answered. 'I think he would…'

'Then it wouldn't hurt that I implied him in the old lady's death without evidence… It is the job of the law force to rule him out! I'm sending in some boys…'

'Boys… wait a minute… boys, why?'

'To keep a watchful eye on my goddaughter and that innocent boy while you are sorting this mess out!'

'I don't think the police would appreciate your boys' interference in their case.'

'There will be none if Maddox stays away from the children.'

'Yeah… fair enough,' he mumbled. He noticed the officer going back to Nolani. She just received a Styrofoam cup of coffee from one of the nurses and some words of condolences, when the officer approached her again. He said good bye to his friend and associate and came closer.

'Ma'am, they are ready to take the body to the coroners to investigate the cause of death. From those pictures on your phone, we just can assume what happened.'

'I know, but nothing rules out the fact that somebody who shouldn't be in my grandmother's room was in her room and took those pictures around the time of her death…'

'That we don't know for sure. We must analyse the pictures to assert something of that nature. Protocol, Ma'am. I can't go to court with assumptions.'

'All right.'

'In the meantime, we need you and your boyfriend to come to the station to have your statements recorded.'

'He's not my boyfriend…' Nolani protested.

'Aha…' was the *'I don't believe you'* comeback.

It was two o'clock in the night, when they returned to his car. The nightmare was not over. They've been told that they will need to come back when necessary *'for a friendly discussion...'* She managed to talk to Jake's father using his phone.

'I talked with my associate in New York, Nolani. Maddox is a fugitive. The trial is soon, and he just disappeared. Brown said he gave a hint to the police where he was spotted lately... as following your son to his football game to be exactly. What do you want to do now?'

His house was full of Talons. Between eight and ten, he didn't know exactly. The father of her boy's friend brought into her house three of his army guys and they were playing poker using a collection of old coins belonging to her as betting chips.

'Go home? Try to get some sleep?' she asked with a low voice.

He drove randomly, checking if they were followed. Then he turned off the engine of his car. She looked around, acknowledging that they were not in front of her house. She was startled, looking at the building, and then she looked at him with defiance.

'I'm not staying here. I need to get home to my son, Terry.'

'Your house is an army camp.'

'Those gentlemen are waiting for my return so they can call it a night!'

'Aha, like your simple presence can protect that boy better than four trained army... They will not be willing to leave, Nolani. If I was them, me neither. Jacaranda is a nest of talons right now. We will not get any sleep, and this is what we need right now. Let's get in there, sleep for a few hours and think about what we will do next.'

Nolani sighed. She was exhausted, she was scared, she just wanted to lay in bed and cry. And against her better judgement, she nodded, agreeing to his plan. She didn't go with him to the reception desk, afraid that she would be seen as a lady ready for a few hours of rolling between the sheets with a man. To protect her dignity, she decided to wait away from the receptionist's sight. Terry went alone to pay for the room and get the key. He returned to her understanding her reserve. He pushed his arm around her waist and guided her toward the room.

None of them said anything. She looked towards the only bed in the room, took her shoes off and disappeared into the bathroom. Then she came out, and he took his turn. When he came back into the room, he found her already lying in bed. The only piece of clothing she took off was her smart jacket. He did the same, took his shoes off, and after he put the light off, he lay next to her. She wasn't crying. With her hair spread on the white pillow and her cheek buried in it, she was looking at him through the semidarkness of the room. His eyes investigated everything, from the sweet features of her face, the shape of her lips, the fragility of her neck, down to the shape of her body. God, she was gorgeous! Then she whispered: 'Terry, I need you to hold me…'

Terry stopped breathing for a short while, and then he lifted his arm with a welcoming gesture. She shuffled over the sheets until the front of the body touched his. She put her head on his bent arm, while he lowered the other arm around her waist. For a few minutes, he could feel her warm breath through the fabric of his shirt, on his neck, while his entire body was celebrating the tight embrace.

Then she raised her eyes to meet his. Terry couldn't say precisely what went through his head before he lowered his lips to meet hers. All he knew was that Nolani didn't protest. It started slowly, gently, and then the intensity of it changed. Their bodies became restless. Their breaths were rapid and interrupted. The sounds of her soft moans and his deep growls were the only sounds in the silence of the room.

He couldn't recall precisely in what order the whole 'Let's just get some sleep' escalated to 'Let's get rid of some of the clothes.' Their movements were erratic and rushed; their kiss went from wild to mind-blowing. Like two instinctual beings, they touched each other, they probed, and they fused. Nolani pulled him tight, clinging to him, crying his name over and over again. She needed that catalyst to consume that grief that was ruining her soul. He left her to use him, wondering who was using who.

Buried deep into her body, after an earth-shaking release, he raised his eyes and looked down at her face. Her eyes were closed. She was moaning gently, lips slightly open, breathing fast. He could feel her tightening around him in erotic spasms lost in the whirlpool of their passion. Gently, it subsided, and her eyes opened slowly, looking at him, acknowledging what had just happened. She didn't make a sound, but the expression of her beautiful face went from ecstasy to pure mortification in an instant. He sighed, caressing her cheek tenderly. With a slow movement, he removed his body from the sweet cradle of her thighs and lay next to her. Ashamed of what she just did, Nolani wanted to put some distance, but Terry rolled her towards him and pulled her in a tight embrace. His hand stroked her back reassuringly, then went down and cupped her bare bottom intimately.

Thinking about what just happened between them, in his opinion, it was absolutely normal. She was as active in making that happen as he was. She needed him as much as he needed her. Why, then, was he overwhelmed once again with bitter guilt? Why was he feeling once again that everything he did was to take advantage of a woman who was down and vulnerable?

When he woke up later in the dawn and realised that she left sometime in the night, he went mad. What were the odds for a man to pass through the same experience twice in his life? He did this once, and he never passed over what happened. In that case, the girl was beaten and bruised and scared to death, close to being brutally raped in her own bed. He took such good care of her that he ended up taking her virginity, for God's sake! He muttered a swear word, dressing up with erratic moves.

Well, this time was not a girl. She was a grown woman with an adolescent son; she knew what she was getting into when she started to pull his clothes like that. Was she? She never seemed to have experienced hardship in all her life, and she didn't know how to cope with it. The sex seemed a good idea in that moment if any of them was doing any thinking. In the light of the day, it didn't look like it…

It was stupid, it was reckless, and she might never look into his eyes again. How much he would have liked to share last night's experience with her in completely different circumstances. After a romantic date? After shared kisses and flirting under the moonlight?

'Yeah, try this, Terry Morgan,' he mumbled with self-deprecation. 'What about after her grandmother's murder, with a criminal stalking her, scared for her life, scared for her son's life… Hm? That's fucking romantic!'

❀ ❀ ❀

Nolani was functioning on automatic. It seemed that way, because when she reached her office, she barely could remember how she managed to deal with the excitement of Tate when Howard told him Terry was at their house last night. What did she answer when he asked her, 'Why didn't you wake me up, mom?' Did she use her grandmother's death as an excuse? The lack of sleep didn't do much good to her appearance. She just wanted to get through the projects and go home and get some sleep.

She didn't know what she said to Marina when she said she called her three times that morning and she didn't answer. She ignored the accusatory attitude, implying that she intentionally declined the calls. She went into her office and started to look through the projects. She called the artist and told him about the cherry blossom framed in cast in Laura's bedroom. She went on the site online and ordered the furniture Laura agreed to for her bedroom.

The hardest thing was to stop thinking about what happened last night. For years, she held him dear in her heart; the moments in his arms on the night when they conceived Tate was the closest to a human caress, the most caring, loving embrace she had ever experienced in her whole life. She felt loved, she felt protected, she felt special that night. The shame and the embarrassment made her run. She embraced his son like a gift of love. Tate completed her. Tate made her whole. Tate made her strong. She loved him for giving her Tate. She loved him for being the protective and caring man he was.

She was disillusioned when they met, that he did not recognise her. She understood, though. Her whole life after was spinning around his memory. He didn't have a reason to feel the same. They didn't

118

know each other's names when it happened. She saw them around, him and Hammer. She learned that his nickname was Stampede. Never a formal presentation took place. They had never talked to each other before he needed to fight his best friend to save her. She was just a girl he never acknowledged. Her hair was short. She had to cut it after some of her high school colleagues almost disfigured her in a prank. She had dental braces. She was skinny and unappealing. To Hammer, she was, she thought, disheartened.

Last night was different.

She sighed and buried her face in her palms. They knew each other's names. There was no way to run away from it. He was still having his office on the eighth floor. He was still living in Jacaranda. She still had to decorate his daughter's bedroom. He was still Tate's dad. And Maddox was still around doing what he was doing for God knows what reasons.

Maybe it was related to that night in Florida. The fact that he didn't have it his way... She shakes uncontrollably. The fact that Tate was conceived that night... Could it be that what was making him mad was the fact that his friend had what he couldn't? Tate was the living proof that they had been together that night. In his twisted way, he could think like that. She dealt with bullies all her life. Maddox was a bully. No finesse. He was a brute, one convinced he was handsome, desirable, and the girls should feel lucky they got his attention. In his opinion, she was rude, avoiding him. He thought he was entitled to have her because she kept away from them. Because she was alone in that holiday and in that hotel room. Because... She shook her head, fighting to stop thinking about it. Who made her a shrink for twisted people? What does she know?

She knew that trying now to hide from Terry that Tate was indeed his son was like fighting an avalanche. At the same time, she knew that in the moment when Terry learns the truth, Tate will become a moving target for Maddox.

Will Terry be mad at her? Yes. Will he think about her that she is just a deceptive bitch? Definitely. Will he protect his son from Maddox's madness? She hoped so.

She raised her head from the paperwork she had spread on her desk, and seeing him standing there with a cynical smile all over his face, her heart skipped a beat.

# Chapter 12

'And we meet again, dolly,' he said with a grin.

He moved his massive body towards one of the chairs and sat down in a nonchalant position, with his hands on his hips, a gesture to put in evidence the bulge in the middle, which was obviously a reason for pride for him. That was the only moment he took his eyes off her, and she tried to make the most of it. Her initial shock transformed into panic, and her heart was beating like crazy in her chest. She felt sick to her stomach. She didn't turn her eyes toward the glass wall. She could hear the joyful chatter of her employees and their careless laughter. Her eyes never moved from his face. He was somehow handsome, with blue eyes and blond hair with few strands touching his eyebrow. He was huge and muscular, like a football star. The expression of his eyes was mocking, and his lips were smiling sarcastically. Her fear was feeding his enormous ego.

Fighting her natural reactions, with Vanda shouting in her ears to gather it together and to lift her chin up, she did. With her hands remaining on the pile of papers on her desk where she fiddled for something, she said with a steady voice: 'God, that goatee of yours doesn't do much for you…'

'You don't like it!' he laughed, caressing his chin.

'You look like a billy.' Blue eyes steady. Cool like a cucumber. Vanda would be proud. 'Now, how can I help you, mister?'

'By all means, I think I helped you, missy. With the old fish turning up her belly, you can get your hands faster on your inheritance…'

'Maybe you helped my mom to get her inheritance, but I acknowledge no service towards myself.'

'Ooh…' he laughed at her poise mockingly. 'Did you tell Morgan that he's got a boy?'

'No, I didn't.'

'Then it remains for me to tell him.'

'Why would you do that? What purpose will that serve?'

'For the fucking bastard to recognise that he lied to me when he told me that nothing happened that night, so I can crack his head open for fucking my chick!'

Okay, he was delusional.

'… then to pull your head off for being a slut and fucking my best buddy!'

Yes, Nolani, try to reason with him if you can. He had his whole scenario in his head. Should she tell him that he had no right to consider her his property? That wouldn't sink well.

'You tell him, or I will. But in that moment, Morgan, you and your fucking bastard are dead meat, do you hear me? And you can put that brave front as much as you want, bitch. I know that you piss your panties, and you wish you would never have cheated on me.'

'Between us two, I am not the one hunted by the police for rape, mister Maddox.' He reacted to the sound of his name with a wide grin. 'I know you can hurt people. You attack vulnerable ladies, and you hurt them really bad. You went even lower than that, killing paralysed old ladies while they are sleeping. I'm sure you are proud of yourself…'

At that moment, Marina opened her office door with a large smile on her face.

'Do you want anything to drink?'

'Fuck off!' he barked, jumping from his chair. 'We are having a conversation here!' Marina was startled visibly in front of such a violent verbal outburst. She started to cry instantly, trying to understand what she did wrong. The girls in the other room jumped on their feet, alerted by his shouting.

'No, Marina, Mister Maddox is leaving now. We finished our conversation,' Nolani said calmly.

He turned on his feet, laughing nervously. Then, it appeared to him that he didn't want to make an entire circus in the office. 'See you soon… Ma'am…' he chuckled, passing by Marina, who was struggling to calm down. She looked after him as he moved his massive body with the easiness of an animal of prey out of their office door, then down the corridor towards the lift. Nolani breathed rapidly and crossed her arms around her middle.

'That was unnecessary,' said Jada, looking after him. 'What was with the barking?'

'He is sexy, though,' laughed another lady in the office. 'I like his goatee…'

'Yeah, you can take him home, Mandy,' she whispered, returning to her office. Mandy came into the door frame with a smile.

'Is he married?'

'No. Marina, I want you to call this number and ask for Officer Flowers, please. Tell him that I need to speak with him…'

'Did we get an arrangement with him? Can I take it?' Mandy asked flirtatiously. Nolani ignored her and sat at her desk, wondering at what moment it was appropriate to just sit down and scream.

Marina came into the door frame with a stoned expression on her beautiful face. 'He asks if it is anything related to the death of your grandmother, boss…'

Everyone looked at her in complete shock. Whatever they were doing, they just froze in place.

'Yes, tell him that the gentleman who murdered my grandmother last night, just paid a visit to my office. Now, Mandy… what were you saying?'

That was cruel. That was unnecessary. It felt, though, better than screaming. She planned a meltdown later. Marina transferred the call to her office and closed the door for her to have her conversation privately.

It was an hour later when Terry entered through the doors at Forever. The atmosphere reminded him of a funeral. The girls were talking about their boss, wondering why she didn't take a day off given the tragedy she was going through. She seemed like nothing had happened. Normal like ever. Then… this!

'Is Nolani in?' he asked, looking towards her office.

Marina came towards him with a sad face. 'Do you know about her grandmother?'

'Yes, I do…'

'She is gone to the police station to talk to Officer Flowers… the man who…'

'I know Officer Flowers…'

'No! No!' she said, agitated. 'The boss alleged that the man who… Oh, My God! I can't believe this happened! He was here!'

Terry's body stiffened and his entire facial expression changed from smiling to angry in an instant. 'Tall… blond… goatee… large guy…'

Marina nodded to every single word of his. 'The boss called him Mr Maddox…'

'Do you know what they talked about?'

'We never…' her voice faltered. 'Everything seemed normal. The boss acted normal… He did bark at me for interrupting them, but he left when the boss said their conversation was over. Just after he left, she said that… that…'

Terry didn't stay to hear the rest. He stormed out of the office and then through the fire exit stairs out of the building.

❀ ❀ ❀

Nolani crossed her legs, looking at all those men gathered in the office, barely remembering who they said they were and from where they were coming. She was so tired and emotionally drained that she didn't even know for sure if she heard right, and some were FBI. Were they?

'I did read your statement, Miss Arrington, and it states that you do have an idea of who sent you those messages… but you have no

125

proof that the person is who you think that is. We did receive a hint last night, let's say anonymous, stating for sure that a certain Richard Maddox was seen in Dallas, and he might be behind your grandmother's sudden death… Now, we did look in the pictures in the phone you gave us as evidence, and to the first assessment seemed what Officer Flowers already alleged, that it may not actually prove that he smothered your grandmother… The computer analyst highlighted though few things that are not visible, just looking at the middle picture… you know, the one with the pillow.' She nodded, trying to understand what he was saying. 'One, there is a small fragment in the lowest part of the picture where it can be seen a small arm with an intravenous cannula inserted… This proves that your grandmother, unfortunately, was underneath that pillow.'

Her heart shrunk. She went pale, and her fingers bent into a fist.

'What that picture doesn't show is that the killer is Mr Maddox. If he is, what would you think would be his reasons? He is a serial rapist, but he has never been accused of murdering someone.'

'You said he was in your office today?' asked Officer Flowers.

'Yes.'

'Do you know him personally?'

'He tried to rape me several years ago…'

Officer Flowers straightened his body. The others looked at one another, finally getting to something.

'So… it was an attempt… he didn't manage, because…' said the man, prolonging his words. He leaned with his back against the desk in the middle of the room.

'He's been followed by his best friend…'

'Did he state what were his intentions?'

'I don't know. He attacked me in my sleep. He punched me repeatedly… He pinned me against the pillows of the bed by the back of my head and tried to pull my clothing off. He was saying that that's not the way a good girl behaves, and he had to teach me good manners. I don't remember much. I was in shock. I was in pain. I was frightened… Then he released me, and I could hear a thump in the room. His best friend was there. Maddox was on the floor. They had a struggle. I think he was drunk, but I don't know for sure. They punched each other hard. He was telling his friend that I tempted him… that I was looking for it… He was referring to me with very… bad words…'

'Bitch… these kinds of words?'

She nodded. 'Then he left…'

'They both did…'

'No, just him. He was bleeding from his nose, from a shoulder… and he was stumbling, like he was drunk… or dizzy… or both.'

'And the friend? He remained…'

Reaching this part, she lowered her eyes. She nodded. 'I cried. I had a panic attack… He remained to look after me.'

'Did he finish what Maddox started?'

'No. I…' Nolani was feeling nauseous. Her throat was dry, and her entire world was spinning.

'Did you have sex with the friend that night?'

'I initiated it. Nothing was planned. It just… happened…'

'Did they have other fights after? Did Maddox come after you? Did he learn what happened? Why are you targeted now? He likes high school girls, and you seem to be an old story of his which didn't finish as planned.'

'After that night, I left. I never knew their names. I knew that Mr Maddox was called Hammer. His friend was called Stampede…'

'So, you ran from Hammer, and you slept with Stampede!' laughed one of the men.

Pale, mortified by their mocking, she looked at each one of them. Their attitude didn't offer her too much trust in law and order. Why did she come in the first place? To have them laughing at her ordeal years ago, like it was something dirty to make their day, it was disgusting.

'What happened, Ma'am?' asked the man in a suit who talked to her about the picture.

'You all are so disgusting; I want to vomit,' she muttered, rubbing her stomach.

'Sorry, it was just a joke. Gentlemen, please!' he made them a sign to stop with the laughing. 'Where are we getting from here? You said you left? You ran? Where?'

'It all happened on a holiday in Florida. I went there for a few days without the knowledge of my grandmother.'

'What made Maddox come to Dallas now?'

'His friend moved to Dallas. He followed him.'

'Why?'

'I don't know why. Why don't you ask that lunatic why he does all he does?' she asked exasperated.

'So, you met the… friend.'

'Yes. We work in the same building…' That answer created another round of smiley faces.

'Did he say anything about what happened after?'

'No. He did not recognise me. It's been over nineteen years now.'

Flowers scratched his head. 'Is he the same guy from the picture with your son, Ma'am? When did he learn he has a son?'

'He didn't. He never met my son. Mr Maddox did. He started to follow my son around.'

'Wait… you have a son conceived that night?' asked the guy in the suit. She was still confused about who he was and why he was doing almost all the talking.

'I'm telling you, White! They are like identical!' said Flowers.

'From there, the message with '*You know, I know, do they know…*' said White with a frown. 'Why would he want you to tell them?'

With a slow gesture, she got out her Dictaphone and pressed the button:

'*Did you tell Morgan that he's got a boy?*'

'*No, I didn't.*'

The lawmen jumped in surprise. They did not expect her to pull something like that!

*'Then it remains for me to tell him.'*

*'Why would you do that? What purpose will that serve?'*

*'For the fucking bastard to recognise that he lied to me when he told me that nothing happened that night, so I can crack his head open for fucking my chick, then to pull your head off for being a slut and fucking my best buddy! You tell him, or I will. But in that moment Morgan, you and your fucking bastard are dead meat, do you hear me? And you can put that brave front as much as you want, bitch. I know that you piss your panties, and you wish you would never have cheated on me.'*

*'Between us two, I am not the one hunted by the police for rape, Mister Maddox. I know you can hurt people. You attack vulnerable ladies, and you hurt them really bad. You went even lower than that, killing paralysed old ladies while they are sleeping. I'm sure you are proud of yourself...'*

She pressed the button, then pulled the tape out of it and handed it to White.

'There you have the entire conversation we had in my office today, Mr White.'

'Is he talking about Terrence Morgan, the Defence Attorney? The guy who refused publicly to represent him and he accused him of disloyalty...'

'Yes.'

'Were you two in a relationship? You and Maddox, I mean. He implies you were together.'

'No. I observed them playing football on the beach with other members of their team, but I kept my distance. A long… distance. He is delusional. Very delusional. Until that night I never changed a word with any of them. This man threatens to kill my son, Mr White. And I'm afraid to tell his father because in that moment, the death of our son would matter not only for me but for him too.'

'Your son is a target because he's been conceived in that night.'

'Exactly.'

'And the grandmother is…'

'Just to show me that he is capable of murder, that he is around… to terrify me. I don't know. You are asking *me* a lot of questions; the answers are unfortunately in the head of a very disturbed individual.'

She grabbed her purse and stood up. 'Can I go now?'

'Yes, sure. What made you record that meeting? Did you expect his visit? You seemed awfully prepared…'

'It is my work Dictaphone. I record all my meetings with it, to avoid clients claiming that they never asked for that or for this… It was just there…'

White nodded thoughtfully. 'Stay around the phone, Miss…' Clearly, he did not remember her name.

'Are you referring to the phone which is in the police custody?' She smiled with sadness. 'I came here hoping that I am going to get support to protect my son from this monster.'

'Trust me, we will protect you and your son, Miss…'

Her look didn't show too much trust. After she left the office, he turned towards his men.

'Do you believe her rape story? She talked very airily about it, White.'

'The demeanour, yes. She talked clear and concise. She's good at hiding her emotions. Her eyes were not lying, though. She made the statement, looking clear into my eyes. The tone of her voice went in an undertone when she talked about the attack. Plus, she had a witness. One who became later Defence Attorney and, for personal reasons, declined to defend Maddox, despite his family claiming that they been friends almost all their lives.'

'Because he knew he was capable of raping girls…'

'Because he stopped his friend from raping one…

'Then he slept with her…' chuckled one of them.

'I would appreciate it if you stop laughing about it, Mr Matthews. The lady was honest about it. Let's stop clowning in here and get to what is really important! We found the primary case. She is blonde, she is beautiful, she is the one he could never have. I don't know why Maddox followed Morgan in Dallas, but in the process, he discovered not only his first victim, but he learned that she has a son. That didn't stay well with him… Now… can anyone tell me what is her name again? She noticed that I don't know it. This doesn't make us look good at all!'

# Chapter 13

Nolani put her forehead on her driving wheel, letting it out for the first time since she learnt about the death of Vanda. Sobbing uncontrollably, she filled the car with loud bawls. Her body was shaking convulsively, as she was struggling to breathe. She was scared for her life and Tate's life. She was lost. She didn't know what to do, where to turn. All her life, she's been alone, she had no one to back her up, no one to protect her. Terry did. Nineteen years ago, Terry was the first one ever to jump in for her protection. They laughed in there, making his act of justice a joke, they laughed at his kindness, and they concluded just what was dirty and spicy from the story. That he had her that night. She growled, feeling helpless and frustrated.

Another wave of crying was because of Maddox's visit to her office. To endure that meeting, to realise how disturbed he was mentally, that consumed her greatly. There was no way to talk logic into that man. Through his own way of seeing things, she belonged to him and the fact that she gave herself to Terry that night was punishable by death. What scared her most was the fact that she knew already how that man was thinking. In that meeting, he just proved her right. It wasn't like she was agreeing with it, but she understood what made him tick.

In that moment, she started hyperventilating, fighting with a tremendous panic attack while she couldn't stop whining. The door from the driver's side opened suddenly. Her heart skipped a beat. Two arms went tight around her and pulled her out of the car. When she heard his voice, she felt safe. His voice was telling her to remember the breathing technique during labour. Slowly, he was demanding her to breathe in through the nose, out through the mouth.

It lasted another few minutes until she gave signs that she managed to relax, and she passed it. He leaned down and grabbed her purse, then with an arm around her, he closed the door and locked the car. 'I'll take you home, Nolani. Your girls in the office told me you got a visit from Maddox. That's the reason you went to the police?'

She nodded affirmatively. Her feet stumbled towards his car. The heat and the fact that she didn't manage to eat anything was making her feel faint. If she managed to get there in one piece and without ending up on the concrete, it was because of his strong arm holding her up.

He opened the door and helped her sit in the passenger seat. He wanted to ask her what Maddox wanted from her, what he had said to her in her office, but she was not in shape to answer any questions. He looked at her. She was pale like a ghost, slouched in the passenger seat. He drove her home in silence. To help her in, he had to carry her.

He got her keys and unlocked the door. He asked her just to push in the code for the alarm. She did it automatically, then her hand fell lifeless next to her body. He laid her on her sofa, and then he took care to close and lock the door. He went to the kitchen and brought her a glass of water. He helped her sit up to drink, and then he sat on the edge of the sofa, looking down at her. He started the day mad at himself for what happened that night and mad at her for running away from him. Now, it didn't even deserve mentioning. The fact that he was upset with her for leaving him in that hotel room was the smallest reason for her to worry.

'Are you better, Nolani?'

'I need to sleep,' she mumbled, fighting to keep her eyes open.

'I'll take you up…'

He pushed his arms under her small body and lifted her up. He had to find the directions without help because she evaded into nothingness. Her room was small and cosy, elegant and bright, but there was nothing to remind him of a princess. Good taste, yes, it was there, everywhere he looked. Too much? Nope. It was classy.

He laid her over the bed cover on her bed and took her shoes with crazy high heels off. He took the pins off her hair and let it spread around like a cloud of silk.

She was exhausted beyond limits; she cried her heart out that day… and she still was looking like a porcelain doll to him. He could hardly believe that what happened between them last night was real. His body was hungrier than ever for her. He would give everything to make love to her, slowly, with both aware of what is happening… Like that, he was living proof that man is the only animal in the world capable of repeating the same mistake twice. If a wolf is burning its paw, it will never get close to the fire again. He touched gently her cheek, with a self-deprecating smile.

His phone buzzed into his pocket, and he decided to leave her room, not to awaken her. He went down the stairs and, from there, into her kitchen. He made himself a coffee and took it into her lounge to savour it slowly, while checking his phone. He had a miscall from Brown, so he called back.

'Tell me, Brown, what's the news?'

'FBI is gone to Dallas. Agent White and his partner should be already there. My boys just checked in at the hotel. I gave them your number to keep you updated if they see anything. They will need the address of the lady with the grandmother.'

'I'm in her house right now. She had a meltdown after an eye-to-eye meeting with Maddox.'

'Oh, shit! How did that go?'

'I have no idea. I will talk to her when she wakes up.'

'Is she his type?'

'Blonde, blue eyes, pretty… yes. But she's not seventeen, Brown. She's thirty-something. I keep thinking that she would have never been a target of Maddox if I hadn't stepped in and had so many meetings, for multiple reasons with her.'

'You like her…'

'I don't know…'

'Ha! How much?'

'She would do well for a future Mrs Morgan…'

'With son and all…'

'I have a little girl… Anyway, keep me posted, Brown. I need to call Wiseman, to see what news he got for me…'

'What is he investigating now?'

'A personal curiosity of his. Some discrepancies in the story Nolani's been told relating to her origins. The grandmother is not the grandmother. The mother is not the mother. Wiseman thinks the grandmother was the mother, but he is still looking for proof.'

'He loves secrets and social stories… It's the office ready to run?'

'It's all on his hands. With Maddox in Dallas killing old ladies in hospitals… I'm a bit distracted.'

'Yeah, fair enough.'

They finished their conversation there, and he called Wiseman.

'Grandma' is the legal guardian of the little girl, but I cannot find any act of adoption, Morgan. What I cannot find either is proof that Vanda Arrington gave birth in 1976… I'm still looking.'

'Did you receive any result from that paper I gave you for tests?'

'Visible prints all over it, seems the job of an amateur. I was planning to call you about that…'

'Did anything come up?'

'Yeah… the prints of Sally Holding… can you believe that?'

Terry paced in Nolani's living room looking out on the window. 'Isn't she one of the victims of Maddox?' He frowns, trying to think rapidly, to get a logic of how a note written by a teenager raped by Maddox a few months ago ended up on Nolani's car. 'We know from our own investigation that Maddox was stalking his victims for weeks, and he was attacking at the first opportunity. It may be something she wrote intended for somebody else, he picked up…'

'Memories? Trophies?' mumbled Wiseman. 'Wasn't he supposed to be a caveman who was raping girls to feed his huge ego?'

'His manners are, Wiseman, but he is not an idiot…'

'How did that end on the car of the glamorous puss in Dallas?'

'Maddox is in Dallas. He is stalking her and the boy. He just killed Vanda Arrington in hospital last evening…'

Wiseman did not say anything. Terry could imagine him scratching his forehead thinking.

'Where is that piece of evidence, Wiseman? We need to hand it to Agent White… who is in Dallas now as well… It is related to his case…'

'I'll pass over to your house this evening, and I'll bring it over. It is perfectly sealed, as it should be, not to add any extra prints to it. What purpose did that serve? The letter on her car?'

'He is threatening her to tell… me… something he is convinced about… that her boy is my son.'

'Is that even possible?' laughed Wiseman. 'I cannot imagine that puss-in-high-heels being your type…'

He wanted badly to say *no,* but he couldn't. She was so vague about it, he needed to discuss the matter with her first, before he could say it out loud to his assistant. 'First, Wiseman, do not misjudge what type of woman I like. Two… this labelling you are doing, starts to annoy me. Three… I don't know if the boy is mine. Everyone who saw him assumes in an instant that he is. Did you see the boy?'

After a quiet moment, Wiseman said, 'Not yet… What does she say?'

'We didn't talk about it. The whole thing started with Vanda Arrington being murdered in the hospital. Since then, she was busy giving statements to the police and receiving the visit of Maddox in her office this morning…'

He didn't give his assistant the whole handover about the situation. Until he was talking with her to learn what Maddox had to say, to risk a visit in the daylight to her office, he couldn't make assumptions about what had been said.

He asked Wiseman to continue looking for her birth mystery to uncover the lies of Vanda Arrington. Nolani deserved to know. Wiseman said he wanted to send one of the detectives they were working with to Louisiana to have a chat with Jessica Arrington. Terry agreed to it, and their conversation ended there.

He thought about the conversation he had just had with Wiseman regarding the prints of Sally Holding, Maddox's alleged fourth victim. He did not talk to the victim or with witnesses, as he declined to represent him, but he followed from a distance everything that transpired from Maddox's case. Sally was the first victim sodomised. Nobody made a liaison between Sally and the first three victims because of the level of damage inflicted on the girl. When Sally Holden recovered consciousness in the hospital and accused Maddox of raping her, then he's been discovered to be the perpetrator of the first three rapes as well.

Maddox denied the allegations, and then he requested to be represented by Terrence Morgan. In all the scandal made by the Maddox family and the media speculating why he declined to do so, it surfaced that there was a fifth victim who claimed she's been raped and sodomised by Maddox. Because the victim came forward weeks after the alleged attack, her case was still under discussion as to why she didn't come forward earlier, but after the media started to write about Sally Holden.

His phone buzzed once again. Terry looked at the screen. It was Mrs Talon. He put the phone to his ear, distracted. 'Yes, Connie, is Laura out yet?'

The woman sounded hysterical. She was screaming into the phone words, which refused to sink into his mind. His stomach transformed into stone; his heart started beating to pass through his chest. A wave of sickness revolted his entire body, and stricken by a surge of adrenaline, he shouted through the phone. 'Can you be clear, Connie? What happened? Did anything happen with Laura?'

'They kidnapped Laura, Mr Morgan!' she bowled.

# Chapter 14

This was the worst day of his life. To learn about his little daughter being kidnapped dived him into a pool of desperation he never lived in before. How he managed to reach the school, without being involved in a car accident, he did not know. The police were there. Mrs Talon was seen by paramedics while she was trying to answer questions to the best of her ability. The hysteria was affecting a lot of that ability.

He learnt that Maddox was at school. With a gun pressed in her ribs ordered her to move down the street towards where his car was parked. From there, the whole story was very confusing because all they could get was that the whole street was *crowded… lots of children and parents, men running in football gear…* and when she turned, Laura was already gone.

Somehow between that and her calling the Texas rangers, police, and God knows others what they were, but they were in uniforms as well, she ended up on the pavement. Maddox used his gun but missed her hip. Mrs Talon was having lots of grazes on her arm and leg; she was bleeding from her forehead, but otherwise, she was all right.

His phone rang, but he ignored it. Between talking with one another… if he had any enemies… yes, he had one, but it appeared he didn't get hold of his daughter either. Thanks, God, for that!

He gave a statement about Maddox, not going too deep about the reason behind their rift, as that was not the most important.

Maddox tried to get Laura. A shiver passed through his spine. Considering what the press was saying that he was doing to his victims, he didn't even want to consider what he was capable of doing to an innocent little girl. And maybe Maddox wouldn't hurt a child in that way, but who could guarantee that everything he wanted was to give him a scare?

It was about six o'clock in the evening when the police told him he could go, advising him to go home and wait to hear from them. If there were any news, he would be the first to find out. He went to the car and checked his phone. He was far from giving up on finding Laura. He needed to call Brown and get the details of 'the boys' who arrived in Dallas, especially for Laura's protection and that of Tate Arrington.

He was intrigued when he discovered he had over six missed phone calls, from an unknown number. He braced himself to hear directly from the kidnapper, requesting money in return to get Laura home safely. He touched the number and pushed his phone to his ear.

'Who is there?' he asked with a growl, leaning against his car.

'Sorry, Mr Morgan, I'm Tate? Tate Arrington?'

Well, he did not expect this one. Now he came to realise that he hoped that it was the kidnapper asking for money. That would make him closer to getting Laura back.

'How can I help you, Tate?'

'Laura is here with us, sir! I took her from him!'

Terry stumbled on his feet, stunned. That first feeling of relief made him feel giddy, drunk.

'I tried to call you, sir, but I did not have your number. Then I thought mom had it, but the police kept her phone, so she needed to look for your number in the Jacaranda deal… I'm sorry if you were scared… I got her!'

'How is she?'

'She just had dinner with us. She knows mom, and they get really well together. Mom gave her some of her drawing and painting tools to play with.'

Terry wanted to cry right then. He understood quickly what had happened. He didn't need the whole story. Tate knew the guy. He told his mom the guy was following him. Then, if he saw Maddox approaching Mrs Talon… his mind moved to an entire group of men running down the street in football gear… in the whole confusion caused by being in such a crowded area, Tate easily could take Laura… but not for a ransom, to safety. He raked his hair with his fingers. He had to decide between running to Nolani's house or back to the police. Knowing how important it was for those forces to use their time helping people, he returned.

He just had to tell them that the son of a friend saw the danger Mrs Talon and his daughter were in when he decided to act. Also, he tried to ring to announce that Laura was safe, but too worried for his little girl, and being necessary to be focused when talking to them, he declined the calls.

When he reached her house, it was about seven in the evening. The emotional rollercoaster he's been through left a deep imprint on his appearance.

He rang to the door, struggling to put it a bit in order. He didn't want his Laura to see him that way. He pushed his shirt into his trousers and raked his hair a few times to put some order in the disorder. The door opened, and Nolani appeared in the door frame. She gestured for him to come in and closed the door after him. He gave her a look. With no make-up, with the blond hair on her shoulders in disarray, she looked just like him. Worn off. Tired. A tragic beauty.

'Will Tate going to be in trouble for what he did?'

'No. The police laughed when I explained to them what rouse he used to pick up Laura and take her away from danger.'

'He is worried about the lady who was kept at gunpoint... He heard a gun being shot...'

'She's okay. She's been taken to hospital and is being treated as we speak. Maddox did not shoot her. I'll go tomorrow morning with flowers to see her. How did Laura take the whole thing?'

'Like a game? She thinks she's playing with the lady hide and seek...'

'Where are they?'

Nolani showed him with trembling hands the door in the back room. 'Just there. Tate is with... with her...'

Terry moved faster than she was ready. Is there a moment when someone is ready to jump off a cliff? Is there a moment when anyone would run to get their death sentence? Is there a moment when anyone would choose to give up a quiet life for incertitude? She knew it was inevitable. Terry opened the door and entered the room where both his children were waiting for him, entertaining one another using her art supplies to draw butterflies and cats. She leaned against the wall, fighting with her anxiety.

As soon as the door opened, Laura jumped onto her feet, shouting happily 'Daddy!'

He wanted her to run to him to give him the cuddle he needed so much, but for her, the whole thing was a game. She was chirpy and sweet and full of energy, still dressed in the school uniform. She collected some sheets of paper from the floor and ran to him to show him what she did in that evening.

'This is a butterfly, daddy. It's made like a rainbow, you see. Here, I made a dragon. I said that dragons don't exist, but Tate said they do, but they are staying away from people. He said that dragons are living in the Fairy Land!' She giggled. 'I thought he was pulling my leg! Daddy, do you like my dragon? It has wings, and here,' she said, showing a huge yellow drawing, 'he's breathing out fire… I made some fairies too… but they are very little because the dragons are so big!'

He wanted to cry right then, seeing her well, so usual self. He needed some time to recover after the scare he got in that afternoon. He opened his arms, and Laura, with the easiness of a loved child, hugged him tight. He pulled strength from that innocent cuddle. Just then, he moved his eyes through the room to the young man sprawled on the floor, surrounded by sheets of paper, colouring pencils and other stuff. He didn't manage to admire the muscular body, his large shape and how well-developed he was for his eighteen years. He looked over twenty.

After the shock of losing Laura, then the relief of getting her back safe and sound, he looked at the young man gutted. Black hair, long enough to touch his shoulders, with few strands falling, rebel over the right side of a very handsome face. The eyes were electrifying, green.

His heart made a jump, taking in all those magnificent lines of a very familiar face. It was, indeed, because he was seeing it daily in the mirror.

His shock was visible, so Tate shuffled with nervousness on the floor, giving him time to assess him well, to pull whatever conclusions, and then to get the hug he was due for over eighteen years of his existence. Laura was still chatting about her dragons and her Fairy Land, but at that moment, he found it impossible to concentrate on her sweet chatter.

'Laura, why don't you come and finish that drawing with the flowers? I will talk to daddy for a little until you finish, ok?'

Terry breathed in, taking in the way the boy called him. He was daddy…

'Ok, Tate, I will add a sky and many colourful butterflies…'

Laura went into a lotus position on the floor and started to organise the sheets in her little hands to find the one she started, while Tate collected himself from the floor and stretched his legs, without taking his eyes from Terry.

'I'm sorry for the shock I gave you today, Mr Morgan,' he said, coming close to the man of his dreams. Only he knew how hard it was to hide his excitement in finding finally his dad. Only he knew how hard it was to find out his dad was here last evening, and he missed him because he was asleep. His heart was beating crazy in his chest, but seeing the man unable to move, he realised that it was not easy for anyone to take in that they have a fully-grown son somewhere. Even more… and that was grumpy Sue at school, some dads are denying their children… His blood pressure raised higher, while he raised his hand towards his dad for a manly shake.

'I don't understand…' Terry whispered, looking at Tate dumbfounded. 'How is this possible?'

He turned towards the door where Nolani was watching him with a fearful expression all over her face. She was not simulating coolness to save face anymore. She could not do that to Tate. She was looking from him to her son, then back, and the duality of the feelings trying her at that moment could make her ill. She was scared Terry would reject Tate. The horror of seeing that happening was devouring her. The damage was done. Maddox wanted so much for Terry to learn that Tate was his son. Well, now he knew. She knew the time had come for him to find out. The police might ask him about his history with Maddox. About the girl in the hotel room. It was better this way.

'Nolani…' he called her with a low voice. His eyes demanded an explanation. She could read his confusion, a desperation to understand. In his head, ideas were flying in a whirlpool, and he was having a struggle to grasp them.

'Florida…' she whispered breathlessly, then she lowered her eyes and looked away.

Florida! Terry blinked a few times, looking at her in disbelief. The girl Maddox tried to rape that night. The girl he comforted so well, he ended up taking her virginity. She was Nolani.

God, almighty, what a mess!

'I always wanted to meet you,' Tate said with a low voice, trembling, expecting. He was aware that his dad would be shocked to find out about him. He was waiting, though for some different kind of emotions displayed. He pictured this in his mind so many times. In all the cases, he was finishing in the arms of his dad, fully recognised, with a smile and a tight hug. The man went into shock and remained stuck there! He had the patience of a tomcat, so seeing that he was not getting what he wanted in the time he wanted, he pushed his arms around Terry and pulled him tight.

It took a while. Few seconds? Seemed more like minutes until he felt the arms of his father raising around him and squeezing him tight. At that moment, he understood that his dad needed time. He will deliver all he wanted and even more, or so he was hoping he will. He lived all his life knowing that his dad lived, breathed, woke up in the morning, gone to sleep at night, somewhere there on the same planet with him. His dad did not have that advantage. He didn't know he existed. He breathed in with an interrupted noise, and he released the poor man with a shy smile. 'We will talk another time, okay? Sometime when you will feel better… I know today was not a good moment, especially after the whole misadventure with Laura… I'll be up in my room. Mom?'

Nolani nodded with a solemn countenance. She had to explain to his dad how… him… happened. Plus, why she did not tell him after they met again.

'Good night, Laura!' he said to the little girl, leaving the room.

'Good night, Tate!'

Hands on the hips, looking towards his little girl drawing in the middle of the room, he wondered what he could say now to her to show his indignation but without being insulting. The options were minimal. His ability to play 'I'm okay' was even lower than that.

He needed to think about this, before he could open his mouth because he would end up projecting his guilt upon her, and he had some nasty words in his vocabulary he put together for the night in Florida with that girl. He needed to know something, the reason why he looked at her. 'On that night, in Florida, you were not eighteen.'

'I was. I turned nineteen in November.'

'Huh…' he grunted. 'Last night… did you plan to have me in between your thighs, Miss Arrington? You knew I was easy…' His self-deprecation was louder than a tower bell in her back room.

Her cheeks coloured in a soft pink, while she turned her head away. She nodded on the sides and turned around. Nolani knew he could be cruel and crude. 'I did not plan last night, Terry, as I did not plan to receive visits in my hotel room years ago. It happened, and I am not regretting it. Not then. Not now. You can insult me if you want, but you loved me then when I've never been shown a display of love. And I loved you for that. After that night… after I had Tate, I have never been denied love again. I had it, unconditionally and pure, from your son.'

'You still ran…' he reminded her with a low voice.

'I was ashamed. I left my guard down twice in my life, with you…'

'And I took advantage of a woman with the guard down twice in my life… with you,' he concluded with a self-deprecating smile.

'You didn't take advantage of me, Terry. I did.'

Their eyes met. In that moment, Laura finished her project and jumped on her feet to show him. As much as he wanted to make a quick exit with a six-year-old girl, it was not easy. He had to congratulate her for a pretty drawing she made. Then Nolani had to express her honest opinion. They had to play nice and civil for the sake of the child. It took him ten minutes to get to the door with Laura by his hand.

Then Laura wanted to hug her and kiss her… then she wanted daddy to invite her and Tate over at the weekend. Neither could remember what excuse they give to Laura or if they accepted. They mumbled something. He took Laura to the car, and then he realised she still did not have hers as it remained in the police parking lot.

'You did not get your car back…'

'I asked one of my employees to bring it for me. It will be here for the morning.'

'Take care. Maddox kept us very busy in the last twenty-four hours…'

'You too…'

'We talk tomorrow. We have a lot to talk about…'

She nodded, and she closed the door after him. She leaned against, and she slid until she sat on the floor. Somehow, she was glad that the first shock, his first reaction was with Laura in the room. People could be very mean when taken by surprise. He had to temper his reaction for his daughter's sake. But tomorrow… she will have to hear him.

# Chapter 15

Nolani managed to fall asleep very late that night. She spent the time turning from one side to the other, trying to plan a way to keep herself and Tate safe from Maddox. Ideally, they should have moved somewhere else, where he could not find them, until he was caught by the police. With her work and Tate's school, that was not possible. Moreover, this whole mess they were in with Laura's kidnapping attempt completely took away the excitement that Tate was accepted by his favourite university. They looked at the papers when they arrived, but they were too concentrated on finding Terry's number to contact him. Nolani sighed. She wished their life could go back to normal, but with Terry knowing of Tate's existence, that would never be possible. And until Maddox was caught, their safety was a priority. She woke up at half past six, and the first thing she did was to check on her son. Just after, she went down and started to prepare breakfast and a coffee for herself, a hot chocolate for Tate…

She was to go that day to buy a new phone. Her phone might remain in the police custody from now on maybe until after the process of Maddox. She needed to be able to contact people and to be contacted by people. It was to be a nightmare to get all the numbers of her contacts, but at least she could start somewhere. She could try to ask that agent for her SIM card. All they could say was, 'It's evidence, I'm afraid…'

Tate came down for breakfast with his hair wet after a shower and kissed her on the cheek before he sat down at the breakfast table. 'Did dad tell you anything last evening? He left very early…'

'He couldn't because Laura was there. He was very surprised, you can imagine…'

'Do you think he will come around, mom?'

'I hope, for you, Tate,' she said earnestly. 'You do not deserve to be rejected… you've done nothing wrong. If there is someone to blame, is me. I made mistakes… your dad did too… I'm not regretting having you, and I will never will, but…'

She sighed, looking at him. 'Give him time, will you? Don't expect anything. I do not know what kind of man he is… in this aspect. I know he adores Laura… but he didn't seem impressed to remember Florida last evening.'

'I'll be patient, mom.' He laughed and added: 'I'll try! I am so happy I managed to see him! I have a dad more handsome than a Hollywood star! He looks better than Tom Cruise!'

'I imagine,' she smiled. 'Your dad is six foot two, Tate!'

'Ok… Mel Gibson?'

She nodded negatively and smiled. 'Better…'

'Yep! He is ravishing!'

'Wow… I thought that only a lady can find a man ravishing…'

'The girls at school,' he explained with a shake of his shoulders. 'Do you? I mean… do you find dad ravishing?'

'Of course I do! He is gorgeous!' she stated.

'Mom! You cannot say about a man that he is gorgeous!' he laughed loudly.

'Why not? He is. Handsome doesn't do him justice. He gave me a gorgeous son.'

Tate blushed and lowered his eyes. Right after, though, he lifted his green eyes towards her and smiled. 'I talked to Jake last evening about dad. He is looking forward to seeing him. Do you think he would come to my games? He used to love football, didn't he?'

Nolani sighed, and her shoulders sloped. 'Tate, don't build up too many dreams, my love. Give dad some time…'

'I know… I know…'

But he continued to go on and on about maybe having dad for dinner or spending the weekend together… He always wanted to see Jacaranda…

Nolani drove to work feeling numb. The last few days drained the energy out of her. Her mind was not having a single moment of rest. She was so caught up in the whole nightmare, she didn't manage to call the care home to announce the death of Vanda. Plus, she needed to talk with Ian Wilson about Vanda's passing and the circumstances of her passing.

She couldn't stop feeling guilty for Vanda's death. Maddox killed her grandmother to get to her. The thought was hard to live with. She positioned the car in the parking lot with precision and looked around. There were other drivers around fact which offered her some safety. Before she left the car, she checked her make-up in the mirror. She made extra efforts this morning to hide her poor night's sleep and paleness.

When she entered in Forever, her girls looked at her like she had grown an extra head. Her look was deceiving, as usual. Nolani Arrington was looking like the nightmare yesterday never happened. In her pale blue smart suit, on her high heels and with her hair arranged nicely on her nape, she looked refreshing, beautiful like a supermodel and behaving like she didn't have a problem in the world.

Marina ran to her with an amazed expression all over her face. 'I tried to call you this morning to know how you feel and if you are coming in today…'

'My phone has been in police custody since the night before yesterday, Marina. Are you all right to go today and buy me a new phone?'

'Sure…' she said with a trembling voice. 'Are you fine? Did that gentleman really do that to your grandmother?'

'I will also need you to get me the number of the Sunrise Nursing Home. I will need to talk to the manager, to let him know what happened.' With that said, she retired to her office, leaving her assistant to understand the message that she was not going to tell her the story of her life.

She could see through the glass how she ran to the others and started to chat fast. She bent her forehead in disappointment. Marina had no sense of protection of privacy. The little she knew, the little she had to share with the crowd… Did Vanda raise her to be an alien? She got out of her bag her Dictaphone. The tape remained with Agent White, but at least she got the machine back. She put in another tape and positioned it on her desk, where she could have it handy. She opened her computer to check her emails. Nothing urgent, thank God. She wouldn't have the energy to deal with emergencies.

The door opened, and Marina entered. 'Sunrise Care Home on line two, boss…' she whispered.

'Thank you, Marina…'

She took the receiver and pressed the line two. 'Hello, Mr Thompson...'

'Miss Arrington! We are so sorry to hear the news...'

'So, you have been informed of what happened...' She looked at Marina, who remained glued to the door frame. She made a gesture for her to understand that she had to leave.

'Yes. One of the police officers came to the Home to ask about Mrs Arrington, if she had other visitors than you and so on... We had prepared all the reports regarding the fall, but that was not his primary interest. Then he said that sadly, Mrs Arrington passed away in the hospital, and it seems that her death was not expected... I told him that other than her mental problem, Mrs Arrington did not have serious health problems. That depends on how she'd been affected by the fall. Do you know anything about it?'

'She fractured her hip and her spine. The doctors were trying to find out if the trauma to her spine was affecting the lower side of her body. She was in tremendous pain...'

'Do you know what caused her death, Miss Arrington?'

'I am afraid I cannot say as it is a police investigation, Mr Thompson, but I guarantee that the fall is not investigated. I did not press charges against the home on any grounds. I know how Vanda was behaving when she was having a psychotic breakdown...'

'It was ugly, Miss Arrington. The carers reported that allegedly she was running 'away from them...' She was screaming, 'I cannot believe you did this to me, Jessica...'

Nolani shuffled into her chair. 'Can I come in and see the reports, Mr Thompson? I don't know what broke my grandmother and my mother apart. I want to see if anything she said or screamed that night can bring me some understanding upon the matter…'

'You said that your grandmother never forgave your mother because she remained pregnant with you being unmarried…'

'This was my own interpretation of the rift between them. My grandmother didn't want to talk about my mother. Nobody sat me down to tell me what was going on… It may be nothing, but…'

'Sure, Ma'am. Also, you can use the visit to collect your grandmother's personal belongings…'

They needed the room. Clearly.

'I will need some time to do that. I do pay for the room until the end of the month, and my grandmother just passed away. I'm sure you are not asking me, in the middle of a police investigation to collect my grandmother's belongings, Mr Thompson…'

'No, Ma'am, that was not my intention. I did specify that because I wanted to save you the pain of having to come to the home again and again. You need time to grieve…'

'Thank you, Mr Thompson. I will make arrangements to have her belongings collected. I also need to talk to Mr Wilson about the matter. So, is that alright if I come in a couple of hours to have a look into the reports of the staff about her breakdown that night?'

'Sure, Miss Arrington…'

She couldn't put a pin on what made her take that decision to look into Vanda's behaviour that night. Same as her, all her life, Vanda was very private; she kept everything in. She wondered if this manner of dealing with problems transformed her into the bitter woman she was or if she had always been like that. Clearly, she loved her grandfather. The way she behaved when she told her she was about to meet him and his family… it was the manner of a girl willing to please, full of dreams of happiness and in love with the man.

Most of all, she was wondering what really happened between her and her mother, which made Vanda hate her so much. That was more than making a child and abandoning it in her hands. She was calling her mother a traitor in her breakdowns.

The conversations she was having with Jessica on the phone did not offer any clues to the mystery. Mr Wilson contacted Jessica first to check if she would deal with Vanda having mental problems and moving her to a nursing home. She declined 'in the worse of manners' as Mr Wilson put it, a fact which made him contact her next. Still, from that moment, she started to receive phone calls from Jessica on her cell phone, inquiring when Vanda was going to die because she wanted the money from the selling of Jacaranda. Mr Wilson admitted that he might have made the mistake of giving her the number in one of their conversations through the phone.

Before, Jessica would call the landline in Jacaranda. The conversations were brief and mostly unpleasant. After she moved to Dallas, she didn't have any contact with her mother. She changed the number in Jacaranda when she renovated the house, so the new owner would not be annoyed with her mother's phone calls. They had no business in the matter of the old owners.

Marina knocked on the door and entered when she made her a sign, she could come in.

'I'm ready to go out and get you a new phone, boss. Is there anything you would like?'

'I need a business phone, Marina. Something like the one you got me last time.'

She handed her the card from the drawer. Marina took it and put it in her purse, but instead of leaving the office, she sat down. 'Did they catch him?'

She looked at her dumbfounded. Catch who?

'Sorry?'

'Did the police catch the man who killed your grandmother?'

She shuffled in her chair, uncomfortable. 'Marina, the less you know, the better. I never made confidants, and I am not going to start now. How much from what I told you this morning do the ladies know?'

Marina looked at her with surprise.

'Do they know that my phone is in the police custody?'

She nodded her head.

'Do they know that I needed to talk to the manager of the care home where my grandmother resided?' Marina bent her head with guilt all over her face. 'I do not appreciate that the lady who was supposed to protect my privacy is gossiping around me. You are not my best friend; you are my employee. This being said, do not ask questions about my private life, to give me reasons to remove you from the position as my personal assistant. Now, please go and buy me a new phone and leave the conversation where it is now. And if

Mr Morgan is coming again, please let him in without spreading gossip about romances under the moonlight. You do not know anything about me, and we will keep it that way. Understood?'

'Yes, boss…'

She stood up from the chair and went towards the doors. She seemed to freeze in the door frame, and she turned towards her. 'Boss, I think Mr Morgan is here to see you…'

Nolani's heart made a somersault. With a very low voice, she said, 'Let him in, please…'

Marina invited him into her office, then pulled the door shut.

# Chapter 16

'She seems… upset,' he noticed, making a gesture towards her assistant.

'I told her off for gossiping about me…'

'Too late. Everyone thinks in the building that we are fucking like bunnies, we moved together, and the wedding is soon…'

Nolani's cheeks caught fire. 'How is your childminder?'

'Fine. She came out of the hospital today. I thought she would give up her job, considering the incident yesterday. She seems more determined than ever to look after Laura, no matter what… I got some men coming from New York. They are some… friends of my associate. One of them had to step in the light and take Laura to school today. The rest of them remained in the shadow to watch over her and Tate, to make sure Maddox does not get close to them again.'

The fact that he extended the protection upon Tate gave her a feeling of relief. Still…

'Are they… legal?'

'I think so. My friend wouldn't access help, which can damage our image and reputation as Defence Attorneys… I hope. I should ask for more details later. For the moment, I feel better knowing that the kids are under surveillance. What Tate did yesterday was crazy and brave… Tate involved in the rouse his entire football team, wasn't he?'

'He has many friends. Close friends.'

She raised Tate to be open, honest and kind to people. The number of his friends he was counting was exceeding hers, with everyone over one. The only friend, true friend she had was Eloise Burton. She was proud of her son. Her manners kept everyone at a distance. In school, she was bullied by everyone for being abandoned, for being lonely, for being shy, and for any other reasons, the kids found to be mean and cruel to her. His manners made him the most popular kid in the high school. The girls were thinking he was… ravishing…

'What does he know about… you know…'

'Everything. I didn't hide the truth from him. I never knew your name. That night would never happen if your friend… let's say, would have been mentally healthy…'

'He is. He is a bully.'

'He is not, Terry. He lives under the impression that me and him had something going on, when you are the witness that nothing like this had happened. He is convinced that I was his… girl… That's why he wants to hurt Tate because he is the proof that you… slept with his girl…' she repeated with an undertone. 'He is mad at you because apparently, you swore to him that nothing happens, when obviously Tate is the proof of the contrary.'

'So, this is what he told you yesterday when he paid you that visit here…'

'That at the moment when you are going to learn that Tate is your son, we are becoming *dead meat*. I had a feeling that this was the case… He was insisting too much on the issue. The pictures he took with you, Tate and the message '*I know, you know, do they know*? I was trying to delay the death sentence by not telling you.'

'And that would be the reason for not telling me about Tate…'

'Not entirely. You didn't remember me. That was painful. You mocked me for having my son without a father…' He moved his weight from one foot to another, realising how inappropriate that comment was. He muttered a swearing word, feeling rotten.

'Vanda wanted to give him to adoption…'

'She wanted an abortion,' she said. Terry startled hating only the thought that his son might have never existed. 'When I refused to do that,' she continued, 'later in the pregnancy, she started to look into giving my son to adoption. When she opened the subject with me, she had all her homework done, contact numbers, connections… She even talked to the social services in my name! I packed my things, and I left. I had no other contact with her until her lawyer approached me with the news that she was suffering from a mental illness and she needed the involvement of a relative… I stepped in, considering that it was the right thing to do. My mother declined the responsibility.'

'Are you sure Jessica is your mother, Nolani?'

She startled. 'What do you mean?'

'Did anyone tell you that Jessica was your mother?'

'My grandmother said that she had a child unmarried, that she was a slut and so on… letting me understand that… she was. I even overheard a conversation when she was telling someone that I was her granddaughter…'

'Did Jessica ever acknowledge that she was your mother?' No, she didn't. Nolani looked at him, baffled. 'Did you ever ask her why she abandoned you?' She didn't dare to do that. She was always so aggressive on the phone and so insulting, she never had the courage to ask her that. She had the impression that Jessica hated her mother and, obviously, her.

'Why do you ask, Terry? What do you know?'

'Wiseman said that Jessica had a baby girl she called Summer. She died in her cot a few months later…'

Nolani pressed her small hand against her chest to slow down her crazy beating heart. 'Who am I, then?' she whispered, looking confused at her desk without noticing anything lying on it.

'Wiseman is working on it. The grand mystery is the fact that you do look like Vanda. He is putting a bet on you being Vanda's daughter… We don't know for a fact, though… I'm sorry, Nolani.'

'Why is he still investigating this?'

'He loves mysteries. For real. He found a subject that is really interesting for him…'

'He hates me…'

'Nah… he hates his ex-girlfriend, who was a high socialite and caught her cheating on him a week before their wedding. After that, he found out that their son was not his. Because he signed the birth certificate, he ended up paying child support for a child who is not his… He has nothing to do with you.'

'I'm not a high socialite…' she argued with a low voice. 'I don't do clubs… I don't do fashion, parties and expensive holidays…'

'I know, Nolani. And I know that him looking into your past upsets you… but on the other side, it might put some light on the lies of Vanda.'

She had to agree with him. She nodded her head, kneading her hands onto her lap.

'The most important here, is Tate. You didn't jump to my throat...'

'I thought about it. I didn't know your name either... You didn't know mine. What happened nineteen years ago was not planned, just as you said. It came back to me what you said last night, that you didn't regret it... How is Tate?'

'Excited? Planning to have you there to his football match next week... Planning to share with you the excitement that he was accepted to his favourite university... he wants to study law and to practice family law...' Terry smiled. He heard that before from her, but until then he never knew she was talking about his son. Now, the fact that his son made all those decisions for his future had an emotional impact on him. His son was making the same choices of hobbies and ultimate career as he did. Nolani continued looking at him with a sad smile: 'He wants to spend time with you, to talk to you like from a man to a man, do with you all the things other boys are doing with their fathers.'

'I think then that we should start by listening to Laura and having this weekend together.' Nolani startled. The time has come for Tate to enjoy his dad, and she was happy that Terry chose to include him in family plans.

'Tate will be very happy, Terry. Will you take care of him?'

'We will take care of him. I'm planning a family weekend. You are coming too...'

'I don't think it would be a good idea. You need this time with him. Tate needs this time with you. I can sort out the stuff of my…' she stopped with a sigh. She wanted to say, grandmother. '…the stuff of Vanda…' was her choice of words after a few seconds of thinking.

'I can do this with you. I must visit Rita anyway.'

Nolani looked at him, feeling a bit exasperated by his intrusion. She didn't want him around when she investigated the reports of the accident of Vanda. God knows what she was screaming that night, and staff detailed the reports. Plus, there was the emotional burden of having to collect Vanda's belongings from the care home.

'I'll stay with Rita while you are doing what you need to do,' he negotiated.

She didn't say anything to that either. She saw him motioning towards the door. 'I'll call Tate to ask if he would spend the weekend with us…' he added. 'When do you want to go to the care home?'

'I have to discuss it with Mr Thompson, when he is available to talk to me…'

He left with a nod of his head. Nolani sat at her desk, relieved that Terry was showing an interest in knowing Tate better and, most of all, included him in the protection plan alongside his daughter. It wasn't much, but it was something. She didn't know what Maddox was planning to do next, but the fact that she would have Tate under surveillance was a relief.

Marina arrived in about another hour with a new phone and a number, and she occupied her time introducing the numbers she had in a small agenda on the phone. She gave a message to Eloise to tell her that this was her new number, then Tate… and ended up sending a message to Terry as well. If he wanted to contact her, the cell phone would be handy.

With Tate having plans to spend a few hours that afternoon with Jack, she concentrated as much as she could to plan the projects *Forever* received. The money from their last projects arrived in the company account, another reason to feel relieved. Her business was thriving. Her life, not so much.

It was a surprise that Terry did not take the news that he was the father of her son very badly. He saw that part of him in their first encounters, and in all honesty, she didn't know if she could manage damaging and insulting comments regarding the son they conceived together. Tate deserved it all, but to that, adding the fact that she ended up repeating the story with him the other night... She sighed. Whatever his opinions, she was happy that he didn't scream or trash the place down.

The last thing she expected for that day was Agent White visiting her at her workplace. He's been introduced by one of her designers, Elena, as Marina just went out for her lunch.

'Any news regarding the autopsy of my grandmother?' she asked while preparing his coffee.

'I have reasons to believe that Maddox upgraded to murder, Miss Arrington. Besides the fact that he confirmed to you that he committed the murder. That cannot be used in court as evidence, as maybe you know, but it is a good hint for me, as an investigator, in what direction to look. We could not find any particles in the airways of... I'm sorry...' he hesitated, 'the body but the hospital staff said that her breathing was very shallow at times. Instead, we did find saliva residue on a pillow after that was positioned on a chair in the room. More, in the picture, the hand that presses the pillow… you can see a Wind Rose tattoo. Maddox has such a tattoo on his left lower arm. He seems to have taken the photo with his right.'

'So, the record does not help the case at all…'

'No, and it does not prove that Maddox is delusional either. You made no comment to set the story straight, Miss Arrington…'

'And how, in your knowledge, a delusional person, big, strong and capable of killing, does react when the story he is convinced of is *set straight*? My instincts told me not to play the red scarf under the nose of a mad ox, Agent White.'

He looked at her with a glimpse of surprise on his face. His dark, intelligent eyes were piercing. Suddenly, his whole expression changed. 'I will need your statement about what happened nineteen years ago, Miss Arrington. And Mr Morgan's statement…' Nolani nodded, moving gracefully around her desk. Coming in front of it, she leaned against it and supported both her hands on the wooden rim of her desk.

'Why did Officer Flowers visit the care home where my grandmother resided?'

'To cover all the aspects of the case. He had to interview the staff there as he had to interview all the staff in the hospital who cared for Mrs Arrington. Procedure, Miss. Now, I did come to inform you that you will be followed by us. Your house is already set under surveillance. Your son, the same. If Maddox wants to put into practice his threats, he's going to come close again. Now… did Mr Morgan learn that he does have a son?'

Nolani nodded, feeling embarrassed at the idea that she had so many people knowing about Florida.

'They met last evening. Maddox tried to kidnap his daughter, Laura, at school.'

The expression on Agent White's face changed. He straightens up in his chair, looking at her with two very dark brown eyes. 'What happened? Did he take the little girl?'

'No. My son did. He asked his friends to create chaos and, in the meanwhile, he took Laura.'

'That was crazy and dangerous,' decreed White.

'Crazy and dangerous is Maddox having Laura, Agent White.'

'He didn't hurt little girls before, Miss Arrington,' he smiled a bit patronizing.

'He didn't hurt old ladies before either, Agent White. How come my grandmother is with the coroners now?' was her quick reply.

He frowned, then leaned forward. 'I will need the address of Mr Morgan. I will need him and his daughter put under close surveillance as well.'

Nolani smiled gently, trying to imagine the party around Jacaranda with agents and the men of Terry's friend while they were having a barbecue on the weekend. She wrote down the address and handed it to Agent White.

'Something else, Miss Arrington… Did you find on your car a letter written with a finger, in acrylic, 'Tell him or I…'? Did Mr Morgan touch that letter?'

'Yes, he removed the letter from the windshield of my car. Why? Is it in your possession?' she startled.

'From this morning. It is sent to the lab, to check for prints. The message was explaining where the piece of paper was found, that has on it the prints of Mr Morgan as he was the one who handled it and that we are in for a huge surprise.'

'That it may be Mr Maddox?'

'I don't know... I thought that maybe you know something...'

'I did not discuss about that letter with Mr Morgan.'

White jumped on his feet and put the empty cup of coffee on her desk. 'All right, Miss Arrington, we will keep in touch.' She wrote on a piece of paper her new number and she gave it to him. 'Do not drive too fast, do not make sudden moves in traffic which would make my colleagues struggle to keep up, highlighting that you are followed...'

She nodded, walking with him towards the door.

'I know Mr Morgan went for law and Criminal Defence as a career. Do you know what Mr Maddox was doing for a living? Did he continue a football career?'

'No, he went for coaching football in a high school. Sally Holden was a student there...'

# Chapter 17

Wiseman leaned with his elbows on the desk in the elegant office set up on the eighth floor of the building and formed a number on the phone. While the phone was ringing, he evaluated some notes he had scribbled on a piece of paper prior to the call.

'Hello?' came through the speakers in the quiet room.

'Hello, Ma'am. Do I speak to Miss Jessica Augusta Arrington?'

'Who asks?' was the reply, a bit snappy in Jeremy's opinion.

'My name is Noel Armstrong, Ma'am. I am investigating the tragic death of your mother, Mrs Vanda Arrington.'

'Tragic, my ass,' came the answer. 'I did speak with Mr Wilson, Vanda's lawyer,' she said, avoiding calling Vanda *mother*, Jeremy concluded. 'He didn't say anything about tragic. She died in hospital, didn't she?'

'Yes, Ma'am. What do you know about Nolani Arrington? She said about speaking to you on the phone several times…'

'What are you talking about?'

'Who is Nolani Arrington, and in what way is she related to you?'

'Ask Vanda,' she answered grumpily.

'What was your understanding about the degree of relatedness with this lady? She had the legal power to look after Vanda's financial affairs and her welfare. Apparently, she was appointed by the court, not by Vanda personally. Seems a bit weird that not yourself, as Vanda's only daughter, but this lady has been appointed as such…'

'Huh… and what was the question here?'

'What was your understanding about the degree of relatedness with this lady?' he repeated, smiling a bit amused by her abrupt approach. 'What was she to you?'

'And the reason you want to know is?'

'Because Vanda Arrington led this lady to think that she was the daughter you conceived as a teenager and you abandoned. To her understanding, Vanda adopted her own granddaughter when her rotten mother didn't want her…'

'That's crap!' she screamed through the phone. 'If that bitch would answer her phone, I would set this bullshit straight!'

'Miss Arrington cannot answer her phone because the item is in police custody, following the tragic passing of your beloved mother, Miss Arrington,' he smiled, drawing invisible circles in the air with his fingers.

He could imagine her seething, infuriated by his words, when he knew there was no lost love between her and Vanda Arrington.

'I remind you that this she was led to believe by your dear mother. What did Vanda tell you about the presence in her house of a Nolani Arrington?'

'That she adopted herself a new daughter, who hopefully will come out better than me…'

'Did you ever meet Nolani Arrington, Miss Arrington?'

'I'm not curious!'

'I'm asking because she is the spitting image of Vanda Arrington. Slim, blonde, blue eyes, posh posture and all. Very pretty lady, I have to say.'

'Are you telling me that she is Vanda's daughter?!' she cried infuriated.

'I'm not saying anything. The mystery is in the air, Miss Arrington because she knows that she is the daughter you abandoned, you know that she's been adopted… and the one who knows the truth is in the coroner's hands…'

'So, you are telling me that she is a legal sister and she has equal rights to inherit Vanda!' she seems to choke. Jeremy smiled. So that was what she was after! Vanda's money!

'I'm afraid not, Miss Arrington. I don't know what it was all about, but something happened between you and your mother, Vanda Arrington, which, and I'm talking from my experience and personal expertise, may lead to you being completely disowned of any rights to Vanda Arrington's inheritance… Do you know what may have caused the rift between you two? We all know Vanda was not easy to live with…'

'Go to hell!' she screamed before she closed the conversation.

He chuckled and scribbled a few words on the paper. In conclusion, nobody knew the truth. Vanda Arrington was telling her own truth to each player in the game according to what she wanted them to know. It was to her advantage that Nolani did not bring up the questioning of her abandonment on the phone with Vanda's daughter.

His mental image of Jessica Arrington was complete. He didn't doubt that Vanda Arrington tried to keep in leash and manage her through strict education as she did with Nolani. It didn't mean that she didn't manage. He could swear that meeting her in unrelated circumstances, would give him the same impression Nolani Arrington left on him. In his opinion, the lady was fighting with all her might against the strict education she received. She was doing everything in Vanda's spite. It was actually possible that she had done nothing but this to cause the rift between herself and her mother. It was enough for Vanda, who was a master manipulator and a control freak. The language was something else. Nolani would crack in embarrassment to voice up such words as *bitch, crap* and *bullshit*. It did prove, to him at least, the level of rebellion against Vanda and her hate towards all her mother stood for.

One thing, though, she didn't hate at all. Moreover, she was dreaming of putting her greedy little hands on… That was Vanda's money.

He considered that conversation a success. Maybe it didn't reveal to him anymore of the family secrets. He did already imagine that Jessica thought of Nolani as being adopted. Through that phone conversation, it didn't transpire the secret of Nolani's origins. Still, he was satisfied.

Now, if he was to bet all his money on one thing, that would be the return of Jessica Arrington in Dallas, to put up a fight for what she thought belonged to her.

❀ ❀ ❀

'Are you sure about this?' she asked, sitting on the passenger seat of a Land Rover car, while he was driving towards the Sunrise Care

Home. 'I need to talk to the manager, and that may take a while...'

'Then Rita will have a long visit from her grandson,' he smiled. 'If you need help with collecting Vanda's belongings, let me know, and I'll come to give you a hand. One over the other, Nolani, this must be done.'

She nodded, then looked through the window to the landscape around them. 'Agent White said he received the note I found on my car... The note was saying that he was in for a huge surprise.'

'Wiseman had the mission to send it to him to the police station. He is the one who is investigating Maddox.'

'Why is the FBI involved?'

'The three girls who accused him of rape were from three different states. Their statements were almost identical to a fault. The beatings, the brutality... the words they are all alleging he was saying during their ordeal... Then the description of the individual... that he was strong, largely built, blue eyes, blonde hair and so on... FBI has been involved when the cases were correlated. He was one on a long list of suspects... until Sally Holden identified him as her attacker. The nature of the attack was different. Apparently, she fancied him. She agreed to meet with him to have sex. She did not expect to be punched numerous times and knocked unconscious. When she recovered her consciousness, he was already committing the act. He kept telling her that he needed to teach her some manners, that she was a slut for causing grief in his team, when she knew she belonged only to him. Then he went on sodomising her. Her ordeal lasted for a few hours. When she recovered in the hospital, and she named him as her attacker, they went to arrest him, but he was nowhere to be found.'

'She could identify him, still, he didn't kill her…' she muttered.

This was proving that Maddox didn't see his acts as being crimes punishable by law. He considered it was his right. In his twisted way, he was convinced she belonged to him and Terry took what was rightfully his… He wanted the girls to remember him, to live with his memory. This was feeding his ego. Terry looked at her shortly before moving his eyes towards the road.

'You don't think he killed Vanda…'

'I'm convinced he did it, Terry. Agent White confirmed it. Also, he said that he placed us and the children under surveillance.'

'Maddox will realise that. He's not an idiot.'

'I don't know…' she whispered.

'Nolani, the guy is more intelligent than you think!'

'I believe he is. I trust though that in his twisted way of thinking, he considers that he does nothing wrong…'

'He wouldn't have evaded arrest, Nolani. He knows he committed a crime…'

Nolani was not convinced, but at the end of the day, Terry had known the man since they were kids. 'Agent White wants a statement from both of us regarding the attack nineteen years ago.'

His fingers on the wheel tensed, and his chin seemed chipped in stone.

'What did you say about it, Nolani?'

'I can't influence your statement, Terry. You have to say your version of how you remember that attack.'

'I'm not asking about Maddox. I'm asking about you and me… conceiving Tate,' he grunted.

'The truth,' she said, blushing and looking elsewhere. 'That I initiated it. That it was not planned. That it was no romance. I was in pain from the punches I received, I was in shock, and I needed that connection with a human body…'

'What did they say?'

'They laughed…' she sighed, slouching her shoulders in a defeated position. 'They mocked me that I ran from Hammer to sleep with Stampede…'

Terry gritted his teeth. He turned the car and parked it in front of the Care Home, then he turned to look at her with his eyebrows frowning.

'They mocked you… Did you tell them you were a virgin that night? That I… practically continued what Maddox started?'

'You haven't done this, Terry. You stayed with me because I was in shock. Because I needed you to hold me… You didn't plan to do anything that night…'

'Yeah… tell this to my dirty conscience,' he mumbled, moving his eyes from her. 'I became successful, I had many merits as a Defence Attorney… I became so good at it that I was a celebrity of some sort. But nothing, Nolani, no success, no recognition of merits could delete that night from my mind when I took advantage of a beaten girl…'

Nolani looked at him with her gorgeous blue eyes filled with tears. 'I never saw it that way, Terry. If I ran away, it wasn't because of what you did. I was embarrassed by what I did… This, plus the fact that he was still around, and I was afraid of him. He could try to finish what he started, and who could ensure me that you could stop him again from hurting me? You gave me the world that night. For Tate, I found the strength to pull myself away from my… from Vanda. In Tate, I found all the affection which comes pure and unconditional between a mother and her child. He was a great kid. Raising him was a privilege. He was always kind, polite, sweet, a little man with his own code of right and wrong. I'm not saying that I didn't bring my contribution to help him identify right from wrong. I'm saying that he is so much like I remembered his father to be. A great man with great ambitions, fighting on the right side of the law…'

'Why Family law?'

'I don't know, really…' she sighed. 'I think it has something to do with a kid he met at school whose mother obtained full custody, just because she was the mother. Apparently, she was horrible to him; she used him to get to his dad, and the boy was suffering tremendously. His dad had to pay child support, but he was not even allowed to visit him from time to time. I think, in his spirit of justice, he wants to make a difference.'

Terry smiled, then sighed. 'Sounds like a person I will be honoured to know better.' After a long moment of silence, he shook his head, trying to clear his mind. 'Okay… are we ready to go in?'

Nolani nodded, then she turned and opened her door.

The discussion with the manager was long. He wanted to present his condolences for her grandmother's passing. He asked about the police investigation. The only thing she could say was what Agent White told her; that was just a procedure. Vanda's death was not related to the fall she suffered within the home. She reminded the manager that she wanted to see the reports regarding the fall, highlighting that she was not looking for staff negligence but to establish in what frame of mind Vanda went down those stairs. From the conversation on the phone, it remained in her mind, something about… Vanda running 'away from them…,' screaming, 'I cannot believe you did this to me, Jessica…'

Who was *them?* What was it all about? Whatever it was, she kept it all in for all the time she could remember. As her mental health deteriorated, Vanda lost that good front she kept all those years. Mr Thompson opened the file and handed her three statements of his staff presented when Vanda had that fall on the stairs. They all stated that she woke up screaming, then she came down the corridor running 'away from them…' The staff tried different approaches, offered her a cup of tea, distraction; all to no avail. Vanda scratched a member of staff who was blonde, and they all knew that she was not keen on blonde female members of staff… she screamed, 'I cannot believe you did this to me, Jessica! You ruined me!' Then she shoots up the stairs, screaming that they were after her. Against all the attempts of the staff to stop her, she went up about twenty steps before she went on her back, tumbling to the bottom of the stairs. From there on was the fact that the staff called an ambulance, the home manager and so on… Nolani felt disappointed. She hoped that Vanda said something else than what Mr Thompson already told her on the phone. In another statement was written that Vanda did not take her medication that day. That was not unusual. She agreed with the health professionals for Vanda to have her medication covertly in her breakfast. In the morning prior to the accident, though, she refused to eat and drink, accusing staff that they were trying to poison her.

Nolani sighed. Vanda was very easy to manage when she had her medication. In the circumstances described in the reports, it was not a surprise Vanda went into a psychotic break.

After the lengthy conversation with the manager, she went into Vanda's room and collected all her framed pictures, her clothes and other items of toiletry, books and drawing materials she bought for Vanda to keep her mind busy. She packed everything, feeling numb. When she turned to leave the room, she was startled to see him in the door frame.

'How was it?'

'Not great…'

'Give me that… I'll carry it to the car. Are you taking the flowers?' he asked, referring to the pots of flowers on the windowsill.

'No, just that luggage and these pictures.'

They all show Vanda in different stages of her life. Her wedding day. Dinner parties. Another event… There were no pictures of Jessica or of hers, as Vanda did not want anything like that around. Apparently, while still living in Jacaranda, she trashed completely the room Jessica used to occupy. When she started to redecorate Jacaranda, she couldn't find any picture of Jessica in one piece. The photo albums of Jessica as a baby were burnt.

'How is Rita?'

'Worried for you.'

'Did you tell her that she has no reason to?'

'No, but I promised her I'll take good care of you.'

Nolani stopped and looked at him, a bit surprised. 'How did you plan to keep this promise?'

'I don't know, really. Remaining the one you would ask to hold you when you are down?' he asked with a cheeky smile on his face.

Her cheeks went on fire. Twice in their lives, she asked him to hold her, and they ended up having sex. Clearly, he made a referral to that and she couldn't stop her reaction. She couldn't come back with any answer. Moreover, she had to keep her composure as the staff surrounded her to tell her how sorry they were for her loss. They asked if she would continue to visit Rita, as they were good friends. Looking at his gorgeous green eyes, she said that it did not depend on her but on Rita's relative if he was permitting her to visit his grandmother.

'Well, my darling,' he commented to her mortification, 'I don't see why not, in one of our next visits, we wouldn't bring our son to meet Rita. I'm sure Rita would adore him...'

To see the staff looking confused at her and the gorgeous specimen carrying her luggage took a lot of effort to maintain her good front. She smiled shyly towards them. 'As it seems, I can visit Rita in the future...' With those words, she rushed to leave the home and all the suspicious looks of the staff at Sunrise. 'Why did you have to say that, Terry?' she asked, feeling uncomfortable. 'You led them to think we are together or something!'

'Why, my love... as we all are on Maddox's kill list, mind as well let them all know we are a couple...'

# Chapter 18

'Is Tate Arrington your son, Morgan?' asked Wiseman that evening, looking at him astonished. 'I mean… when my man brought me the pictures this afternoon, I almost fell from the chair!'

As soon as Wiseman arrived at his house that evening, he invited him out on the veranda. Terry looked at him. He was not looking shocked, he was looking annoyed at it, furious!

'I met him last evening, Wiseman, it's been confirmed. Tate Arrington is my son.'

'You didn't tell me that you and his momma have a story together!'

'I did not remember her,' he said, sitting down in a chair. Wiseman looked at him with the air that he did not believe him.

'When you bed someone looking like Nolani Arrington, you remember…'

'She was not looking like that when I met her.' Wiseman looked at him, waiting. 'For once, she had short hair. Dental braces. Stuff like that. She was petite and withdrawn; I never laid eyes on her. When I did, she was having on her face the marks of the rage of Maddox. He was drunk one night; he went to walk on the beach… I followed because he was behaving weirdly. I had a feeling that he was up to no good that night. He was agitated and restless. I saw him entering on a balcony of a small hotel room. He went over her and attacked her in her sleep. When I entered the room, he was grabbing her hair and pushing her head against the pillow while he was trying to remove her clothes to rape her. He was telling her that that's not the way to treat him, that she should learn some manners…'

'Exactly what his victims are consistently saying in their statements…' Wiseman muttered, looking towards the field of Jacaranda.

'Yes, Wiseman.'

'You knew what he was capable of. That's why you refused his family's request to represent him.'

'I saw him capable of attacking a young girl while she was sleeping and beating her with brutality. I stopped him that night. He was drunk, therefore sloppy, and his balance was not great. I punched him hard, repeatedly, and then I motioned him outside the room. For a little while I remained to make sure that he does not return. Then I went to her, as she was crying, shaking, victim of a panic attack.'

'You didn't call the police…'

'I was biased, Wiseman. He was my best friend. Don't you think that I thought about that night over and over again? In none of my mental scenarios, I shouldn't have just left it that way. I should have called the police and reported the attack. Then, I thought that she would do so in the morning. In none of my scenarios was I supposed to have sex with the victim that night. I did, Wiseman, and I felt the lowest man on earth! What are you going to say or think about me that I didn't already say or think myself? She was a virgin that night if you didn't know…'

He could see Wiseman chewing the inside of his lip, thinking. 'Did she press charges?'

'No, she took her stuff and disappeared. She says she was embarrassed about what she let happen that night…'

'But she was not in the right frame of mind…'

'I know. But even so, thinking back, she says she does not regret that night.'

'She remained pregnant…'

'Yes. Vanda did not react well to it…'

'The friends of the family said she wanted Nolani to give her child for adoption because he would ruin her future…' Wiseman recalled.

'First choice was abortion, but she resisted that fiercely. Then Vanda came up with the entire plan to give Tate up for adoption. She left this house never to return.'

'Damn,' Wiseman said. 'The press in New York will eat you alive when they will find out. This kind of stuff can ruin your reputation, Morgan.'

Morgan was startled and looked at his assistant, frowning. 'Why would the press in New York would find out?'

'Miss Congeniality, here is Maddox's first victim, Morgan. She must give a statement regarding that night. You must give one as well, as you are directly involved. When the press finds out that you took advantage of a beaten girl, it will damage your career, Morgan.' Terry sighed. That he knew.

'I wouldn't say the detail that she was a virgin that night. That would put a question mark on her reputation,' Wiseman started to calculate rapidly, analysing aspects of the story they could use to their

benefit, without changing it drastically. 'If we can make it look like…
I don't know; she didn't like Maddox, but she preferred you. It would
still stink, but it would look like she made her moves on you. You
know what I mean?'

Morgan chuckled and looked at his assistant with curiosity. 'So,
in all the story, I am the victim. The poor, beaten woman jumped from
the bed and performed a striptease I could not resist. She was so
captivating with her swollen eye and with her lip punctured; I had an
orgasm then and there!' He laughed bitterly.

Wiseman looked at him, annoyed. 'I'm trying to save your career
here!'

'And started telling lies will never be the way to fix one wrong,
Wiseman. The lady states that it was not a rape, that she offered
herself to me willingly, and she does not regret our act or the
consequences of it.'

'Looks like a love story…' Wiseman frowned, thinking very
carefully of another plan.

'We have a son together. I am willing to be in his life and to put
my name on his birth certificate. More, we are together now.'

Wiseman's jaw dropped in shock. 'You are… together!' he
groaned.

'Yes, we are, Wiseman. Not like in the movies, dating and chilling
together. Like in real life. We are very active in one another's lives.
We are to spend the weekend together with the children.'

'Make it official. Marry her!' said Wiseman agitated. 'That would
make everyone understand the romance started years ago. This would

conquer the press; the press loves romance. You met after so many years. She was still in love with you…'

'I bet,' he laughed cynically. 'Every woman who loses her virginity enjoys a hell of the night and remains forever trapped in the stupendous act of lovemaking thinking… *Hey, I never lived something like that before!*'

'Can you stop for a minute and see my logic in this one? Ok, I'm not crazy for the lady! Seems that you don't mind, though…'

'I think you are crazy for her, Wiseman… She's exactly your type of woman, minus the flamboyant personality of Kate and her promiscuity… That's why you are digging into her past so fervently. Now…You were saying?'

Wiseman remained for the second time that evening with his mouth opened, looking at his boss in disbelief. 'That you should marry her. Anyway, you have the plan to give the boy your name.'

'That would make Maddox mad like a bull, Wiseman. He thinks I've stolen his girl that night. More, he is convinced that he and Nolani had a thing going on…'

'And it cannot be the truth… why?'

'I was there, Wiseman. Next to him all the time. She didn't even look at him. She was shy, staying away. I never saw her closer than 30 metres. That was attracting Maddox… she was lonely, not part of a group. A perfect victim for him. A bit of alcohol for the drive, lots of opportunity, clearly he saw where she was staying… and then shit happened!'

Wiseman turned around, agitated. 'Okay, that would infuriate Maddox. Wouldn't it be better to live all in the same place rather than worrying if he's going to attack her or your son? Mr Brown sent his brother-in-law's guards in Dallas to protect you and your family. Wouldn't it be in the best interest to be actually a family?'

'Sure,' Terry said with a low voice, nodding his head.

'So… you would marry her…' he said with the air that he couldn't believe what he was hearing.

'Sure, I would. You would be my man of honour, Wiseman.'

'That's way better,' he sighed, visibly relieved.

'Yep… remains only one thing for you to do… if you manage, I'll do it…'

'Oh… And that is?'

'You have the mission to convince the lady to marry me for all the above reasons…'

Wiseman emptied his glass with one swallow. This was not a mission; Morgan was mocking his attempts to keep his image out of scandal. He always knew that he was not working with a saint, and he had his own skeletons in his cupboard. What he did not expect was that his skeletons and Miss Arrington's skeletons were partially shared. Look at them now, after an unexpected reunion, to find out he has a son she doesn't keep hidden and with that delusional rapist swearing to kill them all. What he was wondering was how much all this was to cost Morgan's image and, through association, his as well. He just made a move to make Jessica Arrington return to Dallas and blow the world of Miss Arrington completely as she knew it. Now, this mess could not only affect that Puss in High Heels but could blow out of proportion around Morgan. He couldn't let that happen.

He had to think this through and mastermind a plan in which he and Morgan could get out with their image intact.

❀ ❀ ❀

It was seven o'clock in the morning that Friday, when the bell to the entrance door at Jacaranda rang. Him, Mrs Talon, Laura and one of the bodyguards for hire of the relative of Sean were having fun in the kitchen enjoying breakfast. He made a sign towards the last that he would answer the door, then motioned through the rooms to see who was so rude to call in so early in the morning.

He had some scenarios in mind. It could be Agent White to talk about Maddox. It could be Wiseman to let him know that he became wiser overnight… Maddox and Nolani were further down the lane in his mental scenarios for morning visits. The lady standing in front of the door was none of them.

Blonde hair, straight, blue eyes. Mature features massively covered in make-up reminding him of that show with gangster's wives on the telly. Especially those hips reminded him of the Kardashians…. The short skirt was not a wise choice, and neither was the blouse revealing a set of boobs as a lethal weapon. His looks made a visible impression on her. Her attitude changed from hostile to flirtatious as soon as her eyes scanned him rapidly. Instinctually, he knew who she was. What was she doing though at Jacaranda so early in the morning?

'Yes, Ma'am, how can I help?'

'I am Jessica Arrington Redgrove, the owner of this house…' she answered, lifting her chin up and looking into his dark green eyes for a sign of surprise. Amusement was not what she expected.

'The owner of this house was Vanda Arrington, and Jacaranda was sold to me while she was still alive, Mrs Redgrove. This makes your presentation absolutely ridiculous. Now… what are you doing to my door so early in the morning?'

'I returned to sort this mess out,' she stated, moving her head with conviction.

'Good luck with that,' he delivered, making a gesture to close the door.

'Don't you dare to close that door in my face, mister! I can cause you a lot of trouble as this house, my house,' she insisted, 'was sold to you without my permission!'

'Take this to Mr Wilson who will see to it. I'm not going to have you shouting at me on my doorstep,' he said between his teeth.

'Well, you like it or not, I belong here, and I'm going to stay here until this mess is sorted!' she shouted, making an angry gesture towards the beautiful building behind him.

'That is the most ridiculous statement you made since you rang this bell, Mrs Redgrove. Go to a hotel and come again when everything you planned to do is done!'

'And who is going to pay for that hotel? You?'

'That's not my problem!' he laughed.

'In my opinion, I already have a house in the area, and I don't need to pay a hotel for my stay-in!'

'I challenge your opinion; hence, I have the paperwork to prove ownership of the house, not you. Now take your problems to Mr Wilson and leave me alone!'

'I don't think you will have that smile on that face when you're going to find out that that bitch who you think sold you this house had no legal right to do so!'

'In a matter of fact, Miss Arrington had all the documentation to prove her legal right to sell the house, Mrs Redgrove.'

'Yeah?' she mocked him, shaking her blonde platinum hair. 'And you know that for sure…' she added, implying that the truth was different.

'I analysed the documentation before making an offer for the house. I am a lawyer myself. I think I am sure of what I am stating. As I said before, take your problems to your mother's lawyer!'

He registered in her eyes the surprise, but she was determined to cause trouble, and she wouldn't listen to logic. At that moment, the bodyguard appeared at the door with Laura by his hand. 'Problems, Mr Morgan? Do you want the lady removed from the property?'

The expression on her face changed looking at the huge man with the skin black like the darkest night. He was tall as well and nicely built, but he could not compare with the Terminator allure of his temporary bodyguard. 'I don't think it would be necessary, Devante. The lady got the message…'

'All right!' she shouted moving on a side on her high heels, to make room for the man to motion the child out of the house, then down the stairs towards the car. 'Give me the address of that bitch who dared to sell you the house without my permission and I'm off.'

'I have no authority to give you anything, Mrs Redgrove. Only Mr Wilson can offer you this kind of information. Goodbye!' he closed the conversation, closing the door in her face.

He saw her moving towards her hired car with jerky moves, showing off her frustration and anger. She lacked the class Nolani had in maintaining her composure through any situation. Vanda did not manage to tame this one. Not even a bit.

He got himself ready and drove to work thinking of the impact the return of Jessica Arrington would have on Nolani. No, she had no legal grounds for her statements, but she could cause a lot of emotional damage. Reaching the building, he went directly to the second floor instead of the eighth. Marina was just preparing for herself a coffee when he entered the office. None of the other interior designers were there. 'Did Nolani arrive, Marina?'

'The office was unlocked when I arrived, so I would consider so…'

Marina went towards the office of Nolani, knocked on the door, and then she opened it. Suddenly, she froze in the doorway. Her scream startled him.

# Chapter 19

Agent White nodded in disbelief, taking in the level of vandalism that stormed Nolani's office. He leaned down, touched a portion of her cream carpet, which seemed soaked in blood and moved the finger to his nose. Terry watched him frowning, leaning with his back against one desk. He was feeling sick to his stomach. Did Nolani fall victim to the hands of Maddox? Now, the idea of her moving into Jacaranda with Tate, delivered by Wiseman last evening sounded as being the best for everyone's safety. This was looking like a nightmare. What happened with Nolani, for God's sake? Was that blood on the carpet? Was it her blood? Did Maddox kill her?

The ladies were not allowed to come in. They were forming a frightened group in the corridor. Marina was questioned by another agent and the police. He could watch her frantic moves through the glass of the doors. He could read in her body language that she was talking about the office door being unlocked and the alarm off when she came in.

The team of specialists was checking the office of Nolani, picking up fingerprints and certain items that could be considered evidence. Agent White came out and joined him.

'Is it blood?' he asked with an undertone. Agent White had a single look at him to discover that the guy was in agony.

'Fresh blood, for sure. We don't know whose yet. The good part is that we know whose blood it's not. For our peace of mind, Miss Arrington is at the police station to have her statement recorded.' Terry sighed and pushed his forehead in the palm of his hand with relief.

'Nolani told me about it. I didn't know that was arranged for this morning. When I saw that, I thought for a moment that Maddox attacked her or something... The fact that her phone was set on 'Do Not Disturb,' didn't help...'

'I know, Mr Morgan. That looked like she fell victim to some sort of attack. Now, the serious stuff is... that is blood. Somebody or something did fall victim in the hands of Maddox. What we don't know is who or what? Definitely, that was set to scare Miss Arrington.'

'Marina says the alarm was disabled, and the door was unlocked. Did he become a master at breaking in? I didn't know he owned such skills until now...'

'What skills do you know that he masters?'

'Don't get me wrong, he is a very intelligent person, and I can consider him capable of learning how to disable an alarm or how to...' Terry stopped and looked at the Agent in shock. 'No, he didn't. The building has a night guard who is keeping copies of all the keys in the offices for emergency matters.'

'This means that also the building has CCTV cameras throughout.'

No, that was not what he meant...

Nolani was still at the police station when she learnt that her office had upgraded to a possible crime scene. She felt paralysed to discover that her whole life, now her work, was being put on hold because of the last events. Terry's mental scenario proved to be right in one aspect. The night guard was found dead in the janitor's room, with a bullet in his head. There were no signs of the guard guy being killed in her office, then dragged along through the building a few floors to be hidden in the basement. That meant that the blood on the carpet in Nolani's office belonged to somebody else. She couldn't comment upon the gruesome discovery in her office because she went from home that morning directly to the police station. The officials who were on duty to keep her under surveillance backed her statement.

She was free to go, but she was not allowed to enter Forever as the entire site was under police investigation. She had no control over deciding when she could go back to work. The level of damage was tremendous, and this could affect her business, the respect of her contractors and business associates and ultimately, her image in front of her clients.

Just when she reached home, she saw the computer in a corner, her workshop and all her designs and plans and studies she had completed over the years, she realised that not everything was put on pause. Nobody said that she couldn't work. What they said was that she could not use the Forever offices to do it. With that idea in her head, she went into the kitchen and prepared a coffee. Just after, she put her phone on function mode and called Marina.

'Oh, My dear God, boss! We all thought you were dead or something!' she cried through the phone.

'Well, Marina, I am not. Thank you for worrying for me. Where are you all?'

'We gathered on the terrace over the street. We don't know what to do. We are not allowed in!' Marina added hysterically.

Nolani sighed. 'Can you give me Jada on the phone, please?'

'Sure... Jada? Boss wants to talk to you...' she could hear the mumbled conversation before she could hear clearly Jada in the speakers. 'Yes, Miss Arrington? Are you okay? Marina here is really freaked out! She saw the whole mess in your office. She was with Mr Morgan, who wanted to talk to you urgently...'

'I have a couple of missed calls from him. I will call him in a bit.' She had a few missed calls from Mr Wilson as well. Another one to call in a matter of emergency. 'Question, Jada! Do you have your laptop with you with your projects and all?'

'We all do. Usually, we are working better at home relaxing with a wine...'

Nolani breathed a sigh of relief. She was taking projects at home as well to work on in the evenings.

'The whole idea is that we are not allowed to use the office for I do not know how long it will take.'

'Yeah, I mean... Marina said that your office is devastated and covered in blood, Miss Arrington.'

Her heart shrunk. She didn't know how bad it was. The officers told her that her office had become a possible crime scene and they were analysing every piece of evidence, but her mind did not register how serious that was. 'Oh, dear...' she sighed. 'Jada, do you think you could all come to my house for the time being? We need to send some emails to our clients that for a certain period of time, they should contact us by email or on our mobile phones, but I think we could make this work without skipping contracts and deadlines...'

'Sure, Miss Arrington. Give me the address, and we will all be there as soon as we can!'

Nolani gave her the address and closed there the conversation. It was not ideal. This idea of transforming her house in the workplace could put her employees in danger. With Maddox playing scary games with her and apparently killing people around her, she could not put her girls on the front line of a psychopath. The next phone call she made was to Eloise, to ask if she had any place she could temporarily use as an office. Not willing to scare her best friend with the last events in her life, she just said that her office was temporarily out of use for some building issues. To her satisfaction, Eloise said that she has a couple of furnished rooms on the second floor of her Estate Agency she used to rent out, but which now were ready to use. She promised she would pay rent for the period she would make use of the rooms. Eloise answered in her own way with a 'well, darling, they are yours as long as you need them. The rooms are not rented right now, so mind as well use them.'

After that phone call, she contacted Mr Wilson. She thought that the conversation was about Vanda's funerals. The topic was completely unexpected.

'Well, huh… Jessica Arrington was in my office this morning,' he muttered, obviously upset.

Nolani was startled, looking out the windows to the several cars making manoeuvres to park in front of her house. 'Is she in Dallas suddenly? Why?'

'Apparently, she received a phone call from a certain Mr Armstrong who claimed that he was investigating the death of Vanda and said that she might have been removed from Vanda's will. She came here in scandal mode to assert the fact that you sold Vanda's house abusively when you are not family and you had no right… and you are just a fraud… claiming that you would be her daughter and so on…

'I told her that legally, you are adopted by Vanda, and who your parents are is none of her concerns. I told her that Vanda, not you, asserted the fact that you might be her granddaughter but left an entire mystery regarding your origins. She requested your phone number and your address, claiming that she wants to have you feeling sorry for making such allegations regarding her person… I refused to give her your new number, even less the address. Now, I just wanted to warn you that she's here, and she intends to make waves…'

Nolani nodded her head. She could not believe what she was hearing.

'Now, Miss Arrington, do you know who this Armstrong is?'

'It could be anyone, Mr Wilson. I can state through the phone that I can be the First Lady if I wish to do so. The Officer who is investigating Vanda's death is called Flowers. To my knowledge, there is no Mr Armstrong in the picture.'

'I tried to pay you a visit to your office, but there is a lot of police, and the area is restricted to trespassers. Do you know what happened?'

'I don't know much. My employees are saying that my office was ransacked, vandalised, and there was blood everywhere. The police and FBI are combing the place for clues and are treating it as a crime scene… They are all thinking that the individual who smothered Vanda in her sleep might be behind this atrocity…'

The bell at her door rang, so Nolani walked slowly and opened it. She made a gesture to keep quiet as she was on the phone and motioned them all inside her house.

'What are you suggesting for me to do, Mr Wilson, with respect to Jessica Arrington?'

'Hm, that wouldn't be in the least pleasant. For the moment, let me deal with her and her allegations. I am, in fact, the person who took care of the legal matters of your grandmother, Miss. I'll keep in touch with you.'

'Any news about the funerals?'

'I've been told that they will release the body in a matter of days. I already discussed this with the funeral directors. Vanda never talked about what she wanted in case of death. Do you know anything about what she wanted or wished in case of her departure?'

'No, Sir. She never talked about that. She was not very religious, even if her close friends who were convinced of the contrary would argue on the matter. She was posing a lot. To the church, in society, in visits… She was talking about God respectfully to gain a good image.'

'So, what we will arrange with respect to the funerals is everybody's guess…'

'Very much so, I'm afraid. She didn't comment anything about burials or cremations… One comment she made once was, 'What difference does it make? The bastard is dead anyway!'

'Yeah, sounds like Vanda to me… All right, Miss Arrington. Keep safe and in touch with me. I got this one…'

'Thank you.'

With those words, she closed the conversation and turned towards the six ladies sitting around in her lounge. Marina looked absolutely in pieces. She felt sorry for her, for being the one discovering the atrocity in her office.

'Thank you all for coming, ladies,' she said. 'Does anyone want a coffee?'

'Don't worry, Miss Arrington,' said one of them. 'We just had one on the terrace…'

'First of all, Marina… I think you can take a few days off. I'm sorry for what you had to go through today.'

'Who could do something like that?!' cried Marina.

'The police think it was Mr Maddox, my visitor from the other day…'

'The one you said that he killed your grandmother?' asked Mandy, the lady who found the individual extremely attractive.

'Yes. I need you all to be very careful. If you see him around, alert the police.'

'Did he really kill your grandmother?' asked Jada.

'Yes. And he's been nice to send me pictures of him doing it…'

She could see her employees going all pale.

'I'm sorry, the last thing I want to do is to scare you all, but you need to be warned that he is dangerous, that he is capable of murder, and he swore to kill me and my son.'

She could see the girls changing a look in between.

'Do you… have a son?' asked Marina with a small voice. Clearly, she just realised she didn't know anything about the woman she had been working for the last six years.

Nolani did not answer. 'Now, to turn to the topic of work, clearly, we cannot use the office for a while…'

'Are we going to work here?' asked Jada, looking around, impressed with the way her boss designed her own house.

'I wish, but it is too dangerous. I discussed with a friend of mine who has a couple of rooms on the second floor of her business which she is ready to let us use temporarily.' She gave them all the address and continued. 'We will all meet at the address on Monday morning. Until then, take this day off. You all need time to digest all that's happened.'

'I will go and check on one of my projects,' said Elena, 'then I'll go home, and I'll work on the project for that gentleman in a wheelchair who needs his house changed around to suit his needs. One over the other, I'm not going to sit on my back… If somebody needs time off from all this, it is you, boss. We can take care of the projects and deadlines and everything. You need to keep yourself safe. This thing is dangerous, is scary and it can end really bad.'

'I know, Elena, but if I'm not keeping busy doing something, I'll go mad. I'll see you all on Monday…'

Walking all towards their cars, Marina exploded. 'Do you believe all that? That she has a son? That's the first time I'm hearing about her having a son! Her office looks like in CSI New York, and she acts like nothing happened!'

'And how do you want her to react? Would it give you any peace of mind to find her hysterical and in pieces?' Elena barked at her with an undertone. 'If the woman said she has a son then she has one, even if you don't like that you didn't know about. It seems that it matters more to you the fact that she is a woman with many secrets she doesn't want to share, rather than being worried for her safety! Honestly, Marina!'

'She was talking about funerals with somebody when we arrived. This proves that she has a dead grandmother…' Jada muttered. 'And her office this morning… if it is so bad as you describe, then damn! She pissed off somebody really bad…'

'I cannot believe I liked the son of the bitch,' said Mandy nodding her head.

'You liked others worse than that…' laughed Jada cynically.

'Really? Worse?' asked Mandy, really annoyed. 'What was doing FBI at our office this morning, then? Playing another episode in Criminal Minds, maybe?'

'That guy in the black suit was FBI?' asked Marina, surprised.

'Where was your head when he made the presentation, silly?' laughed Jada.

'To the splatter of blood in boss' office, wondering if she was dead or something…' Marina said with a low voice.

'Well, she's not dead yet, and all she thinks about is work,' commented Caitlin, opening her car. 'And we better get to it, ladies. She doesn't want all this crap to affect the company, and I'm with her on this page. Marina, go and have a bath and try to get over what you found in that office. Play with your kid and be happy you don't have to deal with what's on her plate right now.'

'I would go mad if somebody would threaten the life of my son,' Marina said with emotion, gesticulating with emphasis. 'How can she be so cool about it?'

Jada shook her head stepping in her own car. She asked herself the same questions. Nolani Arrington was something else. When she started to work at Forever, she wondered if that woman had glands. She seemed for sure that she didn't know how to show emotion of any kind. If she knew and she kept it in, then she was very good at dissimulating that she had no worry in the world. She never saw that woman other than impeccably dressed, dealing with everybody with an apparent shy and gentle smile on her face. She never saw her losing her temper, shouting or arguing with somebody. They were all speculating about that relationship with Terrence Morgan, just because they saw them talking on that terrace, and somebody saw him manhandling her right after that. Plus, the fact that he was coming to her office regularly was a reason to speculate about the reasons behind that. This didn't prove that they were in a relationship, though. The guy was gorgeous, but her boss didn't seem impressed. If she was and she didn't show it, that was very bad, because the guy was crazy for her. Maybe they were all a bit too nosey for her liking. Marina told them that the Boss told her off for her indiscretions. She smiled, finding that Marina was digging her own grave. She seemed more distressed that she didn't know the woman had a son than the gruesome discovery in her office.

# Chapter 20

Terry entered her house that afternoon with a serious air on his face. 'You gave me a scare this morning,' he commented. 'I tried to call you, and you had your phone shut…'

'I had to go to the police to make a statement about the attack nineteen years ago. They were saying that I was the piece missing in the puzzle.'

'They think that you are the cause for Maddox's fixation on blonde, shy teenage girls…'

She nodded, motioning him into her living room. 'The girls told me you were at my office the first hour in the morning…'

'I was with Marina when she opened that door. God, my heart jumped when I saw all that blood! Do they know what happened there?'

'They told me they found the night guard shot in the Janitor's room, in the basement. There is no sign that he has been killed in my office, otherwise there would be evidence that he's been dragged across the corridors in the basement. Someone or something else was killed in my office, due to the blood stains all around the room,' she said with a shiver.

'Yeah, looks like it.'

'I got no update until now, though. I managed to talk with Tate half an hour ago. He's looking forward to spending his weekend at Jacaranda… He's fine,' she added with a low voice, a sign that that was what mattered.

'That's the reason I came this morning to your office, Nolani. To tell you that you and Tate should move in with me for the time being.'

Nolani looked at him, taken by surprise. 'I cannot do that…'

'Yes, you can, and you will, Nolani. I'm not talking here about silly reasons, but safety. Not only your safety but our son's safety as well. The Jacaranda became a fortress since Maddox tried to take my daughter. You and our son can take advantage of this. I can't continue going to sleep wondering what would happen if Maddox attacked you and Tate wherever you are.'

'My house is under the surveillance of the FBI, Terry.'

'No, it's not, Nolani. You are. If you are gone for a few hours, they will be after you, not watching the house. Anyone can enter your house in that window of time. You may go to sleep thinking you are safe because you have the hounds outside, and Maddox might be right next to your bed, sweetheart!'

'I have alarm…' she argued, opening her arms widely.

'You have one at your office too. Don't ask me how, but that was disabled, and your company's main door was unlocked when Marina arrived this morning. That was the reason why she thought you were already there, in your office…'

Nolani looked at him in disbelief. 'Can he do stuff like that? Isn't a bit too… too sophisticated for Maddox's style?'

'So, you doubt that was Maddox…' he said, looking at her, curious of her statement.

'He is bold… he charged into my office with no worry of being caught, even if he evaded arrest. He appeared in daylight at school trying to kidnap your daughter. But alarm systems and unlocking doors?' She seemed baffled.

'Well, the night guard might have had the key to your company's main door… it does remain the alarm…'

'See what I mean?'

'I see what you mean, Nolani because if behind what happened in your office is somebody else, you have two enemies playing diabolical games with your mind. I cannot let my son be subjected to this kind of danger…'

'So, your plan would be to move in Jacaranda…'

'This afternoon, Nolani. As soon as Tate comes from school… Pack up, baby, because you are coming with me!'

Nolani sat down on the sofa, looking lost in a blank point. She seemed puzzled, lost, caught in a war with herself.

'Beside this, you have another contender in giving you grief. Guess who knocked at my door this morning!'

'Jessica Arrington?' she asked with a low voice.

'So, you know about her…'

'Mr Wilson rang to tell me that she visited him at his office, with allegations that I sold the Jacaranda abusively and contesting my legal rights…'

'Well, she came at my door this morning, claiming that she is the owner of the house, that the whole process was a fraud and expected me to let her stay in Jacaranda during her stay. I did send her flying…'

'Mr Wilson said that a certain Mr Armstrong, who claimed through the phone that he is investigating the death of Vanda Arrington, stated that she has been removed from Vanda's will. That's why she is here. Now, I don't know any Armstrong investigating Vanda's death. Two, through the phone, it could be anyone trying just to cause trouble.' Morgan turned around with a surprised expression all over his face. 'Do you know this person?'

'No, not really. I think I heard this name before...' he muttered, bending his arms in his waist.

Nolani leaned forward and supported her elbows on her knees. 'I'm tired, Terry. I keep being bombarded from all directions; I feel numb. I didn't even have time to grieve the death of Vanda. Now I'm talking about funerals with Mr Wilson, but I didn't even have time to acknowledge entirely that Vanda is truly dead! It's hard to keep track of what is happening. I'm caught in an emotional rollercoaster, and I just want to evade it. It's too much, and it just seems to happen all at once.'

'Not all at once, but definitely one after the other, sweetheart...' he said in a low voice, sitting next to her. The moment was precious, the fact that Nolani opened up to him, telling him how she was feeling under so much pressure.

'My life it's a mess, Terry. I thought the worse that happened to me was you reappearing in my life when I was not ready to ever meet you again. How wrong I was! I'm scared and lost, and I'm losing my footing. It's like I cannot find solid ground anymore. I'm immersed in something I cannot control... I cannot predict and it hurts more than every hit I ever received in my life. My childhood never prepared me for this. I felt unfit, unloved and misunderstood wherever I went, but mostly in my own house, next to the one who was supposed to make me feel safe, loved and cared for. All of her education impaired me socially. I have no friends, no family, no one to turn to, nobody to count on…' She said vehemently. 'I'm glad my son is not like me…' she added with a small voice.

Terry moved his arm around her shoulders and pulled her in his arms, trying to give her some of his strength. 'You're not alone, Nolani. You do have a family… you do have someone to count on. I'm here.'

'This whole mess can affect you too…'

'More than you think. If it transpires to the media that I took advantage of you that night, everything I stand for is compromised forever.'

Nolani raised her beautiful eyes to him. 'You haven't done that. As ashamed as I am for how I behaved that night… I told in my statement that I initiated what happened between us…'

'You were in shock, Nolani. You were not thinking right.'

'I was thinking right after. I still did not regret what I did that night…'

'Because you remained pregnant…'

'Tate was the greatest gift you could ever give to me, Terry…'

'What about the other child?'

She looked at him, baffled. 'What other child?'

'We did it again, Nolani. And I didn't use protection as I never planned to seduce you in that hotel room. You might be pregnant again, baby…'

Nolani sighed, then lowered her forehead to his chest. He could be right. 'I never thought of that…' she whispered in the fabric of his shirt.

'I'm not trying to shock you. You had enough on your plate today. I'm just realistic. Our history together seems to repeat itself, and damn if we don't play it by the script!' he chuckled bitterly. His palm moved gently on her back, then stopped in between her shoulder blades, where he felt a lot of tension. Nolani lifted her eyes to him. God, she was gorgeous! His lips brushed hers with a gentle touch, then returned, moved over, and pressed a little harder. The kiss intensified with every movement of his tongue, with every answer of hers. Her hand moved on his chest, and then her fingers grabbed the fine fabric, kissing him back breathlessly.

His hand moved on her leg, caressing it from the knee to the top of her thigh. He moaned discovering that portion of fine skin over her suspenders. The next few minutes became a blur for both of them. None could say who made the first move or the second, what item of their clothes was partially removed and which second. They kissed continuously, losing every notion of time, place or reality. They became one on the sofa in a swift motion then they celebrated every complete connection of their bodies with a low growl and a soft moan.

Terry moved his fingers gently on her rosy cheek, then over her lips, looking down at her coming around from the world of intense pleasure their lovemaking threw her. He was weary of seeing her again, ashamed and mortified of what they did. When she opened her blue eyes, he could breathe relieved. He could not find any sign of that. 'God, I cannot kiss you, woman, without jumping on you. What spell did you put on me?'

She blushed and pushed her nose into the cradle of his neck.

'No, sweetie, don't hide yourself from me. You can hide from everyone else but not from me.' He caressed gently her hip, going down towards her suspenders. 'This is so sexy…' he chuckled when she moved her head on the cushion of the sofa to look into his eyes and prove to him that she was not hiding. With a gentle move, he withdrew from her body and planted a kiss on her lips.

'Maybe we should get dressed, Terry. Tate might come home any minute…'

'There's not too much to put back on, my love,' he smiled, rearranging his clothes. 'God, we've been together three times already, and I never managed to see you naked,' he added when he saw her covering herself with modesty.

She didn't offer an answer to that comment. In complete silence, they rearranged their clothes. After that, they went to the upper floor and Nolani started to pack some of her belongings. While he was taking one luggage down, she went into Tate's room, and she collected some of his favourite clothes, toiletries and shoes for a temporary staying. When Terry came back up, Tate was next to him, delighted to find out that they were to move to Jacaranda that evening.

'I'll do the rest here, mom. You can finish packing your stuff. I need some of the books and notebooks for school as well.'

Nolani walked towards the door and then stopped to look at him shyly. 'Are you okay with our decision, Tate?'

'Are you kidding, mom? That's awesome! I am so looking forward to spending some time with dad!'

'Did you have a good day at school? Have you seen that man again?'

'No. There are some new dubious faces around, but I haven't seen him lurking around the school. My friends are all very careful as well.'

In an hour, with the help of Tate and Terry, Nolani left the house in which she built so many happy moments, to return in one which only gave her grief. They left in three different cars to make sure that each one had their own way of transportation.

They reunited in the front of the house, each coming out from their own cars. Terry helped them to take their stuff inside the house. What followed was mayhem. Laura was jumping happily to see them both and even more when she learnt that they would stay with them. Mrs Talon and Devante were extremely pleasant, and Nolani liked them instantly. Tate was over the moon with the idea of living with his dad.

The problem of their accommodation was something Terry never thought about. Tate wanted to offer to sleep with his dad, but he let the adults decide. Jacaranda had only four bedrooms, and three of them were occupied by him, Laura and Mrs Talon. Devante said that he was sleeping down on the sofa anyway. It was Mrs Talon who decided to sleep in Laura's room, to the disappointment of the little girl who wanted to sleep with Nolani. Tate took the empty bedroom and Nolani the one which belonged to Mrs Talon. Terry would have appreciated the lady sleeping in his bedroom, but he didn't want to push his luck. There were too many explanations to give around.

That evening, Laura found it harder to get to bed than usual, feeling too excited to settle. Tate remained in the upper lounge to chat a bit with Terry while Nolani was busy arranging their stuff in the cupboards.

'I really admire mom,' said Tate, looking at Terry with a smile all over his face.

'I admire her too,' said Terry. 'What makes you say that?'

'She hates this house. She was so unhappy here. Still, for our safety, she decided to step on her feelings and return...'

'I don't think she hates the house, Tate. I think it's about the person who owned it. Vanda was not a nice person. It's surprising that she took the trouble to look after Vanda after her health deteriorated, when that woman almost ruined her.'

'Yeah... Mom considered that it was her duty.'

'I'm sorry I wasn't around, Tate...'

'It's ok. It's not like you knew about me and abandoned me on purpose. You didn't know, and mom made sure I knew this, never to put the blame on you. I got used to the idea. When mom told me that she met you again, that she finally learnt your name and you are around... I couldn't contain it any longer. I looked on the internet for everything that was ever written about you.'

'Nolani told me you saw the articles about Maddox, and you recognised him from the school.'

'I freaked out!' Tate whispered, bending his arm over the back of the sofa. Turning back to a problem that bothered him deeply, he asked: 'Are you sure you're not mad at mom?'

'For what?'

'For not telling you about me from the moment you two met again…'

'I can't be mad at her. I thought about it a lot, and in all honesty, I could not be mad at her. I did not recognise her, Tate. That element only it's enough for someone to dismiss the idea of delivering news of such nature. She was trying to push me away, and now I understand why. I was trying to make and maintain any possible connection with her.'

'Why?' Tate asked with a chuckle.

'Huh? Have you looked at your mom? She is a very beautiful woman. I'm not blind, young man.' Tate giggled, happy to hear that his dad liked his mother.

'I think she likes you too. She always said that she loves you for… me.'

'She told me that too…'

'Well, I truly think that she actually likes you for… you, being you.'

'This I very much hope so…'

Nolani appeared from her bedroom with her phone to her ear. She was looking puzzled, pale, looking at him with her blue eyes full of surprize. He stood up and walked towards her, looking worried. 'Who is there, Nolani?'

'Agent White. First, he rang to let me know that his agents told him I literally moved here. He does not consider the move a very good idea as the park offers lots of possibilities for somebody to hide. As about the mess found this morning in my office, he has reasons to believe that the vandalism is the result of a massive struggle and the blood on my carpet… belongs to Richard Maddox.'

# Chapter 21

'I cannot comment on who he had a struggle with. On the cameras of the building,' said Agent White next morning, sitting on the veranda with Nolani and Terry, 'we clearly could see Maddox. He walks into the building without even trying to mask his features. The other silhouette, it's another story. He seems to follow him all the way to the second floor. Also, Maddox is seen on the camera unlocking the door.'

'What about the alarm, Agent White?'

'It seems that it has been disabled with code and all…' he lifted his shoulders. 'One of your employees wrote the code on a piece of paper and stuck it next to the alarm… A move I do not consider too clever…'

Nolani opened her mouth to say something, then sat down thoughtfully. Agent White continued: 'We could see the other one entering after him. What happened in that office is everybody's guess. The second one comes out first. He is moving fast, steady… Maddox comes out in about five minutes. He has a scarf tied around his thigh. He is limping heavily and walks, supporting himself by the wall. We did look again in the office. We noticed that he had an envelope in his hand when he entered but came out without it. At the first search, we thought that it was part of the company's correspondence, but we paid no attention to it. We found the large envelope on the floor by your window, Miss Arrington.'

'What was in it?'

'Explicit pictures of a girl in agony… in the first plan is him… penetrating her unnaturally… Is very gory, if you would ask me…

Blood everywhere…'

'He takes photos of his crimes…' Terry muttered, feeling sick to his stomach, while Nolani moaned a low 'oh, my dear God!'

'That's his trophies. All the evidence we need is on his phone. But we do have enough to prove him guilty.'

'He leaves them alive as well,' Nolani said with an undertone. 'He wants them to live with his memory. I thought about that a lot.'

'Did you read about serial killers, Ma'am? You were right when you said that you didn't want to challenge his delusion…'

'I read about mental health when my grandmother was diagnosed… I got an entire encyclopaedia about it. It offered me an insight of what is going on…'

Terry leaned over the table towards Agent White. 'So, now there is another guy…'

'He's big… looks like a wrestler… I don't know his motivation behind the office attack, but he followed Maddox, he challenged him in Miss Arrington's office and wounded him in his left thigh. Maddox doesn't seem to know he was followed. He doesn't look over his shoulder…'

'That's his style,' she mumbled, looking at Terry. 'What hour was when he broke into my office, Agent White?'

'About half past four in the morning. Now, about the threatening note found on your car, Miss Arrington, besides Mr Morgan's prints, but you admit he handled the note…'

'…and I maintain my statement…' she added quickly.

'The prints belong to Sally Holden. My colleagues in New York are about to talk with her about it. It can be something childish, a row between kids, but obviously, Maddox put his hands on the note and made use of it in the way he did… I don't think he planned you to make an issue of it and have it checked for prints…'

'I think he did. He brags about what he did to Sally Holden. He wants to be acknowledged for what he did. The victim in the pictures… is the victim who came forward after the scandal with Miss Holden?'

'No. She never came forward…' said White, thoughtful. 'I know what you mean with that… He wanted us to know what he did to her. In the meantime, the message says, *Look what I'm going to do to you…*'

Nolani went white like paper and dropped her head under the effect of that threat.

'Now, Miss Arrington, if you allow me… I need to talk with Mr Morgan privately… If you don't mind, of course…'

She swallowed fast, then she breathed in and stood up. Her entire body was shaking. Terry wanted to jump up and hold her, but under the scrutiny of the FBI guy, he just had to watch her gathering herself together before going inside the house to Devante and the other two agents who came with White to Jacaranda.

'Bodyguards…' muttered White, looking at the guy in his kitchen with his piercing black eyes.

'Whatever it takes to keep my family safe,' said Terry lifting his chin up. 'You said about the park of the house which offers lots of opportunities for somebody to hide… The house is in the open.'

'But has so many entries…'

'All locked and alarmed over the night. And in my house, nobody pinned the code next to the alarm, a thing that I think Nolani will need to discuss with her staff…'

'Yeah, that was plain stupid… Now, going to our story, nineteen years ago… Miss Arrington told us that Maddox attacked her while she was sleeping in her hotel room. You were his best friend. You saw him before that attack took place. What was his mood? How was he behaving? What made you follow him that night?'

Terry leaned back in his chair, and with his forehead down and his eyes closed, he accessed the set of memories that he tried for years to forget. 'He drank a lot that evening. He was restless. I saw him moving from one place to another like he couldn't settle. Obviously, he had something on his mind that bothered him… When he was getting so restless, usually he was itching for a fight. When he suddenly said that he needed to take a walk so he could sleep… that was weird. Maddox never had problems sleeping after so much alcohol. He was just going to bed and dropping asleep. I let him have an advantage, then I followed.'

'Was it because you were afraid your friend was looking for trouble?'

'I didn't know what to expect. We've been engaged in many fights before, mostly because of him initiating arguments, being a downright bully… he could find any reason to start a fist fight. He would make comments about someone's girlfriend… about someone's colour or physical appearance…'

'Such as…'

'Not having the teeth straight… or having a big nose… silly stuff like that.'

'Did you notice him paying attention to Miss Arrington at all?'

'She was shy, she was keeping herself to herself. She stayed away… like way away… We never talked to her… We were there with the whole team for training purposes. Messing around on the beach, exercising moves…'

'And you used to call each other on nick names… Miss Arrington said you were…'

'I was Stampede. Maddox was Hammer. Someone wanted to call him Mad Ox. He flipped out big time. I backed him up by calling him Hammer. Anyway, this doesn't really matter, but the truth is that none of us, in those times, would call each other by our real names. Miss Arrington did not lie about this…'

'Going back to following him that night. Did you know where Miss Arrington was staying? Did you know that she lived in that hotel and in that particular room?'

'No, not at all.'

'This proves that obviously, it did escape to your eyes the fact that Maddox had his eyes on her…'

Terry nodded and looked towards the park upset that there were so many signs he missed years ago.

'So, what happened… what did you witness that night?'

Terry rubbed his forehead, not in an effort to remember but to put his ideas in order. 'I saw him jumping the balcony. It wasn't very high, so for someone with the athletic skills of Maddox, that was nothing…'

'Even with so much alcohol in his system?'

'Don't underestimate him,' Terry chuckled. 'The guy started every fight with alcohol in his system and won every single one…'

'With you on his side…'

'That's true… I saw him carefully slide the door and enter the dark room. At that moment, I started to run because my gut was telling me that he was up to no good. When I entered the room, I could hear her crying and moaning in pain. He twisted her in her sheets face down and grabbed her short hair, pushing her face against the pillows. With the other hand, he was trying to pull her clothing off.'

'You saw that even if it was dark…'

'The moon was shining that night. It was not pitch black, Agent White. One could see more than silhouettes…'

'All right. Was he saying anything in particular?'

'That she was to be taught good manners… that that was not the way to behave with him… I saw red in my eyes! I launched against him, and I pulled him off the bed. He was shocked by the interruption. I didn't give him time to realise what was happening. I started to punch him hard. I told him that if he doesn't leave the girl alone, I will call the police myself on him…'

'Did he fight back?'

'I got a punch in my chest. He tried to target my gut, but I moved too fast. Then he launched other punches, exhausting himself in trying to hurt me…'

'And that would be your skill? You never stay long in one place?'

'I was Stampede because of that… and some other reasons…'

'What was Miss Arrington doing at that time?'

'She curled in bed like a baby, crying silently.'

'Did she ever scream?'

'No. I don't think he gave her time…'

'What about after she was awake? Did she ever scream?'

Terry looked at Agent White with his eyebrows united in a V, trying to remember her reaction when she found the note on her car. 'I don't think she can scream, Agent White. Her reaction to shock, to violence is to freeze, not to scream like a normal person would. She cries silently…'

Agent White nodded, taking in the detail. 'Why do you think she reacts like that?'

'Because of her education, I think.'

'Interesting detail. Manners gone too far. So, we reached the moment when you two were fighting in the room. Did the noise alerted anyone?'

'Somebody knocked in the wall to keep it quiet… I pushed Maddox out of the room, and after another struggle on the balcony, I pushed him over in the sand.'

'Did he try to come back?'

'He promised *I will pay for interfering between him and his chick.*'

'Did his statement ever make you think that in between them two was an… let's say… understanding?'

'No. I was with him practically twenty-four hours in twenty-four. He wouldn't have a chance to make a connection with her prior to that nocturnal visit I would not know about.'

'Miss Arrington declared that you didn't leave her room until morning. You decided to stay…'

'At first, it was because I was afraid that he might come back later. He did not. In the second instance, the girl was in shock. She was in pain… I remained to offer her comfort and reassurance.'

'In what moment that night the comfort and the reassurance resulted in having sex with her?'

Terry sighed. That was the question he was dreading the most. 'I never stopped feeling guilty about that. It happened; it was not planned. She clung to me, crying in my T-shirt… I don't know… hands were going wild.'

'Did she start to pull your clothes off?'

Terry nodded and looked elsewhere. 'It was not a rape…'

'I'm not saying it was. Miss Arrington said herself that she initiated that contact…'

'Did she say that she was a virgin that night?'

Agent White looked at him, taken aback. 'I'm not sure she mentioned…'

'I never planned to have sexual contact with her that night. I didn't even know her. She had a swollen eye, a punctured lip, she was in pain and scared and…' He opened his arms, looking truly in pain. 'It happened, and I never stopped feeling guilty about it. It felt like I took advantage of her, in her state of mind. She tells me that she needed that type of comfort and she never regretted it, but still doesn't stand right by me. I'm truly disappointed in myself…'

'A victim of violence, after she passes through such kind of shock, you would be surprised how many are finding comfort in having sex, Mr Morgan…'

'C'mon, White! She was a virgin! She was on the brink of being raped!'

'Still…' Agent White lifted his shoulders. 'I am not here to question your behaviour, Mr Morgan, but Maddox's behaviour. Miss Arrington declared that you had sex that night at her own consent; she never regretted it. There's nothing to it but a son nine months later. For you… nineteen years later… What I need to know is… how did your relationship continue… with Maddox, obviously?'

'We had another fight the next day. He was accusing me of stepping in his business…'

'He declares, on the audiotape Miss Arrington gave to us following his visit to her office… that you lied to him, telling him that nothing happened…'

'He was accusing me of stealing his girl. I did tell him that nothing of that nature happened.'

'He continued to assert the fact that they were, let's say… a couple…'

'He was using words such as *my* girl, *my* chick and so on.'

'Did the argument between you two ever been witnessed by anyone else?'

'Yes. He's been removed from the team following this incident. I broke the friendship with him after that summer, and we both went on separate paths.'

'Obviously, he sees in the fact that Tate Arrington is around, given his age and his appearance, that something *did* happen that night. Miss Arrington agrees with your statement that there was no understanding between her and him and that the guy jumped on her out of the blue when she never laid eyes on him, neither spoken to him prior to that attack. Are you a couple now, Mr Morgan? You said that you want to keep *your family* protected. Do you pursue Miss Arrington as… getting romantically involved, or is it just the past and the fact that you have a son together making you extend your protection upon her as well?'

'How will I explain to my son that I am agreeing to protect him, but not his mom as well?'

'So, that's the only reason why she is here, under your roof…'

'For the moment, that is correct, Agent White…'

The black eyes of the lawman stopped on him, looking into the way he stated that 'for the moment.' After a short moment, he stood up from his chair and shook Terry's hand. 'Thank you for talking to me, Mr Morgan. I appreciate your candour and your honesty, and my advice is not to beat yourself up too hard on the matter. Each victim reacts differently to shock and violence. It's now time to turn back to my hotel. We have a new victim to identify. If she ever reported her ordeal, it is going to be easy to find… I just hope I'm not going to be in for another surprise…'

'What surprise?'

'Miss Arrington was right. He leaves them alive to remember him. Why did he consider it necessary to give her those pictures? Is this victim not able to speak for herself? Is he afraid that he is not going to get recognition for what he did to her? Considering how gory those images are, the level of damage inflicted on the victim was beyond torture, beyond unbearable. He upgraded from rape to murder with Vanda Arrington, or earlier than that, and we just didn't know?'

'And who is the second guy?'

'That's another question. Maddox might question that, too… I will show Miss Arrington the silhouette of the guy; maybe she can recognise him…'

❀ ❀ ❀

Wiseman looked into the paperwork he gathered, not pleased at all of coming out with empty hands. There was no birth registered around the year Nolani Arrington was born to prove his theory that Vanda had another child at the same time as her teenage daughter. He looked into her adoption… it did ring a bell that the paperwork had been signed in Augusta, Georgia, the city of origin of Vanda Percy, who married Arrington. The so-called friends of Vanda Arrington remembered that in that year, after the fallout with her daughter, Vanda went away for months. Obviously, the paper trail was leading him to believe that she returned to Augusta, Georgia, from where she came back to Texas with a baby. Why that specific baby? Why were they so alike?

Her lies were up to the high sky. Her mystery was puzzling him, who managed to solve other mysteries more intricate than this one. Why, on one side, would Vanda tell everyone that they were not related when, clearly, they were? Why would she make the girl believe that she was the granddaughter and her mother abandoned her? She was not Jessica's daughter, so much he figured…

Tumbling through the paperwork, he muttered some swearing words addressed to the mystery in itself. He stood up and made a turn in the lounge of his condo, trying to turn the story inside out and upside down… Suddenly, he remained looking at some notes he scribbled on the whiteboard regarding the case. *What is the truth about N. Arrington?*

The truth… the truth… what if Vanda did not lie but said the truth all the way long? What if Nolani was indeed her granddaughter but not from Jessica Arrington?

It was a long shot, but it deserves to be investigated. He needed to find evidence that Vanda Percy gave birth not in 1976 but before the successful marriage with Congressman Arrington. She did insist on Nolani giving her son up for adoption, to hide the shame of having a child unmarried, to ensure that her future is not damaged and she could still marry God knows whom she planned her to marry. Was it because she had done that herself? In that case, Nolani Arrington could indeed be her granddaughter. It remained to get evidence to sustain the new theory…

With the newfound lead, Wiseman jumped back to work.

# Chapter 22

Nolani called Marina to ask who last left the office on Thursday afternoon. She needed to know who would make the mistake of laying for anyone to see the code to the alarm. Marina said that Mandy was to remain last and she seems to have problems remembering numbers. She left the code on the wall for Mandy to put the alarm on when she was to leave, but she did expect Mandy to take the code with her, not leave it stuck to the wall. It was a good explanation, but by God, that was suspect to discover that once that code was in display Maddox broke in exactly in that night.

She rubbed her stomach, thinking about the succession of events that led to the break-in. She did hope, for Mandy's own safety, that she did not give in to the charm of Richard Maddox, dismissing her warning that he was a dangerous man.

After that phone call, she occupied the Saturday rearranging with the help of Devante the bedroom of Laura. Most of the items she ordered for Laura's bedroom arrived, so she got herself busy redecorating the room. The artist she employed to paint the cherry tree on the empty wall did an amazing job. After a couple of hours of assembling furniture and arranging it nicely, Laura's bedroom started to look as planned. After an entire morning running around with her dad and Tate after a ball, when she entered her bedroom to change, Laura squealed excitedly to discover that her room was unrecognisable. Terry ran alerted by Laura's scream, Tate as well, just to find out what Nolani had done all day in the house. They thought she just wanted to spend the day in bed, to recover after the last events.

To see Laura jumping from one detail to another, telling them how much she liked it and how happy she was to get her princess room exactly how she wanted it… Because she was having a princess room, Laura decided to dress as a princess. She wanted a tiara, fancy shoes and so on just to join them for dinner. Nolani lost count how many cuddles she received… then she told Laura that Devante deserved cuddles as well for being an amazing helper… Poor Devante!

The atmosphere at Jacaranda was animated and generally joyful. Terry absolutely loved that day, then the evening playing board games with his son… There was not too much interaction with Nolani, but considering the circumstances, they were never alone in the room. Sunday wasn't any different. Even if Nolani joined them and helped with the preparation, the serving and the eating of the barbecue, he did not manage to change a word alone with her.

On the next Saturday, Tate had a very important game between high schools, the last game in the junior season between high schools and Terry declared that he wouldn't lose that game for nothing in the world. That brought the brightest smile on her son's face.

She was feeling guilty for Tate not having a dad to be there during his competitions. He was saying he was okay with that, but she knew in her heart that every boy wanted their dad to be there for them.

It was passed midnight on Sunday when, on the silent corridors of Jacaranda, a silhouette emerged from the darkness. It didn't seem to mind the lack of light. It was moving so gently that no noise alerted those who were sleeping in the house. It seemed to know all the arrangements so well that it motioned through the darkness, avoiding the obstacles. It stopped in front of the door of the master bedroom and seemed to hesitate for a few long seconds before pressing the knob of the door, opening it wide. In perfect silence, it went closer to the bed where Terry Morgan lay asleep.

❀ ❀ ❀

He groaned, watching the gesture and understanding what the plan was. 'Oh, don't…' he whined, trying to grab the dressing gown out of her hand.

'I have to, Terry. It's almost four o'clock. We wouldn't want anyone to find out I was here…'

'I don't care, Nolani… Stay with me… sleep with me… let me cuddle you…'

Her breasts had little red marks from the gentle love bites he applied to them in their lovemaking. Her hair was falling in a sweet cascade on her naked shoulders, untidy and seductive. Her lips were swollen from the wild kisses they shared, and the expression on her gorgeous face was that of a satisfied woman. For the first time in their life, what they shared was more than sex for the therapeutic purpose; they made love, shared passion, and enjoyed each other's body for the pleasure of it.

With his hair in disarray, Nolani found him more attractive than ever. His smile was naughty, his eyes brightened up and full of passion. God, she loved this man! It was crazy to creep up on him like that, but since he complained that they never managed to have sexual contact with their clothes off, she thought about this nocturnal visit.

She leaned towards him and gave him a kiss, before getting off his bed. With a simple gesture Terry found extremely graceful she put her dressing gown on and walked towards his door. After she closed the door behind her, Terry buried the back of his head in the soft pillow and groaned, looking at the ceiling.

Terry could usually predict what most people were going to do next, but the one who just left his room. He was giving her that: she was a very good-looking woman, sexy body and all, but a very guarded one as well. The only times he experienced her hidden, passionate nature was when she left the guard down and let him get close to her. Tonight, it was nothing like that. It was not like the other experiences he had with her when she was feeling ashamed or sorry right after the act had been consumed. He didn't experience that feeling of guilt either. It felt right. It felt good, like two secret lovers sharing an amazing night one the arms of the other.

Next morning, when he went down to have some breakfast and drink a coffee, he found her dressed for work, drinking her own coffee with Devante on the veranda. She was reserved but he didn't feel served with the hedgehog attitude he had before. Their eyes met, and she didn't look somewhere else.

She talked about her plans to arrange the temporary offices on the second floor of her friend's place of business. He discussed about his new office and the fact that he was waiting for the last signatures until he could start advertising locally.

It followed a rushed morning with Laura and Tate around the breakfast table, with joyful chatter and plans for the week. After that, four cars left the parking places at Jacaranda, leaving Mrs Talon to clear up like after a tornado.

When he reached his office, he was pleasantly surprised by the good mood of his assistant.

'Did we receive the last paperwork, Wiseman?'

'Not yet, but this is just procedure…'

'And a legal requirement… Then, what caused this great smile on your face?'

'I untied the tangled mysteries regarding the origins of Miss Arrington… I know who she is, Morgan. I got the whole chronologic facts… Do you want to hear?'

Terry smiled bitterly, a bit annoyed now by the perseverance in finding out all the dirt in Nolani's life. He did agree that it would do her good to find out who she was and where she was coming from, but he had a conviction that his assistant had his own personal agenda regarding the subject of his newfound obsession.

'First of all, guess who travelled to Georgia and back this weekend?' he chuckled, sitting then down in a chair.

'Ok, and you went to Georgia… why?'

'To find out if Miss Vanda Percy had any children before her marriage with the great Luke Arrington…' Terry was startled, and Wiseman smiled, realising he had all the attention of his boss and friend. 'I considered the advice she gave Miss Arrington regarding Tate Arrington, such as to give him to adoption, not to ruin her future. We all know that Miss Percy finished marrying very well. A rich girl married a rich man, both high society and whatnot. How I could not get around so many lies, I wondered myself *What if we are dealing here not with lies but half-truths? What if Miss Arrington is indeed her granddaughter, but she is the child of another daughter other than Jessica Arrington?* To find out in Georgia that, indeed, Vanda Percy gave birth in 1953, aged only seventeen, to a little girl her darling parents arranged to be given to a lovely couple for adoption right after her birth. She didn't have a name. She never gave her a name because she saw the little creature just a few hours before she'd been taken away. The paper trail is inexistent with regards to who took the child, but there's a coincidence, and you know how much I love coincidences… in the same family, an aunt of Miss Percy from her mother's side suddenly appeared in the society with a newborn, a little girl she and her husband called Lauren. She grew up like the couple's only child, and her name was Lauren Sparks.'

'And you think Nolani is the daughter of Lauren Sparks.'

'I don't think. About this, I am sure. If there was no one to talk about Lauren being born by Vanda Percy, there was someone who remembers the tragedy of Lauren dying giving birth to a little girl and Vanda Arrington taking the child in adoption. Paper trail long like the distance from Georgia to Texas!'

'No parents? No dad of the child?'

'Mr Sparks died when Lauren was seventeen. Heart attack. The mother died when she was pregnant.'

'And she died giving birth.'

'Lots of complications, apparently. Losing her mom didn't help, I think. Plus… God knew where the father of the child was.'

'So, he's not in the picture,' sighed Terry. He was hoping that this journey of discovery, would bring into Nolani's life one or both of her parents. It was another empty path with respect to the love and the support she could have received from a surviving parent.

'No, I know nothing about a possible father. What I know was that Vanda had been given the child because she was the only relative alive who claimed responsibility, and in the paperwork, she was a first cousin. She was rich, she was young… she was capable of looking after that child. And… she was there! Remember that I told you that her friends said she was gone for a while, and she returned with a baby in her arms? She was in Georgia at that moment. She was in the hospital when Lauren was giving birth! I found some ex-staff from the hospital who remembered vividly how much they looked alike, the heartache of losing the mother… the whole story. So? What do you say? Nolani Arrington is, in fact, Nolani Sparks, and she is indeed the granddaughter of Vanda Arrington. In this light, she wouldn't be in the right to inherit the fortune of Luke Arrington, don't you think?'

'Yes, she can. If Luke Arrington left everything to his surviving wife, it is down to her if she wants to leave it to his daughter, to the church or to the family dog, Wiseman! So, this is what you were looking for? If she was entitled to inherit Vanda Arrington or not? You personally said that she is, in the eyes of the law, legally adopted by Vanda Arrington. This gives her more than one right to inherit whatever is left to her. Not to forget that following her death, the matter is not only about the inheritance of the Arrington family but Percy as well. Or was she not the only daughter of the Percy's?'

Wiseman scratched his head, looking in one place, thoughtful. 'You are right with this one. She was…'

'Now, can you enlighten me with what is in your head? Why follow this trail, trying to highlight whether she is the heir or not? What is this? I am glad you found out who she is and where she is coming from. I would like for you to get some family pictures as well, if you can, so Nolani can get some closure about the matter…'

'Sure…' Wiseman muttered, looking deflated.

'What is clear from the whole story is that Nolani Arrington is a very rich lady. She might be the only heir of the Sparks' as well, of the Percys, and we will see what Vanda wrote in that will of hers. I want you to make contact with the authorities and check if there is any financial arrangement for the child of Lauren Sparks. This is just a matter of fact, not that I think Nolani really cares about stories with family fortune. I was hoping you could find some family members she can rely on emotionally during this period of time. Find the fathers. Who is the father of the child of Vanda Percy? Who is the father of the child of Lauren Sparks? Now, I do have another question, and I would appreciate it if you would answer me honestly…'

Wiseman nodded scribbling on a piece of paper what his boss requested him to do. 'Yeah?' he mumbled after he finished writing down the instructions.

'Can you explain to me what is for you to gain from provoking Jessica Arrington against Nolani?'

❀ ❀ ❀

The six ladies sat around the table, each with a cup of coffee in front of them, looking at one another, waiting for somebody else to start the discussion.

'Ok, Marina, start complaining,' Jada said with a smile.

Marina was startled and looked towards her, surprised. 'About what?'

'That the boss didn't look at all affected today, considering what we all learnt what she is passing through… that she didn't look beaten or hysterical…'

232

'She's a tough one,' commented Elena, looking into her cup quietly. 'I lost sleep this weekend about this and that. She seemed… rested.'

'Cool like a cucumber, my darling,' laughed Jada, shaking her head.

'Stop it, Jada. She doesn't need us all panicking about her stuff. Just because she seems that she is not affected, it doesn't mean that she is not worried. Why did she ask us not to make any evaluations, assessments and visits this week?'

'Maybe she's afraid that that maniac will apply for redecoration?' laughed Jada.

The girls looked at one another, pale like ghosts. 'Who says that he cannot do this, Jada? He shouldn't need much brain to concoct an email pretending he's a family man and he wants his house redecorated. What would happen if one of us walked directly into a trap like that? The guy is a killer! If he wants to hurt boss, her son, and God knows who else and why, that would be a way to lure us, isn't it? How many times did you walk in a house wondering if the client is not a psychopath?' asked Elena.

'Never?'

Marina was looking at one another trying to make sense of what Elena was saying. She had a long conversation with her husband about Nolani Arrington that weekend, and God, she had to hear him when she told him about Miss Arrington being annoyed with her for gossiping about her personal affairs with the girls. As for judging her for the way she was behaving, to have him telling her that not everyone was washing their dirty laundry in public as she was doing, it was painful.

She was looking at those ladies she had been working with for some years and sipped from her coffee. There was nothing with regards to her married life, her husband and son they did not know about. If she cooked something special, they knew about it. If her husband snored that night, they knew about that too.

She knew about Jada that her fiancée was trying to conquer her back. About Elena, she knew that she was desperately in love with a married man who today was swearing that he was going to divorce his lady, then he was back home for a long while... About Mandy, she knew that she liked big guys, and she never said no to sex at first date. About Caitlin, she knew she was a divorcee with two children, and she was considering her ex-husband a *waste of space* and *a deadbeat*.

She had known Nolani for a long time, but she never looked other than professional, cool and, yes, sweet and nice. She knew nothing about her romantic life, about having a son home or having problems of one kind or another. Elena was right. On Friday, she reacted more upset that she did not know about Boss's son than because of the episode with her office. And she had to hear her husband about that, too.

She heard her name, and she lifted her head to discover that all the ladies had their eyes on her. 'I beg your pardon?'

'What did the boss say about the blood in the office?'

'She said that the police have it all figured out and, in a day or two, they may let us redecorate the room and return to work. Miss Arrington thinks that it may take a week, maximum two... Anyway, the question remains: why did Mandy not take the code off from next to the alarm where I stuck it for her to put the alarm on when she left on Thursday…'

Mandy opened her mouth in shock. 'Sorry?'

'You remained last on Thursday. I left the code stuck next to the alarm because you keep forgetting it. I don't know why, but you left it there when you left. The police, the boss and everyone else implied were not impressed that you left the code for the intruder to enter our offices like in his own home! The question is: did you forget or leave it intentionally? We all know you liked the guy. Boss knows it, too. The police know it as well. How are you going to explain that you left the code there for anyone to see it?' Mandy lowered her forehead, overwhelmed with guilt under all the suspicious eyes of her colleagues.

# Chapter 23

Nolani raised her eyes full of questions towards him. They were alone in the elegant sitting room next to the lounge. He was on the side of the sofa. She was sitting on the carpet with her arms folded on the sofa, looking at all the paperwork Jeremy Wiseman collected regarding her mysterious origins. He knew that it was just one matter that would raise questions, one matter Wiseman could not prove: that Lauren Sparks was indeed the daughter of Vanda, not her cousin.

'That would be impossible to prove, isn't it? If everybody from that era has passed…'

'The motivations of Vanda taking you in adoption are questionable, Nolani. She was not an affectionate person. She went for wealth rather than love. She gave up her child for a good marriage. It would prove that she did not do that lightly, without care… fact which would prove after all that she cared about the abandoned child… but otherwise, why would she take the child of her so-called cousin to raise? Then, to stop the dirty minds and poisonous mouths in Angel Marsh, she kept saying that you were just adopted and you two were not related… She cared a lot for what the people were thinking and saying about her… more than loving and caring for the child she took to raise.'

'Yes, Terry, but what makes me question the theory is the fact that Vanda did not prove many maternal instincts. Jessica hates her, and the feeling is mutual. She abandoned a daughter… then she put in jeopardy all her good status and image in Angel Marsh adopting her own granddaughter…'

'I think she thought that only telling everyone that you are adopted would stop the questioning of your origins. I don't think she planned that you, growing up, to look so much like her. This is not a matter someone can predict, having a baby in their arms… how they will look when they grow up and reach maturity. Wiseman is trying to find a piece of evidence to transform what is still a theory into real facts. As you said, it is hard, considering that everyone involved in trading babies passed away a long time ago. There is something that he doesn't have a clue as to who they are and if they are still alive. The fathers. Who was the father of the abandoned child of Vanda Arrington? Who was the father of the daughter of Lauren Sparks? None were listed as fathers on the birth certificates. So, he must dig deep. He went to Georgia again, trying to find out rumours, statements, and gossip around the family.'

'Why is he so… eager to find out?'

'He loves mysteries, Nolani. When I hired Wiseman, he was a very talented private investigator. I found his talents would serve me well in my cases, reason why I needed his services. He was up for a great adventure, to leave behind cases of cheating spouses, for something more exciting. Mysteries, family secrets and deceit were always his favourites. Having stumbled over Vanda's lies, he started to dig for the truth.' He couldn't vouch for his assistant's unbiased opinion on the matter, but he decided to let that part out. He was challenging his assistant every time he had an opportunity to do so, reminding him that his biased opinion about the subject could make him trip and fall on his nose.

Nolani sighed, looking at the paperwork without seeing it. 'You said that you didn't order the investigation…'

'I did not, but I approved it. I thought it would do you good to find out... In all honesty, I was hoping that Wiseman might find some family members for you to meet, to connect... to give you a chance of having an extended family...'

Nolani smiled. 'That's nice of you...'

'I'm a bit disappointed, Nolani. We found out Vanda's secret but with no emotional benefit to you...'

'At least I know...'

'How is work in the new location?'

'I find my employees tiring... They seem more interested in staring at me than their computers. It is like they are expecting me to fall to my knees and start a tantrum about the unfairness of the last events, to scream the place down in fear for my life and the life of my son... Their disappointment is annoying...'

'I think that your girls are enjoying quiet lives, and the thrill in yours is making them consider how they would act if they were in your shoes. Well, this is from the little they know that happened recently. The fact that you are not quite ready to share your life story with them, makes them curious and thirsty for more information.'

'It is my fault that I even let them know so much... That Maddox is a killer...'

'They needed to know to keep themselves safe...'

'The fact that I have a son...'

Terry raised his eyebrows. 'They didn't know about Tate?'

'I'm not talking about my private life with my employees. No, I didn't. Remember how you reacted when you found out I had a son being unmarried? Imagine the speculations between themselves regarding the matter…'

'Well… they are doing it now, wondering why you kept it a secret…'

'I didn't keep Tate secret! I kept them out of my business, that's all…'

'You raised a wall around yourself to protect you from heartache, I understand. Cultivating safety rather than friendships was your goal…'

'I do not consider that a true friend is the one who chatters most and pushes daggers in your back when you are not careful. All they do is gossip. Don't get me wrong, I like them all. They are truly talented designers and they made a name for Forever. I just don't want to mix the postcode from home with the one where I work… Having them at my house on Friday to discuss the next steps, was the first time when I mixed the two. To watch them analysing my lounge with a critical eye…'

'…it's a once-in-a-lifetime opportunity for the girls and part of their job description…' he continued the idea amused. She smiled. The look in his eyes intensified, and he whispered: 'When you smile, you make my heart race, Nolani. You should do it more often, my love.'

'After you told me that my smile can lead you to get a heart condition?' she joked, laying her cheek on her bent arm on the sofa.

'I think love is a heart condition I can live with…' he said, caressing her hair gently with his fingers. Nolani was startled and closed her eyes, trying to hide the emotions and the hopes his words provoked in her. 'Don't hide from me, Nolani. I had to learn to read into you… but now I do know…'

She opened her eyes looking at him puzzled. He knew what? That she loved him desperately? That every hope and dream for the future included him? That he was in every thought of hers? In every breath she took?

He raised himself up and gave her a hand to help her stand from the floor. With a gesture, he closed the file brought home for her analysis and pushed it under his arm, while the other went around her waist. They went up on the stairs in perfect silence and when they reached the upper lounge, he motioned her towards his bedroom. Nolani stepped in with no resistance.

It was night, and the entire house was engulfed in darkness when she stopped the car in the empty parking lot in front of it.

She went to great measures to find out where that bitch lived. Some of them were not exactly in line with the law, but at last, she had the address in her hands. That was what mattered most. She stepped out of the car and pushed it with no intention to keep the noise down. She was intending to raise hell if necessary. She needed to have that head-to-head conversation with her so-called daughter.

'Daughter, my ass,' she muttered, stepping quickly on the stairs leading to the entrance door. She wasn't afraid of the darkness around the porch. She was a woman on a mission, and her mission was to grab somebody's hair and knock her out for good for telling lies about her. How could she state that she abandoned her? The image of her little angel found dead in her crib filled her lungs with anger. It was not something a mother could pass over. She was still dreaming of having Summer giggling in her arms, giving her countless kisses while her heart was booming with joy and intense happiness. To wake up in the morning, every morning, with her arms empty and remembering that her little angel was a long time lost, was taking her breath away.

To have this crazy woman declaring that she was her daughter and that she abandoned her was outrageous. She pushed her fists into the door with fury and kicked the door, enraged.

She could hear the noise of somebody moving inside the house. She continued to push her fists into the elegant wooden door, then stopped, hearing motion behind the door. Finally, the noise of the lock made her feel relieved. The door opened, but instead of a woman, in the door frame appeared a large man, six foot something, wide chest, impressively built, with blond hair falling on his forehead.

'I need to talk to Nolani Arrington. Does she live here?'

'Sure,' he growled, moving to a side and letting her step in. The door closed behind her, and for the first time, she didn't feel comfortable in the plain darkness.

'Where is she? She has a lot to explain to me!' she shouted angrily.

'She has, huh?' was the answer with a mocking tone.

'Who are you?' she asked, feeling a chill down her spine. Just then she realised that she was afraid, she didn't know who the man was, the darkness was not her best friend and she might just have pushed herself into a very dangerous situation.

'That, my darling, you should have asked before you stepped in this house…' was the answer.

There was no pain, nothing to help her understand what was going on. It was just one hit, and she collapsed on the wooden floor like a rag doll.

❈ ❈ ❈

Nolani didn't show any sign of surprise when, the next morning, she received a visit from Howard Godstone and his son, Jake. Jake seemed extremely happy to reunite with his best friend and to meet properly his little sister, Laura. The little girl was chatting happily with both filling the large kitchen at Jacaranda with laughter.

'Sorry to disturb you, Nolani. Jake was really worried for Tate, in the shadow of the last events,' he said, nodding his head instead of a salute towards Terry, who was coming out with his coffee. Terry was smiling, and he commented, amused.

'Laura tries to convince the boys to play with her in her doll house this afternoon…'

Only the thought of the two teenagers who could easily overtake by height and body frame any mature man playing with dolls, was hilarious. The two young football stars of their high school were looking though completely mesmerised by her cuteness. 'I think she has every chance to have them doing whatever she wants them to do,' giggled Mr Godstone. 'Jack doesn't have any brother or sister. He met Tate in kindergarten, and they decided to be brothers ever since.'

Nolani nodded with a gentle smile.

'Are you married, Mr Godstone?' Terry asked, trying to find out if the guy was just a friend or if he signed up for a competition to conquer the ice princess.

'Very much so, Mr Morgan…' Howard smiled, lifting his coffee cup.

'Jake's mom is the head teacher at Laura's school,' Nolani explained. 'Though she took the role after the boys went to high school.'

Katrina Godstone left him a very good impression when he looked for a school for little Laura. She was well-liked and appreciated as a teacher and as a leader of a very well-quoted school. There was something, though, that made Terry look at Mr Godstone a bit sceptical. There was a little something that actually made him charming, same as his wife, and that was not the fact that he was married; therefore, not a competition for him in securing Nolani as a life partner.

As Jeremy Wiseman stated, they did not believe in coincidences. That little something that started to gnaw at him badly, it was too much of a coincidence.

That was not Mr Godstone's large built frame, even though this made him think of another coincidence. It was not his good looks, his blue eyes and shaved head. A smile on that man's face made him consider furthermore that his newly born idea in his head was not so farfetched.

What were the odds that the father of the best friend of his son, and his mother for that matter, had still, after living so many years in Texas, a very strong Georgian accent?

❀ ❀ ❀

Terry sat down next to Nolani in the police office later that morning. Agent White entered the office alongside two of his colleagues and a few police officers. It was visible that the latter were not very impressed with the length of time the Agents were taking over their space in trying to solve this joint investigation. Furthermore, they were very much owning the case and were taking over all the decisions regarding the hunt for Richard 'Hammer' Maddox.

'I was told that you were interested to see the surveillance tape from early Friday morning.'

'You did invite us to have a look and see if we can identify the second intruder in Forever offices,' Terry replied, looking towards Nolani.

'Yes, I did…'

'Did you manage to take any steps to identify the individual?'

'Not very successful ones, I'm afraid. I have to admit that I was counting on Miss Arrington in helping us identify the person…' She controlled a giveaway reaction. Looking completely unfazed by his statement, she nodded that she was ready to see the tape. 'Clearly, the second person is following Richard Maddox into the building, then in that office and challenges him. It seems more a vigilante, rather than a suspect and a danger to Miss Arrington's life. In all honesty, I do hope that, more than I'm sure about it. We cannot build a case on hopes and speculations…'

'Is the person in question charged for any crime?'

'More than breaking and entry and attack and harm another person, for the moment, no, Miss Arrington. He needs to answer for his acts… If you are not pressing charges for entering your private property, he wouldn't have to answer but for attacking Maddox in your office.'

'What if he just challenged Maddox, and he's been the one attacked?'

'Unfortunately, we do not have a piece of evidence to sustain this. We need his statement regarding what happened in that office… Do you know anything about it you failed to share with us?'

'No, nothing more than you know, Agent White. It does seem though as a vigilante, as you said at the beginning of the conversation.'

'Do you know anyone who would take your protection into his own hands, Miss Arrington?'

'No, sir.'

Terry would have challenged that. That was the reason why he wanted to see the tape.

The agent did put the tape a few times, for them to see the second person following Maddox into the building, then into the office at Forever…

'He didn't follow into the night guard office...' Terry noted. 'Maybe he would have avoided the man being killed...'

'He was well behind and acted just when Maddox did enter in Forever...'

Nolani shuffled in the chair, feeling uncomfortable. She did look carefully at the way the man walked; Terry did too. It wasn't what he could see... he frowned because he could not see any resemblance to the only man, tall and large built, with an army career and reasons to protect Nolani. The man entering the *Forever* office that morning, challenged Maddox and then left... was not Howard Godstone. He massaged his forehead trying to assimilate the information, to see the bigger picture and come out with an answer. There was no answer.

Obviously, the man was aware of the cameras and avoided being identified. The cap on his forehead was pushed very low; he kept his head down every time he passed a camera. He had hair. Godstone was shaving his head. He was hugely built, but not so big as Godstone. Plus, he had a start of a belly, if one could judge after the way his shirt was slightly rounded above his wide leather belt.

He leaned forward to see closer. 'What insignia is there on the belt?'

'We looked into that. No significance. Any cowboy in the area has that kind of belt...'

Terry looked at Nolani. She nodded her head. 'I don't recognise the person, sir.'

'Tate's coach?' tried Terry.

'Bald...'

'An employee of yours? You have builders on your payroll…'

'None built like that…'

Terry looked to Agent White. 'Any prints in the office?'

'He wears leather gloves,' White pointed to the camera. 'No prints whatsoever…'

Terry took her hand, leaving the building a bit disappointed. Nolani looked at him, a bit concerned. 'Why is it so important to you to find out who he was?'

'To make clear in my head that you don't have two murderers after you, my love. At least if one is deemed that he done that to protect you, he's in for a few questions, and if you don't press charges for breaking and entry and property damage, he's free. In this situation, we don't know what we are dealing with…'

Nolani nodded and stepped on her high metallic heels next to him, enjoying the feeling of walking with him holding her hand.

'Did you recognise the man, and you just didn't want to tell them, afraid that you might get him in trouble?' he asked, opening the door of his car for her to get in.

'No, Terry. I do not have any idea who that man was. Who wears leather gloves in this heat?'

'A cowboy handling his horses… The only thing was… that man was not a cowboy, my love…'

# Chapter 24

Agent White was badly disappointed by the outcome of the two watching the videotapes. The reactions of Terry Morgan were of no consequence for him. All that time, he looked for a reaction on Miss Arrington's pretty face. To have her looking into his eyes stating that she doesn't recognise the man was tough to chew.

He looked through the window to the Hollywood depicted couple walking holding hands through the parking lot toward their car. Maybe she was less reserved in front of her lover, who unexpectedly returned to her life, but to see her lifting her shoulders was a giveaway. She truly did not know the man.

He sighed and returned to his colleagues. Another reason for his bad mood was the fact that he couldn't find Maddox anywhere. Even though he seemed to play it all in sight, mocking boldly, all the law forces reunited to catch him… now he was hiding, and he couldn't foresee what that brute would do next.

'So, she seems really serious with Stampede…' one in the team joked. White didn't comment but sat down thoughtfully, trying to plan what he could do next to catch that guy.

'Yeah, better rammed over by Stampede than *hammered* by Maddox…' was the comeback of another man in the office, raising giggles between the lawmen.

'She even moved in with him…'

'She did?' answered another in the background, while White almost jumped from the chair to put a stop to all that denigrating talk.

'Are you sure?' asked an officer looking at them surprised. 'When I passed in front of her house this morning, I saw the front door large open! I thought she's really playing with her luck!'

White went white and looked at his colleague. 'Who was supposed to watch her house, agent Blanchard?'

'Her house! We are keeping an eye on her and her son, not the f... house!'

Still, during the exchange, they all rushed from the office, and then out to their cars. 'He likes tormenting her! Of course, I would have expected you to let someone watch her house with her in it or without! It was like her office episode, where he broke in just to leave that piece of evidence!'

'I thought it was about keeping her safe!'

'It is... in what moment will you realise that it is important to make sure that she was not returning home to Maddox waiting for her hidden in the wardrobe!?'

'Damn! Never thought of that!'

They drove those cars like running away from hell, wondering why her front door was opened and, if it was Maddox, what he could leave there for her to find.

The cars went to a halt, and they jumped out, pulling their weapons, expecting anything. The door was indeed large open, taunting them.

'Act carefully. Don't touch anything...' White said before signalling that they could enter the property.

Everything looked untouched to the first sight, when they stepped into the house. Still, with the guns ready for anything, they proceeded to check room by room.

The display left by Maddox in the personal bedroom of Nolani Arrington was so sickening, it managed to affect even agents who thought they saw it all…

❀ ❀ ❀

It was the second time that day that Nolani rushed into the police quarters wondering why Agent White left her a message that he needed to talk to her immediately. She left the temporary office and drove directly to the police.

'Agent White is on the field, Ma'am,' one of the sergeants told her, when she enquired about Agent White. 'He didn't contact us to let us know you are coming… Where did he say he was planning to see you?'

'He didn't. He said there is a new development in the case, he needed to discuss it with me… He didn't say where he is or what was all about…'

'Do you want to wait for him here, Ma'am?'

'No. Just let him know that I got his message…'

'Sure…'

Nolani turned on her heels and left the building feeling rather uneasy with all the last events bombarding her quiet life. What was it now? What was Maddox planning to do next? She sighed entering her car, put her handbag on the passenger seat and started the engine. She breathed in and suddenly knew she was not alone. Her heart skipped

250

a beat, while she was fighting the urge to open that door and throw herself out of the car. His grin was the first thing she saw looking in the rear mirror of the car. The goatee disappeared. She didn't know if it was because she said she disliked it so or because he went for a change of look. Nolani very much doubted that just shaving his beard would have any effect of making him unrecognizable, the reason why she reached the conclusion that he did that was because of her. Only the thought made her stomach harden.

'So… you are not going to scream blue murder, won't you?' he said, producing, from behind her headrest, a gun.

'What would I gain screaming, Maddox?' she asked looking around in the police car park. He was bold. Very bold. Cars were coming in, others were going out, and there he was, hunted by all the law forces, staying in plain sight, with a gun at her head.

'Turn me on?' he chuckled. She went pale, but that was a reaction she could not control. Instead her facial expressions remained still, seemingly unfazed. 'C'mon! Drive, duchess…'

She listened wondering where were the agents that were supposed to follow her everywhere.

Nolani turned the ignition key again, and she struggled to control her trembling limbs, while motioning the car out of the parking place, exit, and then merging into the main traffic. She noticed that during the manoeuvres he laid out of sight, while the gun pointed at her upper left arm from between the front seats.

Somehow, a thought gave her peace of mind. His obsession was mainly with her, not expressly with hurting Tate or Terry. Another calming thought was that, even if she died in this adventure, Tate would not remain alone in the world. Terry seemed willing to take seriously his role as a father. She was trying to concentrate on how to deal with the entire situation, but she didn't have a plan. She truly believed that her safety was in good hands and that the FBI agents were around to keep her safe from harm. Still, he could climb in her car in the middle of the day, in a police car park full of uniforms, and no one noticed him. He was a big guy to miss!

'Were you wondering what Agent White found that he messaged you to meet with you in such a hurry?'

'You sent me the message… How did you get my new number?'

'The paperwork of your new contract was on your desk; you left in plain sight… I managed to take it before your hound jumped on me…'

'He was not my hound…'

'Yeah?' Maddox grinned. 'Why then he barked at me to stay away from his daughter?'

Nolani thought she would faint suddenly. She stopped breathing, trying to understand what that statement meant for her. Her dad?

'I don't have a father…'

'Yeah, you do… and I'm telling you that, he does know how to handle a knife…'

Nolani took the face of another vehicle, making a left without signalling, provoking a choir of claxons in full street. That brought lots of unwanted attention to her car.

'Drive carefully, you bitch. Try to attract attention again, and they will have a cute driver with a bullet in her head!' he barked in her ear, pocking her shoulder with the tip of the gun.

'Do that again, and I'll push the car in the first truck, Maddox,' she warned him, taking a dangerous exit.

'That would fuck you worse than I fucked your mother, bitch.'

'My mother?!' she reacted, looking into the rear mirror in the face of the most handsome monsters in the world. His eyes were daring, his expression mocking, and his smile was deadly.

'I wonder what your daddy would say if he would see the state of his woman after our… passionate night…' Nolani was lost. She could not really grasp what he was blabbering there. 'She screamed for you both, I'm telling you. Don't get me wrong, she was a great f…'

Nolani felt her stomach turning. Her palms were sweating, while her fingers turned white from squeezing hard the wheel. The man was sick. Very sick. She didn't know what mother he was talking about, but the details of torturing a woman, any woman, were sickening. 'I don't think your daddy ever served the lady that way…'

'You are wrong, Maddox…'

'Oh, he did?' he chuckled mockingly.

'I don't have a father and… I don't have a mother…'

'What was she doing at your house last night then? Blonde… stunning… sexy… you wouldn't believe the chick is past her fifties! Nice big ass…' he added, checking on her facial expressions.

Jessica? Jessica was at her house? Oh, Dear God! Reading on her face that she finally realised who he was talking about, he laughed. 'Now, you remember having a mommy?'

'She was not mom…'

'Oh… pretty bad then. I truly enjoyed the thought of f-ing the wife of that dog…'

'Is she alive, Maddox? Did you leave her alive?' she asked, ignoring his language. What he was saying was more than she could stomach, but at the moment, she was more worried about what was going to happen to her at the hands of this lunatic.

'Of course, my darling. How could she tell everyone about how great I was, if she was dead? Now, I have a good question, bitch. Did you cheat on me with my best buddy the last few nights?'

She didn't answer that question, as he directed her on a series of streets in the suburbs. He directed her to stop the car in the back of a little house covered in shrubbery, his possible hideout during his stay in Dallas. He put his gun at her head and instructed her to get out of the car. Nolani's heart drummed like crazy, but there was no one in sight to jump in her help. She closed the door of her car, blaming herself for falling for the message sent from a private number, just because he signed it as sent by Agent White.

He was limping with the hurt leg, she observed. She saw him fumbling with his fingers in a hidden place and produced some keys, unlocked the door and pushed her inside. The smell turned her stomach. The rancid leftovers on the table, the heat and the smell of old beer were not mixing very well. She turned towards him just in time to see the fist on its way towards her head. She didn't have time to react in any way in front of the blunt force that knocked her over. Maddox then threw the gun on the top of the leftovers on the table, then leaned down and grabbed her fragile neck. She was not giving any sign of being conscient.

He moved around the room and produced a dog collar he tied around her neck. He tied the end of the leash, tight to a gas pipe in the corner of the room. Then, he stood up and assessed the situation. The leash was quite tight, and it could suffocate her. That was not a problem, but he wouldn't allow that before he had his part of revenge. He grabbed her limp body and moved her closer to the wall. He got his phone out and shot a few pictures of her being tied up like the bitch she was. There were more to follow because he was about to take his dear time with her. Usually, he didn't mind starting having fun with the girls while they were still out, but her… he wanted to look at her face when he was f-ing the life out of her.

'I will make you scream…' he muttered, throwing his phone on a sorry sofa, the only furniture in the room beside the table with two chairs which were part of the dining area. He went into the cubicle kitchen and produced himself a can of beer. He popped the opener and drank over half in one go.

He was planning to show her all his memorabilia gathered in his phone, for the bitch to know what he did to others because of her betrayal. All he did, although he enjoyed doing, was on her. Especially what he did to her darling mommy… He made a wry mouth, thinking about her reaction to that. She seemed sure she didn't have a mother. Well, whoever she was, they did look a lot alike. Playing with her offered him as much satisfaction as doing that to Nolani. He did consider the reaction on the face of the man who caused him so much grief. With all the alcohol he used on that wound, it still got infected. The son of the bitch will have to pay for that. Apparently, the woman last night was not his wife. Fuck then, he still had fun.

He returned to the room, ready to check if she had come around. One look in the filthy living room, and he came to a sudden halt.

# Chapter 25

Agent White tried almost half a dozen times to call her number. There was no answer, and after a few calls, it was going in, requesting him to leave a message. The sergeant was sure that the lady stated she received a message *from him* that he wanted to meet her immediately regarding a new development in the case. That was not good, not good at all. He contacted his team. No concerns around the high school. None around the primary school. Terry Morgan was at his office. Nolani Arrington?

They lost her, apparently. She drove so fast that, at one point, they lost her.

He barked orders left and right realising that today was just going from bad to worse. He promised that woman he would keep her safe. He promised her that he wouldn't let Maddox touch her again. He shouldn't have made promises he was unable to keep.

She disappeared, and he couldn't stop that monster from hurting her. She was the most ladylike woman he ever met in his life. To think that he was about to find her tortured, disfigured, denigrated to the lowest, and maybe dead, was unthinkable. The state he found the poor woman in her bed, beaten to the point of being unable to open her eyes, covered in bruises, cuts and blood all over the sheets of the bed, was still fresh in his head. She was rushed to the first hospital to receive the treatment she needed to survive that ordeal.

'Track her car! Can anyone find her car? Her phone?'

'We are working on it, White. What went into her to drive like that?'

'I don't even want to think who made her drive like that… Try to find Morgan!'

One of the agents rushed to find the number of contact and passed him the phone as soon as he answered. 'Mr Morgan, have you seen Miss Arrington in the last hour?'

'No, she was at work…'

'She is not there, sir. We have a reason to believe that somebody used a rouse to lure her out of the safety net.'

'What is going on?' Terry shouted through the phone, suddenly realising that something really bad might have happened to Nolani.

'We don't know at the moment, Mr Morgan. I did hope that she might be with you and that is the reason why she ignores the calls. She had been an hour ago to the police station saying that I had sent her a message that there was another development in the case, and I needed to talk with her immediately. I did not send any messages. There was another attack that occurred last night. The victim is treated in the hospital, and she is a possible relative of Miss Arrington!'

'Oh, my God…' Terry mumbled.

'Did she have any plans for today? Did she talk to you about anything she needed to do?'

'All I know is that she went to work. Now you tell me that she thinks you've sent her a message you did not send! You said you have agents watching her and you ask me where she is! Find her, for God's sake! What that monster is capable of doing to her is unthinkable!'

He knew. He saw how cruel and derailed he was on the body of his last victim. Only the thought of her black and purple face, her crying while the paramedics were transferring her battered body on the stretcher and thinking what she must have passed through made him queasy.

'We found an abandoned rented car close to the police station car park, White. The paperwork, it shows that the last person who rented the car was Jessica Redgrove, a lady from Louisiana… The picture… I think she is our victim, sir…'

The officer went white and handed the tablet to White. The picture of the stunning blonde woman filled the screen. White mumbled a swearing word, making a pirouette and looking at his people. 'Anything about the car of Nolani Arrington?'

'Not yet, sir… Working on it…'

'The phone? Did anyone manage to catch the signal?' People were on the phones, checking details and barking instructions.

They were just displaying the picture of the last victim of Maddox when Terry entered, running like chased by devils. At the sight of that picture, he went ballistic.

'Agent White? Where is she? Did you find her?'

'We found the car!' shouted one of the officers, barking instructions through the radio to all the officers on the field. The messages were coming back through the radio that some were five minutes away, some a bit more. 'Be aware, the individual is armed and extremely dangerous. Any wrong move and it may cost a life!'

'He doesn't care if he dies,' said White, running out the door. 'He will make sure though that she is dead before he goes in the blaze of glory!'

Terry's heart went to his throat, then he rushed out after White, jumped in his car and followed closely. All the way, he prayed for a miracle. He prayed that Maddox became sane suddenly; he prayed that all this mayhem was a false alarm, anything but to have to give the news to his son that his mother had been tortured and killed.

Her sweet face passed through his mind, smiling at him from the other pillow, embracing him with her clear, loving eyes. He gritted his teeth when the lovely image changed to another one from years ago, watching his best friend punching her and brutalising her, laughing at her vulnerability. He was hurting people because he could. He remembered her crying softly in his T-shirt, shaking uncontrollably. For years, he fought that memory because of his own guilt. Now, he could not take his mind off her swollen eye and her cracked lip caused by Maddox's brutality. That was nothing compared with what that monster could do to her at that moment, and he was not there to protect her. His feeling of helplessness was eating at him.

He let her down, employing the bodyguards to keep an eye on Tate and on Laura but not on Maddox's main victim, Nolani. He thought that if that monster wanted to hurt them really bad, it was through the kids. He was wrong. Nolani never stopped being his obsession.

'God,' he muttered, driving like a maniac, following the police car in front of him.

Then they stopped the car, and the entire area was cordoned off by the police. He ran after White, to find himself blocked from going any further as it was a police matter.

'I know! My fiancée is in there…' he shouted out of control, trying to fight them off.

'Sir, any mistake can cost your fiancée's life! Calm down, and let us do our job!'

He saw White talking with some police officers, then taking the amplifier to start the negotiations. Maddox was not willing to negotiate. He was not willing to surrender alive, and he was not to spare Nolani's life at any cost. *That was a loss of time and energy.* He said that to the policeman who was blocking his way, but apparently, he was turned the deaf ear.

He listens to White announcing to Maddox that the entire place is surrounded by the police and he has no way out. White demanded that he should release Nolani immediately. He was talking clearly and eloquently, knowing as much as Terry that Maddox was not the guy to negotiate with.

Terry noticed that everyone lifted the guns and was startled, noticing just then that the back door of the small house had opened. His heart started racing when, in the frame of the door appeared the silhouette of Nolani. Listening to some rehearsed instructions, she pulled the door closed. She was not making sudden moves. She had no shoes on. Her hair was falling in disorder on her shoulders while she was walking slowly towards White.

'Miss Arrington, Maddox?'

'He's in there…'

Maddox barked a curse, looking at the dog leash hanging from the pipe. The leather looked like it's been cut through with a knife, and the bitch was nowhere to be seen. He turned around just in time to see the fist coming directly towards his face.

'If you want to play with someone, big guy, play with me!' the voice was low, strong, familiar. He felt his face exploding under the impact with the strong blow. His cheekbone cracked. His nose started bleeding instantly. The next blow followed almost immediately, and his ribs cracked. He growled blindly and launched. He didn't manage to hit anything, and that infuriated him beyond reason.

Nolani rubbed the side of her head where the pain was pulsing, trying to grasp what happened. When she came around, she was lying on the floor at the side of the room and her head was spinning. She thought she was having a flashback seeing the two men caught in a struggle. Nolani collected herself from the floor.

'I warned you to stay away from my daughter,' came the voice from a side, before another blow under his left ear caused agonising pain and made him feel his head was about to explode. Maddox managed blindly to grab an arm and twist it, making the man groan in pain. Nolani didn't have much time to analyse the situation. When Maddox managed to catch that arm, making the unknown man growl in pain, she used the only weapon she had upon her, her shoe. She launched against him, and she pushed that heel where she saw him bleeding on the videotapes this morning. She did not expect the heel to be so sharp to dig deep through the flailed fabric of his jeans and into the flesh. She moved backwards to stay away from him, holding the other shoe, ready to use it.

At that moment, he screamed at the top of his lungs, as the sharp, pointed object hit him exactly in the same place where his wound was pulsing, making him nauseous. He went onto his knees, then fell on a side, while his hands were trying to dislodge the spear out of his thigh. To his shock, the object was a shoe with a very sharp metallic high heel. 'What the f…?!' he cried.

'I will kill you, bitch,' he growled. The bludgeon hit to his head made him go with velocity, his forehead first against the dirty wooden floor.

Nolani looked at the other man, who raised to his feet. His hair was short, dark blonde, his eyes hazel. The features of his face were tough, a series of lines and squares that could define him as a very strict, disciplined man. With her eyes, she measured him as he moved his arm up in the air, then quickly down with a crack. 'Tough bull,' he noted, showing towards the big man lying on the floor. He chuckled with an undertone when he noticed the stiletto in his leg. 'Nice call using that killing heel. Are you ok, my girl?'

She nodded silently while he stepped towards her with a shy smile on his stern face. 'Don't be afraid of me. When Howard told me what was going on, I couldn't stay away any longer…'

'Howard?' she mumbled, taken by surprise.

He lifted his shoulders, looking at her gorgeous face with discomfiture. 'My son? Howard Godstone?'

'He said you told him you were… my dad…' she stuttered, making a very small gesture towards Maddox with the shoe in her little hand.

He sighed, his shoulders slumped, while looking apologetically in her eyes. 'Is that true?'

'I am Clint Godstone…'

'Howard's dad… Jake's grandfather… the General…' She vaguely remembered Tate talking about Jake's granddad. Apparently, he worked all his life in the SWAT division, although it was unclear to her why Jake was calling him the General.

She read about the Special Weapons and Tactics Team. It was a division of the police force, not the army. The man seemed completely lost in examining her beautiful features. He noticed her freezing, her small breath and the horror in her eyes. She didn't need to scream for him to understand what made her react that way. He turned fast and, with a strong kick, crashed Maddox's facial bones.

He moved fast realising that he needed to keep the man under control. He used a pair of cuffs to secure his hands to his back, and then he asked her to give him the dog collar from around her neck. Nolani fumbled with her fingers just then, realising the leather strap around her neck. She undone the metallic buckle and handed it to him. He used it to tie Maddox's legs together.

In that moment a voice could be heard from outside, demanding Maddox to surrender and to let her go.

'Go out, Nolani, but close the door behind you. Don't let them storm this place until you explain what happened. If they do, they would shoot me without asking questions. Tell them Maddox is under control in here.'

She looked at him with her eyes, begging for an answer. 'Just tell me,' she said, touching his hand. 'Are you… '

'Yes, my darling. I am your father.'

She moved as she'd been instructed and closed the door behind her, then walked without rushing towards Agent White.

'Miss Arrington? Maddox?'

'He's in there…' She whispered to his ear with a trembling voice the message, and then she looked into White's eyes with a shy smile. 'It was my father…'

'Did you know about it?'

She nodded with a small smile. 'I didn't even know I have a father. Is he in trouble?'

'We will need to talk to him, but no, Miss, I don't see why… Mr Morgan is here, worried sick,' he pointed, gesturing towards the place Terry was watching her from beyond the police line.

Agent White turned to his men, announcing. 'The area is clear! Maddox is fully under control inside. Let down the weapons, gentlemen!'

Nolani walked towards Terry and threw her arms around his neck. His strong arms pulled her tight in his arms and looked into her face. He could not believe she walked out of there, visibly unharmed. 'Are you all right, my love? What happened in there?' he asked, looking behind her at the police officers bringing out Maddox in cuffs. He was growling, swearing, trying to fight all the lawmen off him. His blood-injected eyes focused on her, in his arms and he screamed, but she could not understand the words, or she tried not to. Walking tall, proud, with his cap in one hand and talking with Agent White, outside came a man. The walk, the way he moved, the way his hair was falling on the back of his head… Terry looked at her. 'The guy on the videotape. Policeman?'

'Howard's dad, Terry… My dad…' she whispered, leaning her cheek against his wide chest.

# Chapter 26

All the TV channels were covering the arrest of Richard 'Hammer' Maddox in Dallas. Even if they didn't learn the identity of his last victim, she could be seen being comforted by the Defence Attorney Terrence Morgan. The last screenshot with her in his arms raised the question of why Maddox, who was known to target teenage girls, moved his victim pool to a lady who seemed to be in her late thirties. Was it because she seemed romantically involved with Maddox's known best friend? The question remained: what caused the rift between them years ago. Terry Morgan always refused to comment, and there were many speculations. One of them was considering that Terry Morgan saw the dark side of his childhood friend and moved away.

Wiseman nodded his head listening to all those speculations presented on the TV. Idiots. Even if they said that those were only speculations and nobody knew for sure, they were making the people watching these programs believe all that. The upsetting part of all, the situation was typical. Maddox and Morgan were crazy for the same woman. The only difference, Maddox was obsessed with her in the right sense of the word. She was the girl he could never have. The fact that Morgan had a piece of that flipped him over the bridge of insanity.

He was in his nice hotel in Augusta, trying to chill out between two meetings. The one in the morning did not seem to take him nowhere information-wise. Now, he couldn't concentrate on the next one because of what he learnt from the telly. Maddox kidnapped Nolani Arrington, and, like years ago, she escaped unharmed. Lucky lady.

He was just prepared to leave the room when the news presented that there was yet another victim of a vicious attack by Richard Maddox. The identity was kept secret by the police, but she was believed to be a relative of Terry Morgan's fiancée, in her fifties.

Jessica Arrington?

He stopped in front of the TV with the air that somebody punched him really hard in his stomach. This one was on him. Morgan was to eat him alive. He brought her in harm's way, feeding her bullshit, just to give Nolani a reason to fear her right to inherit Vanda Arrington!

Plus, this time, they presented Nolani, even if the name was not released to the media, as Morgan's fiancée. With his mind going in overdrive, he shut the TV and rushed out the door.

This could show the media that Maddox had unfinished business with Terry Morgan, targeting his so-called fiancée in all aspects possible. How long will it take them to find out that Maddox killed a paraplegic old lady in the hospital just to get to her? How long will it take them to see Tate Arrington and count one plus one?

This was the definition of a mess. Every single member of this Percy family was blonde with blue eyes. Why Tate Arrington couldn't come out looking like a Percy? Nobody could guess so easily who his daddy was!

The only way around this mess was this fiancée thing. Maddox would look just obsessed with the woman of Morgan, and that was the end of it.

He jumped in his car and looked though the window, one image appearing in his mind. He realised then that in all this, he was the idiot who was losing sleep barking at walls. The image was that of Nolani

Arrington moving between the police officers and FBI agents to find comfort in Morgan's arms. Morgan was romantically involved with the puss in stiletto's! There was never a case to lie about it because that was real! He just didn't get it.

He breathed slowly moving the key in the ignition, trying to remember the conversation with Morgan about him and Arrington. He was protecting her. He hoped that this investigation would bring in Nolani's life, family and emotional support. He was in love with the woman!

Well, he did accuse him of being crazy for her, too. Morgan pointed to him that Nolani was everything he liked in a woman, what he liked in Kate, minus the flamboyancy.

Was all this stunt he was making to bring her down and push her in the drains his way of being crazy for a woman? With Jessica Arrington, it backfired. This could cost him his job. He needed to slow down, analyse all this and find his redemption.

He was in Georgia to find some Percy relatives for that lady, to discuss her inheritance and, at the end of all, make sense of all the lies she was fed by that evil woman. If this was the way, he was taking it.

Nolani was happy to have the discussion with the agents at Jacaranda, rather than at the police station. Howard and Devante were out on the field playing with the children. They were all playing football, and for a very good reason, Laura kept winning. Her knock on the head had been professionally checked, and there was no reason to worry. That was the only reason for her to be happy.

To learn that Maddox did not lie, and he did attack Jessica Arrington in her own bedroom turned her stomach.

She had to repeat a few times the story of finding Maddox in her car in front of the police station and what he said to her on the way to his hideout. She had to recount the attack again and again. The fight between her newly discovered father and Maddox. The way her stiletto ended in Maddox's old wound.

'I left my phone in my purse, in the car, to be easy to track. I was afraid that if I took the purse with me, he would have the phone disconnected. I was hoping that I would have time to drag it, talking him through. The coward never gave me that chance. As soon as I stepped in, he knocked me in the head, and for a few minutes, I lost consciousness. When I came around, I had a dog collar around my neck. I didn't realise that until my father asked me to hand it to him to secure Maddox's legs. They were caught in a struggle. It did remind me of the fight Terry had with him in the hotel room years ago. This time, I refused to be just a victim, crying for help in a corner. When I saw that he had an advantage, I grabbed what I could…'

'Your shoe…'

She nodded, leaning her cheek against a cool sofa cushion. 'I rushed, and I pushed it in the place I saw in the morning that he was having the old wound. I moved as fast as I could out of harm's way, but Mr Godstone had again the advantage. I learnt later who he was. Is he in trouble, Agent White?'

'No, Ma'am. He does talk now to my colleagues. He says he was called by his son to step in, the night when your grandmother died in the hospital, and you asked him to look after Tate that night.'

'He knew all the time where I was…'

'That is for you to find out. It is a great coincidence that your halfbrother and his family were so close to you and your son. In all honesty, I do not think that was a coincidence at all…'

'What will happen now? Maddox was caught… Will he answer for his crimes?'

'His phone is in the police custody. We are following to learn what he has on that phone.'

'I think he has on his phone pictures of all his crimes.' Agent White nodded, leaning his elbows on his knees. Considering the evidence Maddox left in her office with the yet unidentified victim, he strongly believed that Maddox was reliving his crimes each time he scrolled through his phone.

'That alone will be enough to get a conviction. We talk about life without parole.'

Nolani smiled weakly. 'Don't lose him. Next time, I won't be so lucky…'

'Ma'am, I trust you are safe now…'

'What about Jessica Arrington?'

'Redgrave, apparently. She is in the middle of a messy divorce, but she uses the name of her next-to-be ex-husband. She is in the hospital. Two fractured ribs, her cheekbone is pulverised, and she has been brutally abused sexually, but she will survive.'

Nolani shivered, burring her pretty face in the cushion, muffling there a small cry.

'She will blame me for it. She has been attacked in my own house…'

'I do not know about that. For one, I am sure, she had nothing to do in your house, Miss Arrington. Mr Wilson, your lawyer, was very surprised that she found your address, as he refused to hand any information about you to her. Apparently, she was seeking to raise hell regarding your relatedness issues. Her own perseverance turned out against her.'

'Maddox thought she was my mother…'

'It was the reason why he was particularly more vicious in this specific attack. She had more to suffer than any other victim… We are waiting for the medical team to give us permission to talk to her about the attack. All we need from her is to recognise Maddox's picture. We have reasons to believe that your house is full of his prints, DNA and so on. Therefore, if she wouldn't be able to identify her attacker, your statement that he bragged about what he did to her and all the evidence collected in the house would cover all the aspects of this investigation. What we may find in his phone will be just extra. Your house is cordoned off now and treated as a crime scene… I'm afraid you are not allowed to return there very soon, Miss Arrington.'

'Mr Morgan was kind to receive us…'

'Very kind indeed…' he smiled charmingly, looking in her clear blue eyes. She smiled back at him.

Just after they left Jacaranda, she managed to have a chat with Howard Godstone. Nolani, Terry and Howard Godstone were on the back veranda of the house with a nice coffee in front of them. The subject was in the air; in their eyes, the words were screaming to come out. Terry opened it leisurely, commenting that he started to smell something odd when he heard Howard talking with his specific Georgian accent. 'What were the odds?' he smiled. 'My assistant discovered that Vanda Percy Arrington was from Augusta, Georgia… And in the heart of Texas, the father of our son's best buddy has a Georgian accent…'

'We have been here since Jacob was two years old, but no matter how much I tried, I couldn't get rid of it…' Howard agreed, nodding his head. 'So… shall I say what I know about all this business with Nolani and me being half-siblings?'

'Please…' whispered Nolani, waiting patiently to hear what Howard knew about her.

'My mom and dad were high school sweethearts… That was an aspect they both agreed on… They were both born in Savannah, married when they both turned eighteen, and everything seemed like the American dream. They'd been married for two years when I was born … Dad followed the police academy and I was six or seven when he was recruited in SWAT. Mom never agreed with his career choice. Why she couldn't have been married to a businessman? Anything less dangerous than the police or army would have been good for her. This was a continuous reason for them to fight. Every damn mission he was employed as part of SWAT was a reason for her to flip. She hated it; she truly did. She was diagnosed with depression when I was thirteen… then they found a brain tumour two years later. She died in the same year. I was particularly proud of dad. I wanted to follow his steps. Don't get me wrong, I was affected by my mom's death. That was the reason why me and my dad had a fallout when he entrusted me with the secret of your existence. I could understand that mom exaggerated freaking out every time he had a mission, but to find out that he had a fling outside the marriage that resulted in a child, got me mad. I was mad at your mom, mad at you… In another choice of words, I didn't take it well.

'It was late in my high school years when I, myself, cheated on my then so-called girlfriend with Katrina. I was madder that I stepped in my dad's shoes than because of the issue in itself. At the end of the day, I thought that my girlfriend and I, at that time, were broken up and I moved on. I discovered that I got sucked into a messy love triangle, for a teenager who was feeling everything at the highest. At that moment, I opened the issue with dad. His advice was to make a choice. To analyse my feelings and to make a choice before it was too late. I challenged him, asking if this is what he did in the case of the woman he cheated on mom with. He said *yes*. He said that because of his choice, to keep his family together, he had an orphaned child who would never know mother or father. Then I learnt that the lady I hated so much, your mom, who, in my imagination, would have been happy that my mom died so she could be with my dad, died at your birth. I asked dad where you were, and he said he had no idea. I asked him to find you. Me… I went back to high school, and I broke up with both girls. I stopped dating altogether. I didn't like the situation I pushed myself into. I pursued an army career. I met Katrina again after she finished her studies, and she started working as a teaching assistant in primary schools. The attraction was so strong, we ended up together in no time.

'I just learnt Katrina was pregnant, when dad came to me and asked me if I still wanted to know what happened with that child who was in all rights, my sister. He told me that you have been adopted by a cousin of your mom and taken to Texas. In that moment, you were visibly pregnant, and you ran away from your home, to make a future for you and your unborn child in Dallas. He talked with a few family friends to find out what the issue was. Apparently, your adoptive mom asked you to give your baby up for adoption. You chose to raise your child away from her. Dad was particularly proud of how strong you were feeling against giving your child away. He never cared how you ended up pregnant and without a father for your child. As he says often, *Crap happens.* He impregnated your mom without ever planning to play daddy. As I learnt in time, it was not so simple. He did have feelings for your mom. He was torn between loving her and losing his family. You had to pay for his comfortable choice. In that moment, I realised that he sacrificed you for me. It didn't seem right. I took the decision to move to Dallas and meet you. I applied for a transfer and luckily, it has been approved. Katrina didn't have much of a choice. She applied as well for a school in Dallas. We married when Jacob was three months old. She finished her upgrades in Dallas and she became a teacher in full right when Jacob turned three. She ended up being happy with the change. Her family was complaining about having their grandbaby taken so far away from them. Katrina realised that they would have interfered in our family life a bit too much. Anyway, I called my dad when I managed to put Jake in the same kindergarten with Tate. Finally, I had a contact with you. You seemed nice but particularly private, and you were keeping everyone at an arm's distance. I took all the decisions regarding Jake's school to match yours… so our kids would grow up together. I liked being your trustworthy friend. I liked becoming the one you called when you were in trouble. Of course, I did not see all this trouble coming your way. Who would believe that a lovely young lady, private, sweet and with such a boring life, would attract upon herself so much heartache?

'In the night when you called me to come in your house and ensure Tate's safety while you went to the hospital to see what happened with your adoptive mother, I called dad. I saw Terry that evening, and I learnt he was Tate's father. Jacob told me about the guy at the football field. What made me call dad that night was the fact that he was retired, and he could investigate better what was going on, not being visible and in the middle of all of it. I could protect Tate and be there for you whenever you needed me to. Dad could remain in the shadow and do a better deal than me.'

'He did,' Nolani agreed, looking at him with a loving smile on her face. It was his decision to step over his own heartache to get close to her. God, to realise that this man made all the choices possible for their boys to grow together and for him to be as close as possible to her, the thought filled her with joy and sadness at the same time. 'Are you still mad at me, Howard?'

'I realised that I had never been. If I had anyone to be mad at, it was dad, but even so, he could choose to leave me and mom to be with your mother, and he didn't do that. He sacrificed a woman he came to love for his family. He sacrificed you, for me. It was only fair to do my part to find you and be around you, if not as a brother, at least as a friend.'

'Did he keep in touch with you with what was going on?'

'Maddox was playing the game *Look at me! You can't touch me!* As soon as the police and FBI got involved, he kept a low profile, went into hiding. The game changed. Dad said that he was a bragging bully, but deep down, he was a coward. He attacked vulnerable people to prove how strong he was. Everyone's tactic was to keep an eye on you, Terry and Tate, but dad said there were too many victims to watch over and only one criminal. Keeping an eye on his every move would eventually end up stopping him whoever he planned to attack.'

'Why did dad decide to face him, that night in the office?'

'I consider that move pretty stupid, if dad wanted so much to remain in the shadow. Dad said that he used that attack for a few reasons. First, it was to confront the guy and check his strength, techniques in fights, in a situation when no one's life was in danger. Second, he planned to place that wound on him. He was lacking technique, but he was strong like a bull. In a situation when his own blood would have been in danger, he needed that advantage. Third, he told the guy to stay away from his daughter…'

'Maddox told me that…' Nolani agreed.

'Dad knew that if there was going to be a direct attack on you, Maddox would tell you. It was his message to you, *you are not alone; I'm here, baby.*'

Nolani let her forehead drop, and she whispered softly: 'I got the message. I did not know what to make of it. I thought it was another crazy game of Maddox… but I got it.'

# Chapter 27

Terry loved to see her in the middle of her brother and father. After intensive interrogation in the police station, as Agent White promised, Clint Godstone walked out with no charge against him. It was lovely to watch Nolani being in the middle of them, loved and cherished as she deserved. Tate and Jake had a blast to learn that they were, in fact, cousins and they were sharing the same grandfather. Jake asked his dad in shock why he never told him if he knew from ever. The answer was because he wouldn't been able to keep his mouth shut.

Days after the attack against her, they were told by Agent White that Jessica Arrington was stable and she recognised her attacker. Of course, she was accusing Nolani that she was in cahoots with Maddox, given the fact that he was at her residence that night. She got the entire story right from the police and later from the news. She walked into that house, completely unaware of the danger hanging above the other woman's head. She said that the guy thought she was Nolani's mother, and she wanted to make a point that she wasn't. She complained that the woman kept telling lies about her origin and she wanted to take her in court for defamation. Agent White replied to that that Nolani didn't have any opportunity to make such statements to that individual and that Maddox reached the conclusion himself.

At that moment, on the TV appeared the gorgeous picture of Terry Morgan's fiancée, the ultimate target of Maddox. Jessica Arrington could see very little with an eye she barely could open, but it was enough to observe the similarities between that woman and Vanda Arrington. Agent White said that he left her questioning how that was possible. She never saw apparently a picture of Nolani Arrington to realise the cause of all that confusion.

There was no calming period, with Vanda's funeral being arranged at the local church in Angel Marsh. Of course, as usual, her presence was heavily discussed in the closed community. She had never been part of it, and that was Vanda's doing. She made sure everyone knew the girl was adopted, that she never wanted her, but she didn't have a choice, and she did that just because she was a good Christian. She wanted to keep Nolani's pregnancy a secret, so she could manipulate Nolani into abortion and later into giving Tate away for adoption. With Nolani standing tall for her child, Vanda complained to the entire community that the girl was lost and she never deserved to be taken in her care by such a decent woman as she.

Seeing her now with her lovely teenage son next to her, dressed in a suit and looking dashing, with her presented by all media fiancé on the other side, making right by Vanda and arranging a beautiful service in her memory, made everyone gossip a bit harder.

They were all questioning if anything that Vanda said was ever true. Nolani kept herself away from all. She thanked them for their presence but discouraged further development in conversations that would lead to Vanda's truths and lies. Vanda's funeral was the first event they took Rita out of Sunrise Care Home for. With a small arrangement of two carers present specially to look after her needs, Rita could come out of her nursing home a bit more often.

To Tate's intense pleasure, Terry was present at his match that weekend, next to his mom and his newly discovered Grandad and uncle. Another reason for the entire team to be deliriously happy was winning the match. Terry, Clint and Howard joined the boys in the celebrations after the game. Nolani decided to go home and wait there for their return.

Mrs Talon stayed that day with Laura at home. She left when Nolani arrived home as she had an event to attend. With Laura cuddling next to her, she just put the TV on, and her happy bubble broken, when, from the news, she learnt that Richard 'Hammer' Maddox escaped from the infirmary where he had his infected wound treated. The news stated that despite the infernal guard, Maddox managed to break out sometime in the afternoon.

She looked around, in the empty house with horror. There was no guarantee that Maddox was not already in the house when she arrived. There was no guarantee that Maddox just left the matter and fled just to be a free man. In the entire house, it was just her and Laura. Devante left after Maddox had been arrested, same as every other guard employed by Terry's friend from New York. She took Laura gently and made a sign to her to make no noise.

She did have an advantage. Actually, a great one! Between her and Maddox… she knew this house inside out. What she knew, she could use for their safety. 'Sweetheart… now we will play *hide and seek*. And you don't want to lose this game,' she whispered, going low to the floor. With the other hand, she grabbed her mobile phone and turned it on Do Not Disturb. Laura smiled and nodded her head with an accomplice air all over her adorable face. With a louder tone, she told Laura: 'Shall we go upstairs and play with some of my drawings, my love?'

The girl looked at her, a bit confused. The green eyes met the blue eyes which were giving her hundreds of messages. She took the little girl's hand and moved surely through the lounge towards the music room. In one of the mirrors she saw the silhouette shaped on the kitchen's veranda. He was not inside the house yet. That was good to know. She closed the door of the music room and, with her heart drumming on the rhythms of the African tribes, she applied the plan as soon as both disappeared from his sight.

Maddox giggled, discovering that the house didn't have the alarm on. They felt safe a bit too fast to be good for them. Pretty good, at home, was just that slut and the little girl. He moved through the newly refurbished kitchen at Jacaranda, cursing Morgan's good life. Well, he was just about to put a stop to that, he thought, grabbing the biggest blade he found hanging decoratively on a magnetic band on the wall. That pretty house will look good, redecorated in his style. Beside his limping, he moved pretty sure through the lounge where the TV was still on, towards the side door he saw them passing through. When he opened that door, he moaned, really annoyed. That house was a bit too big for his liking. If he wanted a surprise attack, he needed to find them first. He passed through the room with the piano, then through the visiting salon with the veranda. The door towards the garden was large open. He growled, infuriated, looking in disbelief at the open door, then around to the room covered in darkness. He went on the veranda, then around the house to check if her car was still there. There it was, nothing changed. From outside, he could see a room with light on the upper floor. He ran back in, thinking that this might be the sloppiest surprise attack in history!

Maddox moved around into another ground-floor room. The windows were large open. He opened his mouth in shock. 'Huh?' Did he just break through the only locked door of the fucking house?! He turned around and losing patience, he moved as fast as he could to the upper floor. The lounge upstairs was in darkness. He looked to the doors trying to establish which room had light in it. He opened door after door until he stopped and growled like a wounded beast. She knew. They must've said on the TV about his escape.

'I will come to you, and I will cut your head off!' he roared from all his lungs. 'You are dead, do you hear me?!'

There was nothing, but silence. He turned, but he bumped into an armchair. He swore the place down. She could have left the house with the little girl for a long time. She could have gone to the park! Damn, if anyone could find them now! He launched to another door. A bedroom. So many wardrobes, so many places to hide… if… and only if they were still in the big house!

He thought he was losing his mind, moving from one room to another. He returned on the landing tired, hurting, being in the perfect mind set. Mad. He moved down the stairs, looking lost around him.

'Where are you?!' he shouted, agitating the large knife. From all the dark corners of the house, shadows started to emerge, with the guns targeting only one person. Him.

'I don't know where the person you are looking for is. WE are all here, Mr Maddox. Drop the knife,' said Agent White calmly.

Maddox's expression was beyond creepy. His movement was jerky and unpredictable, while with his eyes out of the sockets, he kept turning, looking for a gap in between the reunited forces with different badges and dressed in bulletproof vests gathering around him. Agent White looked at him unfazed. In that moment, Maddox was not the handsome football coach he interviewed a year ago. The features of his face were disfigured by the darkness inside his soul, and for the first time in his life, he looked exactly what he was, a monster. His eyes were bloodshot and full of anger; his body language showed that he was ready to charge, and he just looked for the weak link in the police chain.

Agent White didn't know what would be next, but one thing he knew. Maddox didn't kill again. He rushed to Jacaranda with death in his soul, hoping that he would catch the monster before he would strike again. His colleague said that her number seemed disconnected. Terry Morgan said he was out, and Nolani and his daughter Laura were home that evening. Seeing the car of Miss Arrington outside, he mumbled a prayer. He remembered clearly Miss Arrington asking him not to lose the monster because next time, she might not be so lucky. He was shocked to discover how many doors and windows on the ground floor were opened. The main entrance door was locked. The door between the kitchen and the outside veranda was broken. What was the meaning of that?

'Drop the knife, Maddox, there is no way out! Drop it!'

'You don't understand! That whore cheated on me! She cheated on me with my best buddy! How do you want me to feel?'

'Maddox, she was never yours!' shouted White. 'She was afraid of you. She ran away from you! You went in that room to rape a poor innocent girl!'

'She was my girl! She belonged to me!' he screamed out of his mind.

'Why did you have to teach her good manners, Maddox? What did she ever do to you, for you to teach her good manners? You were idolised by the girls! You could have anyone you wanted! You were handsome. You were a future football idol! She didn't want you! She didn't look at you. Nothing from you impressed her in any way! She didn't look at you like the sun comes up with you. You had to teach her a lesson because she was unwilling to boost your ego!'

White realised that Maddox was dragging it to find a proper moment to make his move. Even if he got out of the circle, outside, the entire place was full of police, firemen and ambulances. Reporters too.

'Drop your knife, Mister, now when nobody is hurt. You have enough to answer for. Don't do anything stupid!'

'Where is she?!' Maddox roared, agitating his weapon.

'I don't know where she is. What I know is that she is not dead. And you cannot die as long as she is still alive!'

At that moment, Maddox charged like a bull, hurting an officer with the knife in the upper arm, hurling to the ground another three and using football techniques and all his strength to reach the exit door. In all that mess of bodies thrown to the floor and others trying to stop his retreat, there were three gunshots from three different directions, all meeting the same target. White sighed. He hoped that the fact his most important victim was still alive would make Maddox get himself arrested.

'I knew this kind of criminal could be stopped only dead,' muttered one of his colleagues. White looked at Maddox lying on the wooden floor at Jacaranda. God, wherever Miss Arrington was going, another crime scene arose. Hopefully, this one was the last one.

'I don't think he planned he would die. I think he just wanted to escape.'

'Huh?'

'I think that Maddox was sure that we would just let him go out that door…' White mumbled.

'That is madness…'

'Well… the guy was not completely in his right state of mind.'

'What makes you say that? He did resist the arrest. He did attack police officers! He wanted to die!'

'No, he didn't. Not before Miss Arrington, anyway… Speaking of…' Then he turned and grabbed his phone, walking towards the main door of the house. He pressed the call, and he waited a few seconds, until the person answered. 'Good evening, Miss Arrington. Are you home, Ma'am?'

'Yes, Mr White. Is it over?'

'I'm afraid that your main lounge needs avoiding for a day or two, Ma'am.'

'I'm sure I can live with it.'

'Where are you? Where is the little girl?'

'In the attic, Mr White…'

❀ ❀ ❀

When the men arrived home, there was a mayhem. Police cars, ambulances, lots of men in uniforms, TV vans, reporters… To have the microphone pushed under his nose when he didn't understand yet what was going on, was nerve-racking. To the question, 'How did you take the news that Richard Maddox escaped from the arrest?' he went from shocked to hysterical. Tate grabbed his arm and asked him what was going on.

In that moment, the doors of the house opened, and they were bringing out a stretcher with a body in a black sack. Agent White was coming out alongside lots of police officers and other FBI agents. An officer was taken by the ambulance crew to have his arm looked at. Terry launched towards White with a roar. 'Son of a bitch. You called me to ask where was Nolani. You could have told me what was going on!'

'I didn't want to panic you, Morgan. I didn't know much, myself. We were already on the way to Angel Marsh. It was the first place we looked for him.'

'Where is Nolani? Where is Laura?' he asked with his heart beating crazy in his throat.

'They managed beautifully, sir. They are coming out now. They were hidden in the attic.'

'The house doesn't have an attic…' said Terry with a rise of his eyebrow. 'Anyway, there is no entry… I looked.'

'Then Miss Arrington is the only one who knows that there is an attic and how to access it. That was brilliant. She left as many doors and windows open… now I know… for us, not to ruin your property. Anyway, it offered us the opportunity to enter undetected. Maddox was inside for a long time, but mad already because he could not find them.'

'Is he dead?'

'He attacked a police officer with a knife, he resisted the arrest… yes, he is dead, Mr Morgan.'

Next to him, Tate was trembling like a young bull, looking at the open doors of Jacaranda, full of anxiety. 'Can I go in? I need to see my mom!'

'Of course you can. Please avoid the yellow band. Tomorrow, somebody will come to clear the area and make the house liveable again.'

Some cameras were taking Tate in their focus, for the first time having a glance of the son of the last victim of Richard Maddox. They could hear him saying. 'Dad? Are you coming?'

Howard, Clint and Jake had already walked toward the house. The lights in the upper lounge had just been turned on. Clearly, Nolani wanted to avoid Laura to see the lower one. They went in and avoided the furniture that was holding the police tape in place. All like one, they rushed up the stairs, towards the upper lounge. They looked like a herd of crazy bulls in a full stampede when they reached the room in light. Laura was on a carpet, excited by a music box, a book and an old doll they found in the attic. Nolani was sitting on a sofa, chatting with her about what else she found interesting in the attic of the house. There was an old crib, lots of books, old furniture and chests with all kinds of old stuff, like treasure chests. Laura looked at them with a huge smile on her face. 'We played *hide and seek*, daddy. There was a man in the house, but he couldn't find us. Do you think he is going to be upset that he lost the game?'

Terry sighed and dropped himself in an armchair, looking at her and trying to calm down. 'Definitely, sweetheart. I don't think he was very good at *hide and seek*…'

# Chapter 28

'Do we really have an attic?' he asked with his cheek deep in the pillow, looking at her still in shock. Her cold blood saved her and his little girl from being killed.

'We do. Vanda never told me about it. I found it when I was about eight. The entrance is through the huge mirror in the ballroom. There are, actually, proper stairs to go up, made of stone. Moreover, when I had Jacaranda redecorated, I applied emergency lights on the wall. I didn't want the building team in the attic, the reason why it doesn't have electric lights. I did leave there some large flashlights for emergencies. It was easy to make Laura believe that everything was nothing but a grand adventure. I just moved opening doors and windows as we got closer. I bolted the mirror from the other side, just in case Maddox would prove to be smarter than all my builders. Then I told Laura that we could whisper, but we are not allowed to giggle or talk loud.'

'I thought I was dying when we got close to the house and we saw all the police cars around Jacaranda. I was furious with White because he rang and asked where you were. I told him that you had gone home to stay with Laura this evening. He said nothing to me then about Maddox's escape.'

'I'm glad it is over. He's dead. It's over…'

'Nolani? They noticed Tate tonight…' he sighed.

'They? Who are they?'

'The reporters, Nolani. Tomorrow, this will be all over the media, alongside the fact that Maddox tried to attack you again.' Her hand moved and touched his, and their fingers intertwined in a very personal way. She squeezed it a bit, and she smiled weakly.

'I never kept Tate hidden, Terry. You said you want to change his name to Morgan. It was just a matter of time for them to discover how alike you two are…'

'He's not the only Arrington I want to change to Morgan,' he said with a whisper.

Nolani smiled with a naughty air all over her adorable face. 'Good, it is time to make an honourable lady out of me…'

Terry giggled and, lifting himself in his elbow, he leaned over and gave her a kiss. 'That, my love, sounds like a good plan… You are though, a terrible house seller… To give a house without telling the new owner about how to reach his own attic…'

'I would have… I think…' she paused. 'The thing is that I was so nervous, I forgot to show you lots of things… The attic is just one of them.'

'Well, I think we have all the time to show me everything you forgot that day… as about you being nervous that day, I think it was my fault I had a go at you about Rita that morning…'

'Was not that. It was the fact that I met again the father of my boy. I didn't know how to react…' she sighed. 'I was mortified that you will recognise me… Then I was hurt because you didn't. I always considered that my strict education impaired my social skills. I was in a situation I didn't know how to deal with…'

'I don't doubt that Vanda had a great influence on your way of interacting with people, my love. I do tend though to believe that she didn't manage completely to write off your will...'

'Are you referring to refusing to give my child away?'

'No, I am referring that you do everything properly. Still, despite all... you are here, Nolani.'

Nolani blushed and closed her eyes feeling ashamed that he brought her night visits up.

'Don't get me wrong, it is not something that I would expect from Nolani Arrington, always proper, always polite, keeping everyone at an arm's distance. It is though, what I do expect from a passional lover. You are, despite your vulnerable appearance, a very strong woman, my love. You raised a son on your own, you have a successful career, and you just survived a month of hell.'

'I couldn't do it without you, Terry. You were my solid ground.'

'I very much doubt that, my darling...'

'You are!' she argued, gently lifting her head off her pillow. 'I always loved you!'

'Because of Tate? You told me that...' he smiled.

'No. I loved you since I raised my eyes and I saw your face. You took my breath away. I know it may sound crazy. I was shaken, I had a swollen eye and a broken lip, I was afraid and clinging to you... When I looked up at your face, my heart went crazy. I never saw in my life such a handsome man... Your green eyes were the most beautiful I ever seen...'

'I'm sorry I didn't recognise you, Nolani. I tried to forget that night. I was feeling guilty for what I did...'

She shook her head with a smile.

'You hugged me. I had never been hugged before. You caressed me. I had never been caressed before. By no one. Not even Vanda. You cared for me. And nobody cared for me before. I fell in love with you in that very instant, Terry.'

'I love you too, Nolani. Sophisticated, glamorous, hedgehog behaviour and all,' he chuckled. 'I'm here now, and our life can be complete. All we need now, that you found a brother, a nephew and a dad, to wait for Wiseman to bring what evidence he could find which might link you to Vanda Arrington…'

'I got it, Terry…' she sighed.

'You got what?' he startled.

'Vanda's secrets. I got it… I found her diaries in the attic. I just need time now to read them through, finally to understand that woman, if that is possible…'

In the following weeks, there was a lot of speculation regarding Tate's existence on the media. The only comment coming from Morgan, Brown and Associates was that Terrence Morgan had plans to marry Nolani Arrington in the middle of August.

Vanda's testament left everything, inclusive rights upon Jacaranda and all the financial benefits coming from it to Nolani. Jessica tried to attack the decision, but Mr Wilson made it clear that due to something she did against her mother, she lost all the rights to ever inherit money or property from her.

Wiseman never managed to put his hands on clear evidence that Lauren Sparks was indeed Vanda's daughter. The evidence was provided by Vanda's diaries. Based on Vanda's testimony, she and Lucas Arrington were in love for a few years before their marriage. The relationship resulted in a daughter she was forced to give away by no one else but Lucas himself because that would cost his political career. He promised Vanda that after they were married, they would adopt their daughter, and Lauren would grow next to them. To Vanda's heartache, that dream became impossible not only because Lauren was adopted by her mother's barren sister and was a *'family business'* but Lucas proved that he never intended to pursue their lost child.

As Nolani kept reading in the diaries, she noticed Vanda becoming more bitter, channelling her efforts and her life purpose in caring for her husband's image in politics. Her new opportunity to become a mother, instead of healing her, it made her feel more obsessed about the child she couldn't rear. Jessica's temper created a rift between them from early childhood. She rebelled against every notion of proper behaviour. Lucas dotted on her. Called Jessica 'the light of his eyes.' Vanda hated that.

She wrote in one diary about the heartache of spending a weekend in Georgia with Lucas and Jessica, then only six, and Vanda was absolutely devastated to have to socialise with her extended family and little Lauren, then about thirteen. She wrote pages about her heart screaming, looking at her, when the entire family seemed to have forgotten who her natural mother was. To have her aunt in her ear talking on and on about how clever, sweet and well behaved was her little girl, made Vanda pass through hell. To see Lucas not giving even a sign of acknowledging Lauren as being their first born and talking with her uncle about the plans they made for Lauren's education made her heart bleed. But she pretended all was well. She already gave up her beloved child to fit the mathematics of a man who put his career first and was less and less the one she used to love blindly. She saw him lying with the easiness others were drinking water. A very convincing lie there, another one here... and his political career flourished. There were many pages about high influential parties, and Nolani was passing over those because she was not interested in who they met at one of those parties or another.

The headaches started at the beginning of the year, and Vanda noticed Lucas taking more and more painkillers and refusing to see a doctor to learn what was producing them. By the end of that year, Lucas passed away. The post-mortem found a massive tumour on his brain.

Jessica took badly the death of the only parent who truly loved her. The only way she could cope with the death of Lucas was to rebel even more against her mother and make every effort possible to make her life a living hell. Instead of looking for psychological support to help her child with the grieving process, Vanda did all she knew to 'make that child behave properly in the house and outside of it.' Jessica rebelled against every rule and decision she was making for her and their house became a war field. Each one became more driven to hurt the other. As strict as Vanda was becoming, Jessica was rebelling against it.

There was a long gap of entries in Vanda's diary, when Jessica just turned seventeen. Vanda wrote that the 'wild goat' became wilder by the day, going out with numerous boys, drinking heavily and becoming the joke of Angel Marsh. On numerous occasions, friends were reporting that Jessica had sex at a party or another, ending up being pregnant and not knowing who her baby's father was. Obviously, Vanda asked her to perform an abortion. The result of it was that Jessica brought into the house her 'herd of unruly friends.' They had been drinking heavily, mocking her and throwing bottles at her, ending their torment with having her 'endure the worst humiliation she ever lived in her life.' It was not very clear what they did. She said she 'was forced to close her eyes and let it happen, while her evil daughter was laughing in her face, calling her names and watching.' At that moment, Jessica left home. Another gap in the diary of several months, before Vanda wrote about her biggest loss.

She was complaining that it seemed a curse of blood for all her daughters to remain pregnant young and without a father to claim for their children. Nolani assumed she referred to Jessica and Lauren. She knew why her father wouldn't step up for the coming child. She needed to know what was in Vanda's head when she took her. A few pages were about Vanda's heartache at the death of her mother. She said that 'telling her who I really am was the first and the last thing I ever said to her...' Vanda feared that the news might have upset Lauren so much it might have led to her death. The doctors argued that there were medical reasons for her death. Vanda was sure she killed her daughter. Taking her child to raise was the only thing she could do for her. Vanda turned to Angel Marsh with hopes for the new child, saying that she would make efforts not to turn out like Jessica.

The next pages were about how proud Vanda was of her. Her results at school were exceptional, and she was such a well-behaved girl! Nolani was reading those lines with a bitter disappointment. Vanda wrote about how talented a pianist she was… how talented she was at painting… but nothing about how she felt about the child she took to raise. The pages abounded by pride but not love. Vanda was annoyed by the gossip in town that the child might be conceived in a love affair she might have had after Lucas' passing. All her efforts were concentrated to dissuade those terrible gossips.

The last entry in the diaries was when she was about eight. What Vanda wrote was an insignificant description of a party organised by a certain person in Angel Marsh.

Nolani was somehow relieved that she didn't have to read about Vanda's feelings when she realised the child; she had so many hopes about remained pregnant, having just turned eighteen, with no father to claim for her baby.

The diaries didn't offer too much emotional reassurance but helped her understand all those involved and why Vanda was so hard on her. It did help her understand that Jessica was a victim, too. She lost the only parent who truly loved her and remained with a mother who, instead of passing all the love she had for her lost child towards her, seemed completely empty emotionally. In her own opinion, Nolani considered that Lauren was actually lucky to be brought up by such a lovely family. Maybe Vanda had maternal instincts, but she didn't know how to be a mother. She described in her diaries that Lauren was pretty, well-behaved and had many accomplishments, making her parents proud. Jessica had a short temper, was a rebel and a lost cause. She was making her proud to remind her of Lauren. No words of love were transmitted through those written testimonies. Vanda was judging kids on behaviour and that was very wrong when being a mother. Jessica lacked love, and she fought in the only way she knew against a despotic parent who thought that all she lacked was rules, regulations and a strong hand to handle her. She didn't recognise in all that behaviour a scream for help, for love. The more she rebelled, the stricter Vanda became. That was a vicious circle with no happy end.

With that in mind, Nolani went to the hospital to visit Jessica. She suffered an advance surgery to reconstruct her cheek bone, and she was healing well. She paid for that surgery as it was very expensive, and Jessica didn't have the funds to have it done. Suffering from post-traumatic stress, Jessica was having regular meetings with the psychiatric team to receive the help she needed.

She was about to be discharged, and she was waiting in her hospital room for the papers to arrive to make her exit, when Nolani entered.

Jessica turned around, and one look at her made her hold her breath. She did see a picture of Nolani plenty of times on the TV, but seeing her in person, had a huge effect on her. It was obvious why anyone would think they could be mother and daughter. Nolani Arrington, soon to be Morgan, was the spitting image of her own mother.

'Did you come to boast over that I got what I deserved?'

'Nobody deserves to pass through what you did, Jessica…' said Nolani calmly, sitting down in a chair, to avoid a confrontational stance.

'I saw on the TV that you've been twice at that animal's mercy,' Jessica said, looking at the window, apparently distracted by what happened in the hospital's parking lot. Nolani recognised the rouse. She used it frequently to maintain an apparent disinterest in the matter. 'Hedgehog philosophy,' Terry named it.

'Three times. Twice in the last month. He tried to rape me when I was eighteen. He became obsessed with me because he was stopped then.'

'He was a criminal in the making…'

'I don't think he thought of himself as being a criminal. In his head, I was his girlfriend, and I belonged to him…'

'Expert in derailed behaviour, huh?' Jessica huffed, with a cynical smile.

'It is the university I followed,' Nolani recognised with a nod of her head. 'As a business, I went towards something closer to home…'

'Organising fancy parties?'

'Interior design…'

'Bad business. Vanda's style sucked!'

'Exactly. I agree with you. To redecorate Jacaranda was my life purpose. I hated the silk and gold walls.'

'Me too…'

Nolani smiled and looked around, to the bags on the bed, the flowers she sent a few days earlier in a vase… 'What are you planning to do now? Going back to Louisiana?'

'Obviously… I have nothing to do around here. I got myself in a huge predicament. There is home. Congratulations on getting all my dad's money… I will still challenge that decision in court. Even if you were Vanda's daughter, you had nothing to do with my dad. You have no right to any of that.'

'I see your point, Jessica. But I was just the adoptive daughter of Vanda. My mom was the daughter of Lucas Arrington and Vanda Percy, before their marriage. They had to give my mother away, to protect the political image of Lucas Arrington.' The pretty face of

Jessica registered a surprise. Then went into an expression of disinterest. Nolani could not be fooled. She smiled and continued. 'I know that Vanda was not a great parent. I've been myself raised by her, and she almost ruined me. You adored your father, and he adored you. That made the situation even harder for you to deal with the loss of the only parent who showed you love and remaining with a tyrant mother who judged everyone upon their good behaviour.'

'Vanda was a manipulative bitch. You put it well there... tyrant...'

'I agree with you, too. I did talk to Mr Wilson. He said that the will does name me as the only heir, but also, what I choose to do with the money and the property resulting from the cumulated fortunes of Lucas and Vanda Arrington, is down to me. To avoid further heartache for both of us, further expenses in court hearings and so on... I discussed with Mr Wilson that I want you to have half of the money left to me in the will and, as related to properties, half of the value on the market today. I never managed to touch the money transferred into the accounts from selling Jacaranda in Vanda's care, as she passed away before. You would get half of that money as well...'

'Why is that?' Jessica asked with a sarcastic expression all over her face. 'Because you are afraid of me that through court, I might take everything?'

'No, because through court, you wouldn't get anything, Jessica. It would mean lots of money paid on lawyers and court expenses, to no result. I would take the offer if I was you...'

With those words, she extracted from her bag all the documentation she had completed with Mr Wilson and handed it to

Jessica. She took it and had just a little peek at the cumulated sum on the last page. Nolani signed it to be passed over to her. 'I don't know what you did to Vanda. I don't know if your friends raped Vanda that night, and in all honesty, I don't want to know. You were hurt because she asked you for an abortion. You flipped. Vanda wrote you off her will for what happened that night.'

'Raped?! No! I wanted her humiliated! They got her naked and writing all over her what a bitch she was! They touched her everywhere, you know, but there was no humping going on. I wouldn't permit it!'

'Lots of drunk teenagers could go easily out of control, Jessica. You risked a lot… Anyway…'

'No! You don't understand! The bitch tried to get me forcibly to a woman she knew in town who was doing all kinds of stuff! She wanted to kill my baby!'

'I know, Jessica. She wanted to kill mine, too. Then, when I resisted the idea, Vanda talked with what she called *the right people* that I wanted to give him for adoption. That's when I left home. Believe me, what she did to you, she did to me as well. That's how she knew to be a mother! You are not telling me anything new…'

Jessica looked at her with a frown on her forehead. 'How it all went around that I was your mother?'

'To begin with, she was saying that I was just adopted, and we were not related… Then, because I was looking so alike her and people started to gossip that I might have been her daughter from a love affair after her husband's death, she changed the tune to something more credible. I heard Vanda saying that I was her granddaughter to someone in town. She literally told them that I was your daughter and lost how you were, and they all knew… you abandoned me. I was seven. What was I to believe? That's all I knew… She wouldn't say to anyone that she had another daughter before marriage, so she poured all the bad decisions and shortcomings on you, the black sheep of Angel Marsh. It was easy to manipulate people to believe it. It was easy to manipulate me to believe it. Imagine how hard it was for me as a little girl to hear you on the phone being so spiteful… and you never told me that you miss me… that you are sorry that you gave me away… I needed to hear that, but how were you to deliver what my heart desired, if everything was just a lie to suit Vanda's need to keep her head up in society? I lacked love more than you did, Jessica. You did have a father who loved you unconditionally. All I knew was Vanda…'

Nolani stood up from the chair and gestured over the paperwork. 'Look at it. It is the best offer I can put down for you. I know it means a lot for you, not only financially but as something coming from your beloved father. It is what I consider that is right.'

'You will make me laugh if you are going to cry here that you want us to be a family!' Jessica said sarcastically.

'I won't say that, Jessica. Whether you like it or not, we are sharing the same blood…'

She left Jessica with those words.

# Chapter 29

Returned to Louisiana, Jessica had just an attempt to discuss with a lawyer if she would have anything to gain from making procedures to turn Vanda's will completely in her favour. She heard that she was lucky that her mother's heir was willing to share with her the inheritance. Vanda had the right to leave all her money to the family dog if that was what she wanted, and there was nothing she could do to turn that decision. Her sanity was not put in question at the moment when the document was completed.

Nolani had to travel to Georgia where Jeremy Wiseman announced that there was an heir for the fortune of Percy's and Sparks'. Maybe it was impossible for him to bring evidence that Lauren was indeed Vanda's daughter, but there were documents to prove that she was the daughter of Lauren Sparks, adopted legally by Vanda Percy Arrington. The lawyers who were administering the money of the family and who were looking after a surviving legal heir got their huge break when they met Jeremy Wiseman. Nolani never offered them the image of a lady who won the lottery. Composed and shy, she declared she was there because it was the right thing to do. She decided that the money was well administered the way it was, and more than being kept updated about the investments they were making and changes, she didn't want much to deal with it.

Her relationship with her brother and her sister-in-law became stronger than ever, and with her dad in the picture, Nolani finally felt that she was growing strong roots. To have a dad to walk her to the altar in her wedding day it was very important to her. Dressed in the bridal dress on the morning of her wedding, with Katrina arranging her veil, Nolani was shining.

Everyone was gathered at Jacaranda that day. Terry's family from North Carolina, his associate and many friends from New York were all here to witness Terry's wedding. She wanted to go for an elegant outfit just to look bridal, but Tate and Terry really wanted to see her dressed as a bride. She gave in easily. The beautiful white dress was any woman's white dream.

The ceremony was about to start when Wiseman managed to break into the room; she was almost ready.

'I just want to apologise for the way we started, Miss Arrington. I left my personal problems affect the way I handled our acquaintance…'

'No hard feelings, Mr Wiseman. Thank you for all the efforts you've made to untangle the mystery of my family…'

'It was my pleasure, Ma'am. Just to be aware, there is a lot of media out there… They are trying to milk as much as they can on the love triangle between Terry, yourself and Maddox… I told Morgan that it would be a good idea to feed the media with a romance story. This way, his image wouldn't be affected…'

'His image?' she asked, looking at him carefully.

'They would eat him alive if they knew what happened the night when your son was conceived.'

'Oh… and you consider that us… marrying… is just for feeding the media a love story… or a thriller story with a happy end…'

She sat in a chair and caressed the beautiful fabric of her dress, while her sister-in-law looked at her panicky. 'That is just pure lie,

Nolani. The guy loves you. He wouldn't marry you just to protect his image!'

Wiseman looked at her with a smile, waiting for a reaction. He put in all his artistic talent to make a good front. 'Sorry, Ma'am, I thought that the matter has been discussed openly between you and Mr Morgan, and the accord for the marriage came as a solution not to endanger Mr Morgan's career…'

'As you can see, Mr Wiseman, there was never a conversation that Mr Morgan's career would be endangered because of our past story… I cannot see it that way. I know Mr Morgan feels that he took advantage of me that night, but he is the only person who sees it that way. He knows my feelings and that I would never make a comment to the press to lift the mystery of what happened years ago.'

'People are speculating, Ma'am…'

'And they will always will… Mr Morgan did laugh about your panic regarding his image and your proposal of marrying me for keeping up a good front. What I do not understand is what you are gaining from trying to pry in my mind the idea that Terry would marry me to save his image. If your boss would benefit so much from marrying me, why would you endanger this by telling me that he doesn't marry me for love?'

'Ma'am, believe me, that was not my intention at all…'

'Yes, it was, Mr Wiseman,' she smiled, standing up from the chair and lifting her beautiful eyes. 'Maybe you do see in all the scandal around him, a great way of advertising. A great defence lawyer proved with no morals would bring a pool of clients lacking morals as well. That is where the money is. In all honesty, I don't know, and

I don't care. What I do know for sure is that Terry will not appreciate your intervention in our private matter. If you think that I am going out there raising hell for fooling me into making me believe that he loves me… well, that is something I am not going to do…'

'You told him, girl!' Katrina said, giving Wiseman a killing look.

'Did he ever tell you how he ended up having the full custody of Laura? I know you are pregnant! He confided in me that you are. If this is ending in a bitter divorce, are you ready to lose your child how Vivian lost hers?'

Nolani stopped at the door and turned around with no expression on her face. She didn't know much about that matter; that was the truth. She did question how Terry ended up having full custody of Laura. She knew as well that, as good detective or investigator Wiseman was, he had ulterior motives to make her walk out of her wedding. Why did he choose this particular moment to tell her all this? He just said that there was a lot of media outside. Did he plan for her to make a show and leave Terry at the altar in front not only of his family and friends but all the big news channels as well?

'Did he tell you that because of me, she failed the drug test? That I made up witnesses to bring testimonies that she was an alcoholic?'

'That's what you did… Did he know about all this?'

'Of course, he knew she was not an alcoholic or a drug addict! He paid for all of it! The witnesses, the drugs, the whole lot! He personally declared that he was capable of doing anything to gain the custody of Laura!'

Nolani smiled. 'Did he know what he paid for? Did he know what you did to make his wish come true?'

'You don't know him like I do!'

'Of course, I don't,' she replied, walking out, hearing his vague answer. 'I know him better!'

She met her dad downstairs. He looked dashing in his ceremony suit, with his hair nicely brushed towards the back, freshly shaved and smelling nice. He noticed in the behaviour of Katrina that she was like a barrel of gun powder ready to explode. 'What happened?'

'I'm not sure, Clint. Are you okay, Nolani? Do we go ahead with this?'

Nolani nodded and passed her arm around her dad's. 'I don't believe a thing he says. I don't know what he has to gain with this, but he chose a very interesting moment to bring up all these matters. Dad? Is it time?'

They walked out through the opened French doors of the salon, and she looked at the beautiful arrangement on the grounds, the chairs arranged on one side and the other, covered in white satin and tied with blue ribbons. Laura was waiting for her there, dressed in a beautiful white dress with a basket of blue flowers. 'You look beautiful, Nolani…'

'Thank you, sweetheart…'

Terry was waiting, looking like the dream groom next to his son. They looked at her, exchanged some words, and they both smiled. The music started, and she made her way at her father's arm, while little Laura walked nervously in front of them. She saw the cameras and reporters commenting with microphones the event. Passing the first row of chairs, she smiled behind her veil recognising Agent White and few other agents present there. There were very few people invited from Angel Marsh. The rest of the guests were coming from very far away to witness their marriage. In a wheelchair, Rita smiled at her with all her heart. She stopped and touched Rita's hand with all her love. Katrina walked behind her and sat down next to her husband and son, a pack of nerves. She whispered to his ear a few words, and he frowned. Wiseman walked out as well but remained standing behind the last row of chairs, with his hands crossed on his chest. He was smiling. He knew that he had managed to push doubt in her head. There were two matters he brought up, and none was to be ignored. Yes, she was putting up a nice front, but he knew for sure that no woman would ignore the warnings.

Terry noticed the expression on Katrina's face. He shook hands with Clint and took her hand with a smile. 'Is everything okay, Nolani?'

'Wiseman made a stunt in there… He said that he planted evidence and paid witnesses for you to gain full custody of Laura… He also implied that you knew all about it.'

His expression changed from the smiley groom on his wedding day to shock in a matter of seconds. 'Why would he say that?'

'Just tell me. How did you get the full custody for Laura?'

'Vivian is a war pilot and she's been in Afghanistan! I do not have the full custody of Laura. She remained with me because I am the parent who doesn't put his life in danger every day fighting somebody else's causes! You see that woman in the first row to your left?'

Nolani looked in that direction subtly. She saw the beautiful woman dressed in ceremony uniform. Laura was on her knees, and they were whispering endearing words. 'She managed to take a twenty-four-hour leave to attend my wedding. There was no such thing as paid witnesses and planted evidence!'

The reverend whispered towards them if everything was okay. 'Yes, sir. Please proceed,' Nolani answered, taking Terry's arm. The delay was too short to be noticed. As they chatted in a very low voice, people thought that they exchanged compliments.

Nolani closed her eyes and leaned her head forward, listening to the beautiful speech the Reverend prepared for their ceremony. Wiseman really managed to ruin her wedding day. For a woman who's been denied love was hard to hear that her groom might take her to save his public image.

What she was wondering was what hidden agenda Wiseman had to say all that to her, on her wedding day. The scandal? Really? The controversy? When she turned to say her vows, she saw him with the corner of her eye. She took in the expression on his face. There was no more pretence, no more falsity. Then, she finally understood.

# Epilogue

The situation with the mother of Laura became more than clear on the day of her wedding. Nolani managed to talk to her for a while. All the rubbish Wiseman tried to push in her head before her wedding was clarified and over. The two men had an argument in private as soon as they had an opportunity. It turned out that her suspicion was correct, as crazy as it was. The man was in love with her. She found that he had a very funny way to love somebody. Despite his attempt to ruin his wedding, Wiseman remained in the services of Terry. The only warning he received was to stay away from his private life.

It was Nolani's idea to rearrange a room on the ground floor at Jacaranda with a ceiling hoist and all kinds of equipment, to meet Rita's needs. With Jacaranda mostly being wheelchair friendly, the next step was to bring Rita home first for a weekend, then for a little longer, then… permanently.

Tate and Jake started the Universities. Tate followed his dream in law. Jake went for an army career same as his father, which was expected.

Even though her private life became a public interest for a while, Nolani's employees did not witness any change in her behaviour towards them. She didn't start to share with them any details of her private life. It did prove that she was pregnant, and she kind of had a suspicion that she remained pregnant on the night she learnt of Vanda's death. It couldn't be proved in any way, but her life seemed governed by a weird symmetry. Even Terry was laughing about that. He said that whatever that was, mistake or karma years ago… he was the only crazy man to repeat the story to a fault.

Vivian managed to come home for two days for Christmas that year and remained in the middle of them because she didn't want Laura to miss out on such an important period of the year with all her family reunited.

She gave birth to a gorgeous girl at the beginning of February, they called Christina. In the year after, they welcomed between them another baby boy, Julian.

Life at Jacaranda became a dream come true, with a beautiful park for the children, an adopted shepherd dog, with Rita in the middle of them, with laugher and love, exactly how a house should be.

With their business thriving and their family life depicted in a storybook, Nolani and Terry were happy.

Wiseman tried to have a moment with her, possibly to apologise for his stunt on her wedding day, but Nolani avoided any chances for them ever to be alone. She knew that that kind of man was not to be trusted. Also, she knew that that kind of man could cause a lot of damage in her life, no matter how careful she was. Avoiding him was the only way to make sure that she was not giving him an opportunity to strike. He resigned from his job lately that year, willing to open an investigation agency.

With media running after sensational, and Maddox's case becoming an old story, they've been less and less in the public attention. Soon after, they were highly regarded as successful in their businesses more than being linked with the vicious Maddox. There were moments when it could not be avoided, but Nolani did understand that she would never get rid of that shadow completely.

It was late in the night, the children were all asleep when Nolani finally could put her head on her husband's chest and sighed.

'Tired, my love?'

'Hm… It was pretty hot today. I might consider that idea of yours to have a pool at Jacaranda.'

'I think we would all benefit from it.'

'I'll call my team tomorrow. We need to be extra careful with the kids around, but I'll see what the costs for a pool would be.'

He kissed her on the top of her head and then moved with his lips on her forehead and nose before ending on her lips with a passionate kiss.

'God, I have the most beautiful wife one could ever dream of,' he moaned gently.

'And I have the most handsome man one could ever dream of having…'

'I cannot believe I did not recognise you, Nolani. This doesn't stand well with me…'

'It's okay,' she smiled, caressing his cheek with all her love.

'You changed so much…'

'Give me a swollen eye and a broken lip, and you will remember me instantly,' she giggled.

'Don't even joke with that!' he growled. His lips travelled down on her slender neck, then lower.

'Hm… I think I like this plan better…'

'Better than what?'

'You said you are tired, and you are looking forward to going to bed tonight…'

'The only plan I had for tonight was to make love to my wife…'


THE END